I0638778

For Lesley.
You are the fire in every race.

I know the very moment I fell in love with Dustin Bridges. It wasn't the first time my brother's best friend and I were alone together on a dusty track under the assault of the cruel Arizona sun. It would be far from the last, too. So many weekends of my life were spent in the infield of some endless loop, inhaling gassy fumes while I sheltered in my parents' truck camper shell. It was always the three of us—me, Dustin, and my brother, Tommy. They were two rowdy boys, hell-bent on making me miserable and reminding me that no matter how hard I fought back, there would always be two of them and one of me. They would always be older, bigger, and capable of far more devious pranks—like the time they filled my duffel bag with slugs they dug up at the creek's edge during one of our overnight trips.

We were the ultimate love-hate triangle. I've never blamed Dustin for taking up for Tommy all those times. It was his best-friend duty, in all honesty, and I was the annoying baby sister. I lived up to my moniker, too, busting in on their private conversations, tattling every time they lit things on fire out in the desert, and pretending to cry just to get them busted when they play-punched me in the arm. *It never actually hurt.*

When it came to race time, though, I was one-hundred percent on their crew. Team *Eat My Dust*—that's what they were called—always crossed the finish lines first. And if they didn't, my loud mouth was the first one shouting about the cheaters who stole first place. I was a part of their squad on the weekends, and even though I never touched a tool to the kart in my family's garage, I still somehow had a stake in their race. I don't think a person can spend that many hours riding in cars and traveling together without feeling that kind of kinship. The three of us fought like hell sometimes, but we were also friends. Best friends. *Family.*

But something changed that March morning when I just turned thirteen. Dustin dropped his invisible armor, and I saw straight into his defenseless and wounded insides. It was the first time I felt desperate to soothe his pain and help fight his demons, both real and imagined. Maybe it was the first time I fully understood. Not a day goes by that I don't think about my thirteenth birthday and how hot Dustin's tears were when they landed on my bare, sunburnt shoulder as I held his quaking body tight.

Even now, four years later, on the verge of my seventeenth birthday, those few moments haunt me. I'm surrounded by dozens of friends and family and more gifts than any girl truly deserves, yet all I feel inside is emptiness and ache. Because while my eyes scan the crowd gathered around the outdoor picnic table to serenade me with the happy birthday song, I keep coming up short. The only person I want to celebrate anything with . . . ever . . . at all . . . didn't bother to come.

---

4 YEARS AGO

The trip from our hometown of Camp Verde to the track south of Tucson is always miserable. It's a long drive, yeah, but it's also littered with traffic, even at the crack of dawn. The constant starting and stopping has made my stomach turn over at least a dozen times, and Tommy keeps trying to force me to sit up in the cab of the truck with our dad. I probably should, but if I move up there, I won't be able to hear my brother and Dustin talk. The growl of the roadway is too loud to hear people in the camper through the small window from the cab.

That's probably exactly what Tommy wants. My brother is fourteen and a freshman, so he's into girls and smoking weed and looking at porn. The last two things he doesn't know I know about. He's been going back and forth with Dustin for the last hour telling super dirty jokes that my dad would hate. I think the two of them are trying to make me blush, but instead I keep laughing, even at the ones I don't understand.

I don't get embarrassed. Not easily, at least. I think I owe that to the fact that most of my life has been spent under the wings of these two. If I'm a hard nut to crack, it's only because they made me one.

Tommy's phone battery ran out about halfway here. He never leaves his phone on the charger overnight, and he always asks to borrow mine when this happens. My brother would never *take* my phone from me, though. He's actually very protective when it comes to anyone threatening me physically. That doesn't mean he won't resort to a classic guilt trip. He almost had me giving in about fifty miles ago, with his sad puppy eyes and promises to let me drive the kart through the dirt hills at night next week. Dustin made him stop pressuring me before I gave in. As protective as Tommy is over me, Dustin's sense of duty is even stronger. I think it's because he sees me as an extension of his best friend, and he'd do anything for my brother.

The truck chassis dips and I knock my head into the back window from the harsh bump in the road as we turn off the highway, finally reaching the track. The sun is up, and we're later than my brother and Dustin like to be for the event.

"I told you we should have left at four," my brother shouts, pounding his fist against the glass that separates my dad from us. My father turns to the side and glares at my brother with a weighted brow, a warning shot to get his temper in check if he wants any semblance of freedom this weekend.

"You know he hates this drive," I say in defense of my dad, and maybe a little to admonish my brother.

"*You know he hates this drive.*" The voice Tommy uses to imitate mine is shrill and nasally—and nothing like me. I flip him off as my dad lowers the tailgate.

"You see that?" Tommy points over his shoulder at me as he slides out of the back.

"Yeah." My dad sighs. "I'm sure you deserved it."

I pucker a smile at my brother, but it fades under my dad's shadow as he peers under the camper shell to stare at me.

"Sorry," I mutter.

He shakes his head and leaves the back end of the truck open for me to gather my things. I've learned to bring my own chair for these races. I end up following my dad and the boys all over the place, but mostly, it's a lot of standing. I learned fast that I prefer a lot of sitting.

I pile my blanket and backpack on my chair inside the foldable wagon we use to haul our cooler and water for the day. The boys are already disconnecting the kart from the trailer and prepping it for check-in. This is one of the few times I will get to wander around this place completely on my own. I don't waste any time, and scope out the best places to watch the race.

Most girls my age would probably be pretty bitter about spending their thirteenth birthday in the middle of a dirt track with their brother and his best friend all day, but I can't think of any place I'd rather be. Besides, I like the hot dogs the food trucks make at these things, and my mom's making my favorite cake for when we get home. This is kinda my dream birthday lunch and dinner.

Despite the long drive to Southpointe Raceway, this place will always be my favorite. Maybe because it's the first place my brother and Dustin ever raced. They were seven; I was six. We've come a long way from the kiddie karts they started in. They've graduated to the biggest tracks they can get on before that next big step—stock. That's always been the dream. I'm not even sure who came up with it first, Dustin or my brother. I only remember they started messing around with an old kart my dad picked up at a rummage sale and days later, this long-term vision was locked in.

There was also never any question that Dustin would drive. Not that my brother can't drive; he just doesn't have the edge it takes to win. Dustin, though? He's all edge. My dad told me that most people are born with their own limiters, just like cars. His and Tommy's, and even mine, are set a little higher than average. We like to compete. Dad says his passion for winning is what makes him such a good attorney. But in the Judge family world, we always obey the rules.

Dustin? He lit the rulebook on fire the moment he was born. If the rule is "no running," he's going to sprint. There's no such thing as a quiet library when he's inside. And if a car can be made to go a little faster, or be driven a little bolder, Dustin is going to push the pedal to the floor and find a way to hug the curves and come out ahead. Anyone in his way is simply another object, and if he can't get around them, he'll go right through. Even if he gets burned in the process.

"Short-sighted." That's the one phrase I remember my dad lecturing him about when he came in third last month. My brother tunes out the things my dad says during our drives home, but not Dustin. He's engaged the entire way, even if he's mad as hell about losing a race. That's what gives him his edge—he's willing to listen to what he did wrong. He's not willing to change, though. Sure, he'll shave off a bad habit here and there, but when a race comes down to the wire, his instinct to become ice cold takes over and nothing can stop him from driving his way.

"Hey, you're that kid's sister, that Tommy kid or *whatevah*, right?" I turn toward the voice barking at me from above. There's a huge bar in the middle of the racing complex with seating around the outside. It's a great view, but every time I try to sit up there someone kicks me out.

"I'm Hannah, yeah." I squint as the reflection of the rising sun glints off the window behind the man. He leans forward over the railing and spits out what looks like dirt. I think it's tobacco.

"You tell Dustin I showed up . . . like I said I would." The man looking down at me has a shaved head and a long beard that twists to a point at the base of his throat. He pushes his reflective sunglasses down his nose to peer at me over the tops with his deep black eyes that somehow look like holes under the dawn light. His white T-shirt isn't very clean, and neither are his jeans, kinda like he's been walking around the track in them for a day or two. Maybe he lives out here.

"Who are you?" I bunch up my mouth and cock my head to the side as if I'm actually the tough girl I pretend to be. I certainly dressed the part today, wearing a pair of Tommy's old jeans with holes in the knees and my gray Thrasher hoodie. My muscles are primed to drop my wagon handle and sprint toward the boys if I have to. I wish I had gum in my mouth; I look tougher when I'm chewing gum.

It takes the man a few seconds to answer, the slow drawl of menacing laughter spilling out before his words.

"You tell him it's Colt." He winks before pushing his glasses back up over his eyes. My stomach rolls like I'm going to be sick.

I hold my stare on him to keep up my act, nodding before turning back to retrace my path and hunt down Dustin and Tommy. I don't walk any faster than I did on my way up the path, but I want to. I want to very much.

"It's ready, dude. Relax. We'll pass; we always pass." My brother is never stressed before a race, but Dustin becomes a ball of nerves. He's pacing around the kart as I walk up to join them.

"We're up next, boys," my dad says, standing back to make room for the race inspector.

There's a lot of cheating in kart racing, or at least in our region. People like to mess with the speed governors and make small adjustments that will get them one mile per hour over the next driver. My brother has a mechanical brain and he knows how to push everything right up to the line. Dustin always worries that he's pushed a little too far. What's funny is how opposite they are when it comes to driving. When Dustin's in the kart and working to pass people, lines don't even exist. I've heard people say he drives dirty, but my dad says he drives *aggressive*.

A quick glance over my shoulder confirms that the mystery man is still standing on the bar ledge, waiting for me to deliver his message. The glow from a cigarette flares briefly near his head. I turn back to face the kart as the inspector paces around it, then he kneels to measure tire pressure. Dustin's knees pop in and out, the kind of dance a little kid does when they have a potty emergency. My brother is the exact opposite, his mouth rotating the toothpick he almost constantly chews. Dad is on his phone, probably texting my mom, so used to this process by now that he's just counting the hours until he has to drive us all back home.

"Start her up." The inspector glances toward my brother first, but Tommy nods at Dustin, who glides his way into the driver's seat. Eventually, he gets the kart rumbling.

"You came back fast," my dad says at my side.

I startle a little because I was deep in my thoughts, worrying about the message I have to deliver. I don't have a good feeling about it, and I'm not sure telling Dustin before he hits the track is a good idea.

"Yeah, I ran into someone." My expression probably looks confused, but it also must show my nerves because my dad turns me to face him and inspects me for injuries.

"Not, like . . . literally. I mean, someone is here . . . for Dustin."

The color leaves my dad's cheeks at my words, and his calm demeanor is replaced with a tightness in his jaw as his eyes harden their focus on me.

"Is something wrong?" Clearly there is.

"Stay here," he says, squeezing both of my shoulders as if he's physically planting me in place.

My dad leaves the boys to handle the rest of the check-in process and moves to the front of his truck, his eyes scanning the growing crowd to get a better view of the area around us. I glance back toward the bar where I left the stranger, but the area is filling with people hungry for breakfast before a full day at the track. When I turn back to alert my dad, he's already gone. I ignore his orders and move from my spot to the front of his truck, where I hoist myself up on the hood for a better view. I spot my father a few race groups down, policing the area for a guy I'm pretty sure is bad news.

The boys clear inspection easily, as they always do, and prep the kart for their heat. I want my dad to come back. The uneasy feeling I got from the bearded man has only gotten a stronger chokehold on me since my dad left. It's a little cool out this morning, but that's not the reason I feel the hairs on the back of my neck standing. Something isn't right, and the fact Dustin and Tommy are heading out to the track under this dark cloud kinda feeling has me seriously on edge.

I stand on the hood of my dad's truck to gain a better view, turning slowly to scan the heads in search of my dad's dusty orange hat. When I don't spot it on my second pass over the crowd, I decide to hop down and drag the wagon up the hill to our regular viewing spot, away from the bar.

When I die, I'm sure the coroner will find proof of years of octane-infused air in my lungs. I don't do much to avoid it. Rather, I like the way it smells—the burn of gas and oil, the pungent scent of tire tread smoked along rough asphalt. Other girls can have their bath bombs and body sprays; racing aroma is my fragrance of choice.

I get my chair set up for the best view and pull the binoculars out of the bag my dad packed with snacks for the day, taking a granola bar for myself while I'm at it. I nibble at the oats and honey while I study my brother and Dustin as they inch up to their starting position. They have a good spot, not near the front but high for the first turn. Dustin will work his way out of the middle by the first two laps, easy.

"I see you found the snacks," my dad says from behind me.

"Sorry I left. I didn't want to miss the start." I hold the binoculars up for him to use. He shakes my offer off, still more interested in studying everybody but Dustin and Tommy.

"Yeah, it's okay." He's not paying attention to me and I can tell. I didn't even tell my dad what the man looked like. I wonder whether he thinks this is about someone else, or if something is worse than it actually is.

"He had a beard," I say, giving my dad details he hasn't bothered to ask for.

"Yeah, I figured." He nods but his eyes don't shift to me. He's still on guard.

"Who is he?" I focus on my dad's face, looking for a sign

as his mouth tightens and his eyes wrinkle at the sides. He hesitates to answer me, but he knows I won't let up. I've never been the kind of kid who accepts what I'm told. I question everything. I'm going to be a lawyer one day.

"Kiddo, Dustin's family isn't like ours. You know that much, right?"

I nod because yeah, I know more than he probably thinks I do. Dustin has always gone to the same school as me. He can be a handful in the classroom, and when we were little, he got in fights on the playground all the time. He still throws a lot of punches, but he's bigger than most of the other kids in junior high, so he doesn't get hit so much himself. Somehow, though, his arms and sometimes his face, they always look bruised.

"That man you saw. That's Dustin's dad, I'm pretty sure."

My instinct is to respond with *Dustin has a dad?* It's just that none of us have ever seen him. When we all hang out, it's always at our house. I've never asked why, but as I got older I assumed he was embarrassed about living in the trailer park. We have a pretty nice house with a pool, so it makes sense that when friends want to do something, we do it there.

"Does Dustin know he's here?" I glance up to meet my dad's waiting gaze as he hands the binoculars back to me with a shrug.

"I'm guessing no," he says.

I suck in my lips and think about all the questions I could ask but don't really need to—and maybe don't want to. Thankfully, Dustin is driving in the first heat, and the announcer is making the last call for racers to take their positions. My dad pulls the cooler out of the wagon and takes two Cokes out, passing one to me when he sits on the closed lid. We crack them open as the motors vibrate from the track below.

"How are they going to do today?" I ask this question about every race. I grin as I take a sip of my soda, anticipating my dad's usual answer.

"With Dustin driving? I'd sure hate to be in one of the other cars."

I chuckle against the can and meet my dad's sideways glance with my own. He winks as the race kicks off and we both consume ourselves with the track below. Fifteen laps for qualifying. It's twenty-five for the final. I know Dustin and my brother are going to be doing this with bigger cars one day, the sponsorship sticker-covered kind that get hauled around the country on eighteen-wheelers. I bet Dustin will have his own life-size cutout one day, too.

As expected, Dustin cuts his way to the front of the pack before the second lap is done. He's sitting comfortably in fourth, and though one more spot might get him a better start for the final, he doesn't need to do more than finish where he's at. Dustin likes starting from behind, though.

"Kid's a chaser, and he likes to have an enemy," my dad always says.

I always thought that made sense with the competitive side I've seen of Dustin at school during recess kickball games or when we got older and he played flag football with my brother. He's always an impossible defender, fast enough to run anyone down. But now that I've seen the guy who might be his dad—and stared into his dark, coal eyes—my dad's words conjure a different meaning. Maybe Dustin has *one* enemy, and I'm not so sure he's chasing him as much as running away.

This is the part of the race when I can usually sit back

and relax, but my dad is still poised, leaning forward and surveying every camp spot around the track. It's making me do it too. I'm not sure whether it's good or bad, but as Dustin finishes his twelfth lap, my eyes land on our target.

"I found him. Dad!" I point as my dad leans against my shoulder to follow my sightline, and as soon as he sees the man I'm signaling to, he hops over the short embankment wall in front of us and jogs down the hill to where my brother is cheering on his driver.

I glance around at our stuff. We don't have anything worth much except the binoculars, so I stuff those in the front pocket of my hoodie and head down the hill in my father's footsteps. The sun is finally warming things up, and my dark hair sticks to my neck and face. I'll be melting under the sweatshirt soon, so as I walk I pull the string from the hood and use it to tie my hair back before freeing myself of the sweatshirt, opting to carry it like a bundle. I step up next to my dad and set my things on the ground between my feet, looking up as Dustin whips by at the final curve.

"Go, Dustin!" I shout as he passes. He doesn't balk. He says he can hear me, though, even with his helmet on and the rumble of the track drowning out the world, so I always cheer.

My dad digs his feet into the gravel and folds his arms across his chest. His sunglasses are the kind that wrap around his face, which makes it hard to tell what he's looking at. Based on the flex of his biceps and the way he positioned himself between me and the bearded man walking our direction, I have a pretty good idea where his eyes are fixed.

"You must be Tom," the man says, reaching to one side and hitching up his slouching jeans as he walks. He runs his palm along his hip before holding it outstretched. My dad pauses for a second before gripping it.

"Colt, right?"

My dad's forearm is flexed.

"Riiiiiight," Colt answers, dragging the word out as a smirk takes over his face. Both men let go from their shake, their faces reflected in each other's lenses.

I lean forward to look around the standoff at my brother, hoping he has a better idea about what's going on, but he's more focused on Dustin's route. I have a feeling he's trying to ignore our guest, and I wonder how much he knows about Dustin's parents.

"You living down here now?" my dad asks, pulling my attention back to their conversation. I tie the sleeves of my hoodie around my waist and pull the binoculars out to make myself look busy while I listen. I follow every curve Dustin takes, all the inches he shaves off of the next guy's lead with every line he makes on the track. I could get lost in watching his details but I'm only halfway invested because of the conversation happening a few feet to my left.

"Oh, here, there, a little bit of everywhere." Colt coughs through his laugh and I note that my dad doesn't make a sound.

"I hear Trisha's got a job," he says.

"Mmm, yeah," my dad responds. Trisha's Dustin's mom. I've seen her a few times at school for pick up and drop off. Seems she's always working because every time Dustin spends the weekend at our house it's because his mom has a shift. She works at the gas station convenience store right off the highway. It's the only thing open twenty-four hours a day along the route up north.

"That's good. Good," Colt says.

I hold the binoculars out a fraction, giving myself enough space to look to my side and study Colt and his movements and expressions. He's jerky, his face constantly moving with these slight ticks, and he keeps stretching out his jaw, moving the bottom half of his mouth around as if it's some independent piece he can snap in and out of place at will.

I miss Dustin's next pass at our curve because I'm so busy inspecting the man who's supposedly his father. I refocus my attention to the track but my ear stays tuned on the conversation taking place next to me. My dad sounds angry. Not *irate* angry, the way he gets when Tommy comes home with an F or when one of us leaves the milk out on the counter, but a low-key kind of simmer . It's obvious my dad doesn't like Colt. But his tone says more than simple dislike—I get the feeling my dad doesn't trust him, which makes me not trust him either.

"He's making a move," Tommy shouts back toward us over his shoulder. My brother's moved closer to the track and I join him, abandoning my eavesdropping in favor of rooting on my friend.

"Come on, Dustin. Come on!" I growl loud enough for Tommy to hear but nobody else. Not even Dustin, this time. He's going too fast to hear anything other than his own voice telling him what to do, where to cut, and how to get what he wants.

This is when he's at his best. Two laps. Eleven turns on the track. Three cars in front. In theory, he's only racing the clock right now. It's a qualifying heat. But for Dustin, there's always someone to fight, to be better than.

My dad moves into the space next to me, and I breathe out a short sigh in relief. Short, because Colt steps in on my father's other side. He hasn't moved on or gone to watch from somewhere else. He's settled in. Attached himself. As if he's maybe staying awhile.

A long stretch of straightaway points right at us, and I count in my head the turns Dustin has left before he heads our way. My brother's fists are clenched, as if he's guiding the kart himself, holding the steering column taut and praying the tires hold their path.

"Come on, Dusty. Come on," my brother grits out.

I hold my breath as our friend finishes the final turn and manages to gain half a length on the kart in front of him. The euphoria is fleeting. Dustin never makes eye contact with us while he's driving. It's been that way since he hopped behind the wheel in their very first kart and practiced driving down our street. He's always been a natural, focused to a fault. But something has his eyes today. Through the slit in his helmet, I can tell his eyes are not narrowed on the road. They're locked on us—or rather, the man standing alongside us.

My brother somehow knows Dustin's speed and angle are off and calculates the situation with only a second or two to spare.

"Fuck!" Tommy breaks into a sprint just as Dustin's tire clips the back end of the kart he's chasing. He lost the ground he'd gained the moment he saw Colt, but he didn't ease up on the gas to avoid the wreck. It was inevitable, almost purposeful.

Our kart rides up the back end of the leading kart, taking it out of the race along with Dusty. His arms flex and his body fights to right the spinning vehicle that's now cutting through dry grass and kicking up gravel on its path toward the protective bank of hay bales. The impact is swift, sending hay in all directions and the scent of burnt rubber and fuel into the air. The race managers are on-scene a second before my brother reaches the kart, where he works quickly to yank our friend free of the safety harness. I must have been rushing toward them without realizing, because by the time Dustin's pulled his helmet from his head and thrown it, I'm close enough to pick it up from the ground.

"Dude, what happened? Was it the tire? Something on the track?" My brother hits Dustin with a barrage of questions, but it's a ploy to stall him from what I'm sure we all feel is coming.

Dustin breaks into a run, charging the man who calls himself his dad, this stranger named Colt who showed up out of nowhere and claimed he was invited. Colt doesn't even flinch as Dustin closes the distance between them, his palms landing in the very center of the man's chest. The impact knocks Colt off balance, but rather than get angry and come back at Dustin with a shove of his own, he stretches his arms out wide and begins to laugh.

"This isn't good," Tommy says at my side, moving his eyes from me to the scuffle happening a few dozen feet away. Most of the track is watching us now—watching Dustin. His neck burns red from the blood flowing through his veins, and his cheeks puff with heavy breathing. His dark hair pokes out in crazy curls that jut in all directions thanks to the sweat caused by his helmet, the helmet I'm glad I'm holding for him. I think if it were in his hands, he'd launch it right at Colt's face.

"What's this greeting, son? I thought you *wanted* me to come watch you race?" Colt's hands are still out at his sides, as if proving to all of us witnesses that he's the innocent good guy.

"That was when I was seven!" Dustin shouts.

"Dust—" My dad reaches out to touch his shoulder, to

calm our friend. Dustin cuts him off and slaps my father's hand away.

"No! Who invited this guy? Who told him where to go? Was it you, Tom?" Dustin rocks on his feet as his eyes dart from Colt to my dad, as if he's holding a gun on everyone who feels a threat.

"I did." Tommy speaks up next to me. It's times like this when I realize how much we look alike. Our freckles seem to pronounce themselves when we're guilty, and it's hard to hide the red that flushes our cheeks when we're nervous.

My stomach sinks at my brother's confession. There is clearly so much I don't know. I instantly feel betrayed and left out. Our triangle is not equal; my brother is included in parts of Dustin's life that I'm not. There are secrets they keep, and there are promises my brother has broken—is breaking. Right now.

"You . . . what?" Dustin's head falls slightly to the side and his eyes droop even as his chest puffs violently with a new panicked round of breathing.

"I didn't mean to, Dust. I wanted him to go away. It was last week, when you were at the shop, and I was waiting with your mom. I—"

Dustin's eyes grow wild, the centers dark and his focus roaming around the space between everyone but never stopping for long on someone's face.

"You . . . saw Mom?" he finally manages to question, stepping close to Colt again.

"I mean, it's my house, isn't it? I paid for it and all," Colt says, reaching to his back pockets and pulling a cigarette pack from one side and a lighter from the other. Holding the pack to his teeth, he pulls out a cigarette and holds it between his lips while cupping his mouth to block the breeze from the flicker of his lighter. A few short puffs generate a circle of smoke that he blows into Dustin's face.

"Why would you tell him about the race?" I mutter to my brother.

"Shut up! You have no fucking clue about any of this," Tommy says, turning his sour expression on me.

"Hey!" my dad pipes in, poking his enormous finger into the center of my brother's chest. The move sucks all the boldness out of my brother's act, but he's still too set on not admitting to anything wrong to apologize to me. My dad grabs the shoulder of Tommy's sweatshirt and pushes him back several steps, probably to create space between us. The two of them try to focus on the wreckage instead.

"Paid for it," Dustin finally laughs out. His hands are still balled into fists at his sides, but a smile has spread into his cheeks, the dimples deep on both sides, a complete opposite expression from the tears welling in his eyes.

"Yeah, I *paid* for it," Colt puffs out through smoke, only using one side of his mouth to talk. "Some fuckin' race there, sport. You're a little too old to be playing around with cars, aren't you?"

"What, should I be selling dope like good ol' Dad?" Dustin fires back.

The words silence those of us close enough to hear. They silence the air around us, the bugs and birds living in the grass blades, and the thin branches of the desert trees nearby. They silence my heart. They break it, for my friend.

The only preface to the hand landing on Dustin's cheek is the quick flex in Colt's jaw just before he cocks his arm and swings his palm at his son's head.

"You gonna make a living doing this shit? Take care of your mom with this? Riding on lawnmowers?" Colt punctuates each insult with another slap of his hand. Each time, Dustin takes it. His knuckles whiten at his sides as his fingers curl tighter with every strike.

"Stop it!" I cry out as one more blow lands on my friend's face. His eye is already swollen from the one before.

Colt laughs at my plea, but it's enough of a pause to give Dustin the breath he desperately needs to catch. Shoving past his father, he storms up the hill, swinging his feet over the embankment and past my wagon on his way back to the camper and trailer—back home.

I blink away the vision of him ducking between the cars parked closest to the track and let the panic I've been holding off settle into my chest with a quaking breath.

"Probably a good time to move along, Colt," my dad says to Dustin's father. The two of them stare at one another, my dad's face hard as stone and his mouth a perfect line while Colt merely smirks as his cigarette collects ash where it dangles from his lips.

Not wanting to be the reason my dad holds in his temper, I decide to chase Dustin for once. I pick up my hoodie and binoculars and sprint up the same path my friend took, climbing over the small wall and dropping my things in the wagon. Nothing I own is worth more than the hurt I think my friend is feeling right now.

"Dustin?" I shout his name as I cut through the lines of trucks and minivans. I step over hitches and when I reach our truck, I step up on our trailer to get a better view of the parking lot or the road leading back to the highway. I wouldn't be surprised to see Dustin walking home—despite the two hundred miles that walk entails.

"Hannah." Dustin says my name as if he's about to ask me to pass the rolls at the dinner table. I leap down from the trailer and follow the sound around to the other side of our camper where my friend is sitting on the wheel well with his forehead in his hands. He lets go as I step up, his fingers widening enough for him to meet my gaze through them as his palms slip away. The whites of his eyes are a bright pink and his cheeks are streaked with muddy lines from the tears he doesn't want anyone to know fell. They cut over deep bruises, and his busted lip weighs heavy on the bottom of his face.

"You're hurt," I say, such a dumb and obvious observation. He chuckles, but within seconds the shaking of laughter turns to sobs. I step up to him in time for him to stand and wrap his arms around me. Dustin holds me so tightly that his arms seem to wrap around me twice, his lips quivering against my bare shoulder. I'm sure the blood from his lip is staining the strap of my tank top, but I don't care. Tommy may know more of Dustin's secrets, but I know the important ones. I won't ever tell anyone he cried like this. Just as I won't let go until he's done.

FOUR YEARS LATER

"You ready to blow out your candles?" Tommy holds a pan filled with yellow cake and fudge icing in front of me. Behind him, my parents, cousins, and friends are all gathered, singing to try and embarrass me. My brother is just tired of holding my dessert.

I force my smile in place. I'm seventeen today—the same age as the boy I love, but only for the next six weeks. Dustin turns eighteen at the end of next month, and then I'll go back to being his best friend's baby sister. Flirting will be inappropriate because some law somewhere states those ten and a half months make kissing someone illegal. I'm probably imagining things between us anyhow—the lingering hand on my arm, the thigh pressed against mine in the back of the truck during long rides, the few times I've caught him staring at me in the one class we have together.

If there's anything there to believe in at all, Dustin would be here right now, standing alongside everyone else important in my life. He'd be up front, in the most important place. But he's not. He hasn't been around for days. And I'm a foolish girl with a crush caused by years of proximity and shared experiences. I'm the victim of biological and social science, and that is all.

"Happy birthday, dear Hannah. Happy birthday, to youuu!"

I close my eyes and blush with my smile as everyone drags out the end of the song. I inhale and pause, filling my lungs to blow out the seventeen candles Tommy randomly spread around the cake Mom made. I open my eyes and blow while my head swivels from side to side, spraying the fudge topping with my germs. This is an incredibly stupid tradition, but since it's my cake, joke's on everyone else, I guess.

"What'd you wish for?"

His familiar voice sends a rush of goose bumps down my spine, up my neck, and over my shoulders, pouring down the center of my chest like warm liquid. I've gotten good at hiding this reaction from the rest of the world, but I savor the way it feels. As for hiding the playful banter that's become a habit between Dustin and me, that's another thing.

"Aw, now, if I tell you, it won't come true," I tease. I

catch my brother's glare as I turn to face our friend. Tommy is constantly reminding me that Dustin is not the sort of guy I should doodle about on my notebook with hearts and arrows. He's right; Dustin's not. He's the guy who keeps me up at night with worry, the one who makes every other boy at North Highland High look juvenile and weak, and the only one I think about when I make wishes over fire and cake.

What my brother means is the three of us are friends and that's as far as everything goes, not that I'm much of a part of their anything anymore. High school, it changed those dynamics. So did Colt moving back in.

"Happy birthday, Hannah." Dustin holds out a small plastic bag from the drug store, a last-minute purchase that he probably grabbed before racing over here for cake. I should be offended, but I'm just glad he showed up.

My eyes slide up the length of his chest, up the wrinkled collar of his button-down shirt that only barely masks the deep red marks left behind from someone's hand—a chokehold, I'm guessing. I've taught myself not to linger on these marks. It only pushes Dustin away when I notice them. I don't *dare* speak of them.

"For me? You shouldn't have," I say, putting on a fake southern accent as I touch my free hand to my chest, a gesture to show how touched I am.

The contents of the bag jingles, so I figure it's something like an Arizona keychain or a flashlight-slash-glitter pen. My parents have taken the cake away, and most everyone in the room has lined up to get a piece. Even at seventeen and eighteen years old, cake is a hit. My brother is just over my shoulder, so I keep the act up as I reach into the bag and pull out my gift, which it turns out is nothing I expected.

Tiny copper pipes are tied together, each one dangling from a swirled blue and gold metal wire that's balled up to look like the moon. A faint, haphazard melody sounds as the small pipes clink into one another. The entire piece is the size of my palm, but the sound it produces is magical.

"Do you like it?"

My eyes drift from the miniature chimes to the boy who brought them. Hazel eyes, tired from never getting sleep, sit deep amid the sharp lines of his face. The baby fat that I used to pinch on Dustin's cheeks disappeared two years ago, and now his skin is smooth, minus the rough scruff that grows in every two days. His lips raise on one side, pushing into his cheek and carving out the dimple that reminds me I know this boy. It's the one thing that has remained the same on a face that has grown and survived and changed.

"I do," I answer.

This wasn't some gift bought at a drugstore last minute. I don't have to ask him to know. Dustin made this. He made it for me. The moon and stars and the sound of angels. Something I bet he's proud of and embarrassed by all at once.

Maybe I am not imagining things after all.

2

Dustin
Bridges

My house smells like toxic acid and smoke. Like embers ground into old carpet and covered with baking soda bought at the dollar store. I can't stand sleeping here, and I rarely do. When I'm not spending the night with the Judges, I'm usually in my car. I'd rather take my chances sleeping in the back seat of a Supra than sleeping under a cloud of whatever shit Colt's cooked up.

Sleeping in the car takes care of two things, actually. One, I've got some distance from Colt and my mom, and two, I can keep a close eye on my car. Colt's "friends" tend to steal shit, and they're savvy enough to know my car's worth more than it looks like it is. Especially in parts.

Colt isn't here today, and it's the only reason I can slip inside my own damn home to take a shower. I usually end up taking those at school in the locker room or at the Judges'. Lately, though, it's gotten weird with Hannah only a room away. We had a bathroom run-in last week when she opened the door I'd forgotten to lock. I couldn't care less that she saw me naked, but Tommy sure cares a lot. I never would have told him about it because it legit only lasted a second, but he happened to be walking down the hall at the perfect time to catch it for himself. He says I did it on purpose. I didn't. He's just being the protective big brother.

"That you, Colt?" My mom's nodding in and out of consciousness on a sofa that's so rotted and stained by her bad habits that homeless people would reject it if I took it down to the shelter.

"It's Dustin. Just taking a shower. Don't worry, I'll be gone in two minutes." I don't bother to stick around for her response because I know she's just going to ask me to make her a shot or grab her pills.

My mom's an addict. I don't know her as anything other than an addict, besides the few short years Colt was gone and she was semi-sober. She never fully pulled it off, but she was at least able to hold down a job and be present for me, make me breakfast and shit. She smoked a lot, and I hated that everything I owned smelled of nicotine. I'd trade that for the constant chemistry invading my clothes now. I keep most of the things I wear in my duffel bag in the back of my car, and I have a lot of clothes in Tommy's room. Sometimes when I'm there overnight I run a load of laundry. I've gotten good at squatting.

Yesterday was Hannah's birthday. I could tell she was a little pissed I was late, even if she pretended it didn't bother her. A person can't know someone for most of their life and not be able to read their expression. For me, Hannah's pretty much a large-print book, and she wears her emotions clear as day, no matter how hard she tries to hide them. I had a deal on a new intake for my car and had to meet the guy at a diner halfway between home and Flagstaff. I'd forgotten to take Hannah's gift with me when

I left so I had to stop back home to get it before making it to her party. I probably should have kept it in my car anyhow; there are a lot of copper strips on that thing and if Colt knew I had it, he'd sell the scrap.

It took me a month to find those pieces at work, and my hours at the tow and scrap yard are limited, so the good finds are pretty well picked through by the time I get on shift on Sundays. I think the piece turned out nice, though. I'm not sure Hannah remembers, but there was a wind chime like that at the cabin we stayed in when we raced in Colorado last year. Some artist made it and called it *Moon and Stars*. Hannah said it sounded like angels, and Tommy and I made fun of her for being so sappy. I felt bad and wanted to buy it for her to make up for it, but the thing cost like two hundred bucks or some shit. Mine's not art, but I think she got the sentimentality.

I speed through my shower, lathering up and not even bothering to rinse all the shampoo from my hair. I'll shove a hat on my head and take a dip in the Judges' pool later. Whatever it takes to get out of here before Colt comes back.

I don't even bother to walk through the house on my way out, instead opting to stuff what I need for the next few days in my backpack and crawl through my window. Good thing I do, too, because I see the back of Colt's piece of shit truck idling at the side of the house the minute I toss my stuff in the passenger seat of my car.

My phone buzzing in my back pocket, I round my car and make sure I get inside before answering. I hate that I'm still somehow afraid of that son-of-a-bitch. I quit calling him Dad when I was three, the first time I saw him put a fist in my mom's face. That little act of defiance earned me the first beating I can remember.

Key comfortably in the ignition, I answer my phone on speaker while I crank the engine.

"Yo, you're late," Tommy says. He has a thing about punctuality. I think it's because he's never faced much adversity in his life. It gets harder to be on time for things when you have a lot of crazy shit in your way.

"I stopped at the house to grab a shower. On my way now," I answer, flinching as a half-empty bottle of God knows what crashes against my windshield, busting it into a spider web of glass.

"Fuck!" I shout, my blood's temperature instantly hot enough to burn me from the inside.

"Dude, what was that?"

"Hang on," I say, tossing the phone in the passenger seat. Tommy's questions are going to have to wait.

I get out of my car to pick away the green bottle remnants from my hood while I survey the damage. A few scratches and chips in a paint job I plan to redo aren't the worst of it, but my windshield is trash. I toss the biggest shards into the gutter and turn to catch Colt's wasted smirk as he wipes his sleeve across his nose then extends his arm and points his finger at me. He holds it there, and all I want to do is run up to him and break it off —break *him*.

"I have to pay for that!" I shout, as if he gives a shit.

Leaning forward and off balance, he spits into the gravel and falls back on his heels before turning toward the house where he'll take my mom down to even lower depths of hell. I've quit trying to be her hero. It's not my job. I wish the Judges would take me in full-time, adopt me or some shit, but I get the feeling Tommy doesn't want that. We've never talked about it, but it's the feeling I get, and going down that path might mess things up. Whatever.

I'll be eighteen in six weeks and then I can rent my own place, work on the car, and build my brand.

Tommy's hung up already, so I leave my phone in the seat and take off fast enough to spit gravel at the trailer I've come to hate with a fiery passion. It takes less than twenty minutes to get to the Judges'. Life twenty minutes away from the highway is a lot different than the trailer park I live in under the service station's neon lights. Tommy's already working in the garage when I pull up, so I follow the curve to the side of the house where the floodlights should let us work into the night.

Tommy holds his palms out as I pull up, his face bunched up as his mouth hangs open. I kick open the car door before coming to a full stop, slap my work boot to the ground and let it slide to a stop along with the car. I push the gear in park but leave it running, my body still hot from my encounter with Colt.

"Dad's home," I say, waving my hand at the busted glass. Tommy's already leaning forward to look at the nicks on the hood.

"Dude, bigger problems than the paint," I huff, threading my hands behind my neck while I pace around my car.

My friend tilts his head up with a scowl. He hates when I take my anger out on him. It happens a lot, so I guess he has a right to be sick of it.

I walk a few long paces toward the street, bend forward with my hands still gripping the back of my neck and let out a deep growling scream. There's a crack in the Judge driveway that zigzags right between my legs, so I stare at it while drawing in several deep breaths before righting myself and heading back to Tommy and my busted windshield.

"Sorry." I apologize a lot.

"We're gonna need to get it fixed. I mean, unless you want to take Hannah's car to the drag races Friday night." His famous honest, straight line cuts across his mouth, and I roll my eyes.

"It might cost less to rig up her sedan than do everything I need to do to this thing," I say, kicking the rubber of my back tire. My foot rebounds hard because the tires are new, something Tommy reminds me of as I do it, as if I'm actually considering taking Hannah's car out to the straights.

"Looks like I'm selling the intake to pay for some glass. Unless . . . ya know . . ." I leave the hint out there, already knowing the answer.

"Are you serious? I'm not buying a windshield for a car I don't even drive, Dust. I'm sorry, but I'm staring down at college."

"Yeah, yeah." I wave my hand and flash a short smile. "No, I get it."

Tommy swears he's sticking with me for the racing season. We're a team. But the more he brings up school after this summer, the less I feel I'll be able to count on him. My stomach tightens at the thought of Tommy bailing on me, but I try hard not to let it color how I see him. He's not Colt. My dad left because he's a ruthless asshole. Tommy's smart and has goals. It's just . . . our goals were always in sync until last year. He brought up business school out of nowhere. Makes sense, though. If we get big and incorporate in a couple of years, he can run the business end and I can focus on driving and hiring a crew.

I round my car and flip open the trunk, pulling out my bag and the intake manifold so I can clean it up nice and get it ready to sell. I catch the oil rag Tommy tosses my way just as the air fills with the sound of heavy bass. My mouth curls from the sound of Hannah's car thumping its way up the driveway. Tommy and I installed the stereo system for her when her parents bought the Buick for her at an auction last year. It's the only thing about her mom-car that kicks any ass, and has not gone to waste—the girl has no shortage of tunes queued at all times. I swear she does it just to drive her mom nuts when she pulls in.

I drop my bag to the ground and set the manifold on the towel so I can hold my hand over my chest and thump my palm against my body with the beat of her latest musical choice. She leaves the car running for a few extra seconds when she spots me, rolling her window down and pumping her fist.

"Come on, Dustin. Show me your moves!" She tilts her head back in laughter, and her friend Bailey leans over her lap to shout at me through the window too.

"Dance! Dance! Dance!"

It's impossible to ignore the request, and frankly, the attention is a nice distraction. I flip my Pro Racing Gears hat around backward and bust into the only moves I've got. I've always had a natural sense of rhythm, and girls seem to be into the way I dance. Tommy says I look like those asshats on Magic Mike. If I do, I'm fine with it because those dudes raked in the money.

Hannah jets from her car to join me for an impromptu driveway dance-off, turning around to pull off the ultimate distraction. Girl might be *like* a sister to me, but she's not *actually* my sister, which means when she bends forward in her ripped up denim shorts and curves her back as she stands and leans her shoulder blades into my chest, I react in all of the ways any male who's into girls would.

"Ohhhh!" I say with a tilt of my head, backing away and

fanning myself with my hat. It embarrasses her when I tell her she's hot. It also pisses Tommy off, which is the real reason I do it. I guess that move was too far, though, because the music cuts just before I threaten to tug my black tee up and over my head for the full Channing Tatum. I let go of my collar and jerk my head around to catch my friend's death stare.

"We gonna sell this part or what?" His eyes flit from me to his sister as he marches toward her and tosses her keys at her chest. She claps them against her body, frozen in place with a locked jaw and open mouth.

I lean forward and brush my fingertips on her elbow.

"Sorry," I mouth when our gazes meet.

Her mouth falls shut and her eyes blink rapidly as she shakes her head.

"It's fine," she breathes out, shoving past me to join her friend, who is now getting out of the passenger seat.

"We going?" Tommy asks. He's already got the part in his hands and has shined it up decently with the rag.

"Wow, got a hot date or something?" I'm deflecting because I know *exactly* what that's about. Thing is, I'm not the guy he needs to protect Hannah from. Plenty of dudes at our school are into her, and none of them are worth shit.

"Something like that," Tommy lies, getting into my passenger seat, leaving my duffel bag on the ground by the garage. I kick it into a corner so nobody runs over it and get into the driver's side, thankful for the rumble of my engine and the blaring music I quickly crank up.

There's only one decent place to sell parts in this town, and I'll be lucky to get half of what I paid for it. Just as long as I can cover the windshield. My stripped-down bare bones insurance policy barely lets me take this thing on the road. I pull into the back lot for Earl's Garage, a total racket that takes advantage of people who get stuck off the highway on their way heading north. I'm about to get out when Tommy reaches over and grabs my arm.

"What the fuck was that?" he demands.

I pause with one leg out of the car and my eyes squint at the busy oil bays overcharging people a dozen feet away from us. Sucking in my lips, I prepare myself for his lecture and roll my head to the side to meet his stare.

"You need to relax, you know that? I was just trying to chill out and have fun, dance a little and goof around. I don't know, maybe get rid of this black pit burning a hole in my gut?" I rub my hand over my stomach while my face sours.

"Right. Right," he says through an unamused chuckle. He glances down at my part held in his other hand, his jaw flexing.

"You don't "goof around" with Hannah. That's not what you and Hannah are about." While I appreciate that he's not gripping my arm anymore, I don't love the air quotes he makes in my face.

I pucker my lips to hold in my own unamused laugh.

"I know, Tommy. She's family. That's all," I say.

He locks onto my eyes, studying them for a few breathless seconds.

"Is it?" he asks.

"*Pffft*," I spit out, not interested in indulging him further. I get out of the car and slam the door on him and this conversation. Unfortunately, he's persistent and has already gotten out of his side before I have a chance to put distance between us.

"What was that whole birthday gift thing about? You make that?" He's pushing me, and my patience wears thinner by the breath.

"Yup," I respond, lengthening my strides toward Earl and his crew of numb nuts.

"So, you took time to make, what, some piece of art or something? For my sister. For her birthday. Because . . . she's like family, right?"

Okay. This has to stop.

With an abrupt stop, I spin on my heels and shove my hands into my jeans pockets so I can form fists without Tommy commenting on them.

"Yeah, Tommy. She's like family. And she deserved something special from one of her oldest friends for her birthday. Hell, girl deserves diamond earrings and designer clothes and all that shit, but I can't give that to her. I got nothin', Tommy. I barely got this car. So yeah, I grabbed a bunch of metal at the scrap yard during work one night and made something out of it, because I literally couldn't give one of my oldest friends anything else. But thanks, Tommy. Thanks for shitting on it. Can we go sell this thing now so I can pay for a windshield?"

I grab the part from his hands and meet his eyes before leaving him several steps behind on my way into Earl's. If I looked at him any longer, he would have called my bluff. That's what Tommy does. He *reads* people. Reads situations and options and always makes the right choices. He'd see through my bullshit if I gave him the chance. Thing is, though, I've been buying into my own bullshit too. I spent weeks making that wind chime. And if we weren't dancing in a driveway in front of her brother, maybe—*maybe*—things would have gotten carried away. I've thought about it. But I always remind myself that Hannah Judge is family, and nothing else. And me? I'm Colt Bridges' bloodline. Nothing good could ever come from that.

3

"My brother can be a real asshole."

I swear my face still burns from his little show of power out in the driveway. At least Bailey's used to it. She gets a front row seat to most of the shit my brother pulls at home. When Tommy tries to put me in my place and play "big brother" in front of a group of people, like at school or a party, it stings a whole lot more.

I don't like the way he's gotten about me and Dustin hanging out. I feel as if he's trying to drive a wedge between us, and despite the feelings I've kept locked up in my chest for years, Dustin and I have always been incredibly close. Friends. There are truths that boy says to me that he cannot say to Tommy, or rather *would* not say. I know which bruises are from fights he starts and which are the result of sucker punches from Colt. And I know how much those lashes hurt inside.

"Tell me this, though." My friend collapses on her back into the billowing pile of comforters I never make on my bed. "Why is Dustin Bridges so goddamn sexy?"

I breathe out a laugh and turn my attention to my closet so I can strip out of my T-shirt and shorts and crawl into the soft joggers and oversized hoodie I'm more comfortable in. I can get away with agreeing with Bailey when she says stuff like that because there isn't a single person in a hundred-mile radius who would argue with it. I'm careful to always throw in the occasional "yeah, but he's like a brother to me" comment when it feels as if she suspects anything more is going on in my heart and head.

"You think they'll get that windshield fixed in time for the Straights on Friday?" Bailey asks.

I shrug, but I know there's no way they'll skip a race. Dustin would hotwire someone's ride to "borrow" for the night if he had to, just to show up and defend his streak.

Bailey loves tagging along with us when the boys drag race. She comes from a pretty strict family that doesn't believe girls should be exposed to the wonders of the world. She's been wearing makeup for the last year, but only because she puts mine on in my car every morning then scrubs her face clean before I take her home in the late afternoon. She's never spent the night at my house, at least according to her parents. She's gotten good at breaking out of her bedroom window after midnight and riding her bike to my house. It sucks that we have to sneak her back in before the sun rises. Her mom is always up by six, and she inspects every inch of that house as if waiting to bust her daughter. *If only Bailey's family knew the shit she gets to see when she sneaks out with me.*

"That's cute," Bailey says. I turn to find her pointing to the chime Dustin made me that I've hung from the curtain rod over my window. I temper my grin as I react.

"It is, isn't it? Dustin made it for me," I say, moving toward my window. I slide the glass open to let in a breeze and the chimes make a soft jingle, like tiny spoons tapping against glass.

"Think he'd make me one?" Bailey asks. I bristle and keep my back to her.

"I don't know, maybe." I close my window. I don't think he would, but that's because I think I'm special. The thought of him making her something he made for me turns my insides into a boiling, gooey sludge. My childish jealous side rarely rears its head, and I *never* let people see it.

"You should ask." Heat courses down my chest and swells my belly. I can't believe I said that out loud. What's worse is I know the reason I did. I want to test him, and I'm already internalizing all possible outcomes, including the crushing feeling of not being special at all to Dustin Bridges.

My friend and I spend the next few hours crash-studying for our biology mid-term that's coming up. Actually, for the first half hour, I'm lost in my thoughts, self-diagnosing my behavior and talking myself back into the neat little box I keep my feelings in. Even if my wildest fantasies came true and Dustin kissed me and told me he saw me as more than a friend, too, we would have to hide all of it from Tommy. My brother is barely supportive of me hanging out in public places with the guys in my grade. If he found out I had major feelings for our best friend, he might drive Dustin up north to the Grand Canyon and boot him from the passenger side while taking a tight curve.

With the dinner hour growing close, Bailey and I close our books and hope we've crammed enough into our brains to pull out B's on Mr. Ormand's test. He doesn't believe in giving A's, which is awesome for students like us who are trying to earn academic scholarships. And by awesome I mean a seriously dick move.

"You want to see if you can stay for dinner?" I ask, knowing Bailey won't even want to ask. She's already tucking in her T-shirt to make sure she looks presentable and up to her parents' standards when she walks in her front door. Her makeup came off the minute we hit my room. She doesn't even bother to answer, instead tilting her head to the side and leveling me with a straight mouth and heavy eyes.

"Your mom knows she doesn't get to go to college with us, right?" I help to pull back her bright blonde hair into a perfectly smooth ponytail at the base of her neck, the style she left the house with this morning. She laughs at my joke then glances over her shoulder. Our eyes meet briefly and widen; both of us are a little unnerved by that thought.

The house smells of garlic and oregano, my mom's pot of sauce already boiling on the burner in the kitchen. It's a rule in our house: we make time for family dinner at least twice a week. Weekends are so busy for the boys we usually shoot for weekdays. My mom loves to cook, and we all love to eat, so nobody messes with this unspoken law.

"Say hello to your parents for me, Bailey," my mom says as we pass through the kitchen.

"And tell them I said to lighten up," my dad jokes, earning a semi-swift right hook from my mom. "Ow! Kidding!" he adds.

My dad can't stand Bailey's parents. Not so much because of the way they raise their only child, but more because Bailey's dad went up against my dad in court a couple of years back and won. My dad says he's crooked, but I think that's probably just him being a sore loser. Mr.

and Mrs. Tingle are by-the-book on everything, even their church attendance. They never miss a Sunday.

My family? We'd be burned to a crisp by a swift bolt of lightning even stepping foot on the church campus. Not that that's why we don't go. We don't go because we'd rather be out at the track, and while we're all at the races, my mom is in her office doing mayor business. Someone has to run things in this town with a population of eleven hundred and four.

"You walking Bailey home?" Dustin cranes his neck, looking at me over his shoulder as I pass behind the sofa. He's in the middle of a video game with my brother, and he must be the one in control because the screen is paused and my brother just sighed.

"Yeah, I'll be right back." I slightly pinch my brow, wondering why he cares.

"I'm— I'll go with you. I gotta check something." Dustin tosses his controller on the sofa in the spot he vacates.

"*Psshh*, we're in the middle of a game!" My brother points to the screen, the scene some jungle area lit up with special night-vision goggles.

"Hey, Dad! Take my controller," Dustin yells. He's been calling our dad by that name since the day his own dad showed up at the Tucson track and made him crash. At first, I think it was simply a way to rebel and make Colt angry. Now, though, it's habit.

"On it," my dad says, abandoning my mom in the kitchen and hopping over the back of the sofa to join Tommy in the game.

My brother's stare lingers on Dustin as he heads through the front door, only shifting focus because I walk into the path of his gaze. He blinks away, and my stomach tightens like it does when I'm on the crest of a roller coaster's big drop. I shake the feeling off and shut the door behind us, noting the shine coming off of the new piece of glass on Dustin's car. He jogs ahead and works off the tape holding it in place, forming it into a ball that he tosses in his hands a few times before throwing it at me.

"Hey!" I squeal, jumping out of the way. Bailey picks it up and chucks it at Dustin to get him back for me as we walk down the center of the road toward her house. My friend has even less athletic talent than I do, though, so the makeshift ball sails off course, landing in the brush to the side of the road.

We keep the game going for the quarter-mile walk, Dustin finally shoving the tape ball into the back pocket of his jeans as he hangs back a few steps and lets me walk Bailey up the driveway.

"I hate that he thinks my parents don't like him," she says under her breath. Dustin knows his reputation, one he's labeled with mostly because of his family. But he hasn't helped it along with his string of suspensions and run-ins with the sheriff's department for fighting all over town.

"I'll remind him that your parents don't like anybody," I joke. My friend laughs, but it's a token one and I feel bad for picking on a reputation she doesn't deserve to be labeled with, either. "Hey, you know what I mean." I suck at apologies.

"Yeah, I know," she says. "It's just, if they see me with him, they will put cameras up in my room and probably hire a drone to follow me everywhere I go."

She gives me a sideways smile and we hug before she dips inside and refuses her mom a chance to greet her in the doorway. I skip back down her driveway and find Dustin leaning on one of the neighbor's many cars, hands in his pockets and ankles crossed.

"You thinking of buying that next?" I nod toward the rough-looking Crown Vic. Dustin's bought a few parts from the older man who lives at this house. The guy used to be a mechanic but now it seems he just collects automobile ghosts—shells of vehicles that were once great but have lost their verve and soul from either a wreck or major owner neglect.

Dustin pushes off from the car and rests his hand on the roof, patting it twice before letting his finger trace one of the rusted spots worn bare in the paint.

"Nah, not unless I want to enter a derby one day." His slight smile inches into his cheeks, making faint dimples that catch my eyes. My own smile itches at my lips. The only way I can make the feeling stop is to look away and even then, it takes a few seconds before I'm sure I won't turn bright pink.

"Thanks for walking with me," I say, timing my steps to line up with his. I falter purposely and brush into his side. He fakes a stumble and does it right back. This is how we flirt. It's been a year of this, maybe more. I live for it.

Our pace back to my house is half of what it was to Bailey's. We're stalling. Well, *I'm* stalling. Dustin isn't urging me to speed up, though. After a few silent, amazing seconds, he reaches over and lifts a lock of my hair, holding it out and letting it slip through his fingers until it falls back to my shoulder.

"You curled your hair today," he remarks, his eyes still on the wavy strand.

"Braids, actually. I slept in them."

"Ah." He nods.

I flit my gaze to the other side of the street so I can suck in my bottom lip and soak in the attention. It's cool enough outside that I'm glad I wore joggers and a sweatshirt, but I also wish I still had on the shorts I cut up last night. I liked the reaction I got from Dustin while wearing them. Not sure the cotton Hanes collection is going to earn me the same response. In fact, I can almost guarantee it won't. Still, this quiet attention . . . it's nice too.

"So, your windshield." I let the topic linger as we walk, desperate to keep talking to him about anything. The longer it takes him to respond, though, the more I regret focusing on something that probably stresses him out.

"Yeah, that's a bummer. I had to sell the intake to replace it." He glances to me sideways and lifts his shoulder, playing it off, but I can tell it's a big deal.

"That sucks. Dad's always getting nailed with rocks that the truckers kick up on the highway."

Dustin chuckles, straightening his arms as his hands push deep into his pockets. He tilts his head to the sky as his mouth hangs open with a hint of a smile.

"Yeah, I wish it was a rock. Would have probably lived with it for a while. Can't see through shattered glass left in the wake of one of Colt's cheap-ass beer bottles, though." His gaze falls back to the horizon as he puffs out a short, defeated laugh.

"Oh, Dustin, I didn't know. I'm sorry. I wouldn't have brought it up." I reach toward him and squeeze him at the elbow. His tight muscles soften under my touch, and the rigidness of his arm relaxes. I let go, but remember the way his warm skin felt on my fingertips.

"It is what it is." He says that phrase a lot, at least to me. It's the way he's always summed up his circumstances, and I used to argue with him about it, or encouraged him to find a way out. But as much as he says he doesn't care about his mom, she's the reason he hasn't run away completely. It breaks my heart to see him try so hard to save someone who doesn't want to be saved. Maybe that's also what makes me love him so much.

"Hey, so, you coming Friday?" He turns to walk backward so we're facing each other for the few hundred feet left before we reach my house. He's managed to ward off the tension forming a divot between his brows, instead lifting them high to match his forced smile.

"You know I don't miss a race," I say.

His lips pull in with a tight smile, bringing back the dimples.

"Good," he says, swinging an arm around my neck as he shifts to my side. I tuck my cheek against his chest and breathe in, memorizing my favorite smell of oil and body wash, hoping to capture enough to last me until I dream.

He pulls his hat from his head and pushes it down on mine while I walk alongside him, held to his side by his casually draped arm. If we were a thing, we would walk around like this all the time. I would demand it. His arm slips away, though, the moment our feet hit the gravel leading up to my house. I start to pull his hat from my head too, wanting to erase evidence before Tommy has a chance to call us out on it. Dustin doesn't let me, though, laying his palm over mine and gently nudging his hat back in place on my crown.

"Keep it. You look cute," he says with a wink.

I tug the bill down and glance at him from the shadow it makes over my eyes just as he pulls the tape ball from his back pocket and throws it at my chest. I manage to bat it away and rush toward the house, but he catches me by my midsection and swoops me into a circle before setting me on my feet, a little dizzy and full of butterflies. He abandons me where I stand the second my brother steps outside, and the two of them gather around the car to inspect the new windshield before climbing inside and revving the engine a few times.

I've watched Dustin act the way he does with me with other girls. I could easily talk myself into believing it isn't the same, but really . . . it kinda is. And that's the biggest reason I don't let myself get carried away. Pissing my brother off to be with Dustin would be one-hundred percent worth it, but only if I have a guarantee that I wouldn't break my own heart and lose a best friend all at the same time. So instead, I'll have to be satisfied with a cool trucker cap and a work of art that catches the breeze through my bedroom window.

4

Sometimes I crash on Tommy's floor. Tonight, I couldn't seem to make it off the Judges' couch. I'm not sure when exactly I fell asleep. Last thing I remember is getting into it with Tommy over some junior high kid who was trying to blow up our compound on *Combat Warrior*. He threw his controller and turned the game off in the middle of play then stormed off upstairs.

Someone turned the TV off and threw a blanket over me. It was probably Tommy's mom. When I was little, she used to tuck me in and call me her little burrito. I'd lay on the rollout in Tommy's room in that lock-tight position all night, not wanting to undo her work. I'd never felt so safe.

I roll to my back and kick the blanket away as I feel around for my phone to check the time. It's dark in the house, so I doubt it's past five. My phone flops to the carpet and I tap the screen to see 3:30 and a flurry of messages before my screen goes dark.

"Shit," I mumble. I haven't charged it all day.

I manage to get to my feet and stretch my arms toward

the still blades of the ceiling fan, brushing the wood with my fingertips as I grunt under my breath. My body is forever crooked. Just one night I'd like to experience sleep on an actual mattress with a real pillow and all of that memory foam crap. With my luck, my body would rebel and insist on curling itself into the twisted nightmare my spine is accustomed to.

I rub my eyes, my phone clutched in one fist. There are usually a couple of chargers plugged in around the kitchen, so I slide in my socks along the wood floors until I'm close enough to feel around the counter. My hand lands on someone's phone screen, stirring it awake, and the glow lights up the room enough to help me unplug it and start charging mine.

"You reading my text messages?"

The pink glittery phone case registers in my brain as Hannah's voice sounds behind me. I jump and spin around anyway, my heart racing to a thousand beats at getting caught.

"O-okay, we are going to need to put a bell on you," I whisper through nervous laughter. I hold her phone against my chest, my arms and legs still numb with the burst of adrenaline.

"Like a cat?" She holds a palm out for her phone. I hand it to her and match her crooked smile.

"Yeah, something like that."

My pulse settles back to its natural rhythm, but the beats still echo in my head. She's wearing an oversized T-shirt from one of the tracks we went to in Nevada. That shirt—it's it. That is all she is wearing. Her hair is split in two halves, each taking a shoulder. My hair? It's standing straight up in the air. I can feel it. And Hannah can see it. Her eyes have traveled slowly up my face, the corners of her mouth rising when my wild hair comes in view.

"Oh, I bet that's all kinds of crazy up there," I say, palming my head with one hand before running the fingers of the other through my hair in an attempt to tame things.

"It's electric," she says, her lopsided grin still in place.

"Yeah, I bet." I run both hands through my hair a few more times then give up. It is what it is.

"Trouble sleeping?" I lean against the counter, folding my arms over my chest. Hannah lifts herself up on the counter opposite me, sitting with her ankles crossed and her thighs exposed. My eyes can't help themselves, making a small trip over her bare skin before coming home to her face. I swallow hard and dig my nails into my sides as my arms grow more rigid around my own chest.

"I forgot my phone was out here. I woke up in a panic because I couldn't find it."

I nod and smile at her honesty.

"Sad how dependent we are on these things, right?" I tap my screen to the right on the counter, showing off the red battery icon.

"Yeah," she breathes out with a short laugh.

Her eyes hit mine and hold on for a few seconds. I'm not sure when looking at her became so challenging, but there's no denying that chemistry between us is different now. It's been this way for a while, and I'm not sure whether it crept up on me slowly or happened all at once.

Hannah is family. I have to keep reminding myself of those three important words.

"Were you warm enough?" She finally breaks the awkward quiet.

I furrow my brow, not sure what she means.

"You fell asleep on the couch. I covered you with my

blanket." She shrugs and her shoulders stiffen, almost as if she's nervous and wants my approval that my stay here on the sofa was top-notch.

"Yeah, it was cozy. Thanks," I say, relaxing the death grip I have on myself, moving my hands to the counter's edge. Hannah covered me up. I wonder how many times it's been her all along.

We exchange a few more awkward, tight-lipped smiles and she swings her legs forward and back with the building nervous energy. Her phone vibrates in her palm, giving both of us an out. I check the progress on mine while she reads her message. I'm trying to give her privacy but the heavy sigh that leaves her body brings my attention roaring back to her.

"What's up?" I say, setting my phone back down on the counter. Four percent isn't going to get me anywhere.

She's cupping her phone and staring at the message, so I step closer and nod, silently asking permission to read her text. She turns the phone around and holds it out for me. I pause right in front of her and take it in my hands. I'm not sure who this BOSA guy is, or why he's offering her fifty bucks, so I glance up with an arched brow.

"He wants me to take the bio test for him tomorrow. He sits right next to me." Her shoulders sag as if she has no choice in this matter.

"He's willing to give you fifty bucks to let him look at your paper?" Seems like a pretty sweet offer to me, but school's never really been my thing. Hannah's always been the smartest of our trio, which pisses Tommy off because he likes to think he's the one with the brains.

Hannah's head falls back with another heavy sigh, exposing the pale and tender skin of her throat. I catch my mouth hanging open at the sight. I right that shit before her chin falls forward and our eyes meet.

"It's not that kind of test. I'd have to write things. Like, I'd take his paper and put it under mine and do both tests at the same time, in different handwriting," she explains.

"Wow. That's— You can do that?" I joke.

She kicks her feet forward, her toes punching me in my thighs. I grab her still-crossed ankles in front of my body, but I'm careful to let go fast. Her gaze slips anyhow, so I take a step back to build in some distance. I keep her phone, though.

"I've done it before," she finally admits, glancing up at me through heavy lids. Her eyes slope at the sides with shame.

"Hey," I pipe in, swinging one hand forward and brushing my fingertips lightly over her knee cap. "Don't do that to yourself."

"Do what?" She shrugs.

"Beat yourself up for making a profit on your skills." I meet her gaze and hold on to it this time, unwilling to let go until she softens. Her lids flutter eventually and she blinks her focus off to the side.

"You think I would be hitting one-fifty in pitch black in the middle of nowhere every Friday night if I had smarts I could sell off instead?" I tilt my head to the side and wait for her eyes to come back to mine. When they finally do, we both quake with a short laugh and she nods.

"Yeah, Dust. I'm pretty sure you would," she teases, kicking her legs forward again. I'm too far away for her to do more than taunt me.

"You're right." I shake my head. "I probably would."

I glance down at her phone in my palm again.

"So who's BOSA?"

"You know him. Michael Bosa." She rattles out more details. "He's been in my grade since fourth. He's so lazy, but he plays baseball and if I didn't help him pass classes he would never be eligible."

"Oh. So this has been a long-term business arrangement." I meet her guilty eyes again. I hold up a palm when her shoulders begin to lift. "No, no. I'm not judging. I just think—"

"What? That I'm a pushover?" she blurts out. She's getting defensive.

"Hell, no!" That was probably a little loud, but I want my point to get across.

Hannah's eyes widen and she presses a finger against her smiling lips.

"*Shhh!*"

I glance around the corner to peer up the stairs, holding my breath for a couple of seconds. When I don't hear a sound or see lights come on, I come back to Hannah, letting myself stand a little closer than I was before.

Hannah's palms rest on either side of the counter and she's uncrossed her ankles. I probably would have noticed anyway, but she keeps flexing her feet then pointing her toes, drawing my eyes down. I wonder if she can tell that I'm not looking at her phone screen but instead the soft pink polish on her toenails.

"You just think . . ." she echoes my words from a minute ago. I shake out of my trance and glance up. She's leaning her head to one side and chewing at the inside of her cheek.

"Do you want to get out of this? Or do you want the money?" I lay her options out there, the way Colt would. I hate hearing myself talk like this but it's maybe the only good thing to come out of my unfortunate birthright. Colt doesn't get pushed around when it comes to business, and when he's done dealing with someone, he lets them know. What's strange is he isn't even that big of a guy. He just has these crazy eyes and wild behavior that signals he isn't the guy you mess with. I have those same vibes in me, when I want to show them.

"The money is nice." Her admission squeaks out and her cheeks redden as her shoulders lift back up to her ears and her gaze falls.

I touch two of my fingers to the soft spot under her chin and lift it gently, coaxing her focus back to me. Sliding my feet forward a few more inches, her knees part to let me in closer. Heat races up my chest and down my legs, my cock flexing with that familiar hunger. I'm not supposed to feel that with this girl, but goddamn, do I right now.

I hold my tongue against the back of my teeth and steady my breath, letting my eyes drift to her lips for just a second. How fast I could ruin everything. Her legs part more. I don't see it but I feel it at my sides. I know I'm smiling. Not like a huge boyish grin, but like a drunken high kind of smile. I feel it in my cheeks, even with my tongue pressed firming against the sharp edges of my teeth.

"I think it's time you raise your price," I utter.

My fingers slip from her chin to the phone I'm holding in the small space between us. I glance up to catch her waiting eyes.

"May I?" I ask.

"Mmm, yes," she rasps.

I'm not sure if either of us knows whether my question and her answer are about me kissing her or me typing a message on her phone. Part of me meant it both ways, and I'd bet my Supra so did she.

Hannah is family.

My tongue passes over my top lip and I drop my eyes back down. This is getting hard. *I'm* getting hard. My thumbs feel like swollen grapes, and I have no idea if they're going to work, but my brain tells them to type. Thankfully they get the message and sweep over her keyboard.

My price is $75 now.

I hit send and Hannah sucks in a sharp breath. We both stare at the flashing dots on her screen, and when this BOSA jackhole finally comes back with a short *OK*, we exhale in relief.

"Ha." She breathes out a short laugh in disbelief.

I let my grin stretch the width of my face and hand her phone back to her, proud of my negotiating skills, not that there was a lot of negotiating to do. It was common sense. Hannah must be the only game in town for cheating, at least for this dude. If he's desperate enough to pay five hunny, he'll pay six.

"Thank you!" she whisper shouts, flinging her arms around me and squeezing me in a bear hug.

I let her, but I'm all too aware of how this looks and the inevitable moment coming in five, four, three . . .

Her arms loosen but don't let go. She's still clutching her phone in one hand but the other is free, fingers able to unfurl and stop at the base of my neck, which they do. We separate but don't part, and her fingernails tickle against long hairs that curl at the base of my neck just as my hands part behind her back and retreat to her sides, then her hips and the tops of her thighs where her extra-large T-shirt suddenly feels incredibly small.

The sweetest breath escapes her lips as they part, and our eyes search amid the few inches between us until they meet. I feel the moment in the pit of my stomach, the kind of rush that I only ever get from crossing a finish line before everyone else.

Hannah is family.

My fingertips flirt with the hem of her shirt, rolling it up once, then twice. I'm testing how far she'll let me go. When her thumb traces a straight line down my neck, dipping under my shirt and scratching my skin in a way that is so far from two friends embracing, I know that at this very moment, there is no line for me to cross. That line doesn't exist. Not in this kitchen. Not right now.

The harsh reality of a door closing upstairs is the only thing that breaks us apart. And it happens fast.

I step back until my ass hits the counter's edge behind me, my hands diving into my pockets for safekeeping—like jail. Hannah slips down from the counter, her shirt rolling up enough on her way down that I glimpse the lacey pink panties she's wearing and the place where the fabric meets in the middle.

Fucking hell.

"Probably Tommy taking a piss," I say, running my palm over my face while she scurries around the corner. She pauses with her hand on the wall and looks over her shoulder, her eyes not completely coming to me, though. Her mouth hangs open, and I swear that bottom lip quivers.

"Thanks, Dustin," she finally utters.

"For what?"

Her eyes flit to me briefly, and she smiles on the side I can see.

"For getting me what I'm worth." She winks then ducks around the corner, racing up the stairs before that bathroom door opens again.

I wait until the upstairs is completely silent again

before I unplug my phone, borrowing the cord to take it out to my car to finish charging. No way I'm going back to sleep now. I'm too jacked to sort through and settle the bets coming in via text for Friday's races, let alone sleep. I turn my key partway and shift my car into neutral, extending my leg out the door to kick my way backward down the driveway without rumbling the entire household awake. I stop when the tires dip into the street and I flick the headlights on to check the status of Hannah's window. Curtains are drawn, and I'm not sure how I feel about it. It's better if she doesn't chase me, though, because I'll get caught. Willingly. And that will fuck everything up.

I turn the key fully in the ignition and shift into drive, leaving the Judge house in the dust. Hopefully, I didn't wake anyone on my way out. Even if I did, that's a small price to pay to keep myself from blowing up the only family I have.

5

Seventy-five bucks feels good in my hands. It also feels dirty. Michael Bosa didn't do shit to earn that C I got him on the bio test today. And yeah, I earned him a C instead of a B because this scam only works if I make it believable. I don't think he's ever gotten a grade higher than C in his entire life. The B is for me, and only because A's don't happen in here.

Honestly, what does it matter? Is forcing him to understand the differences between DNA and RNA going to somehow make him something other than a shortstop destined to flunk out of the college that picks him up? Probably not. And now, I'm seventy-five bucks richer.

I don't know why that intake thing is important, but it meant a lot to Dustin that he was finally able to get it, and have it installed by Friday. *This* Friday, for whatever reason. The idea to get it back for him struck me after I left him in the kitchen last night.

After he helped with my negotiation.

After we almost—

Bailey is always the last one out of class, which means my car is the last one out of the school lot. Normally, it's fine, because we don't have anywhere to go. But today, I'm kinda in a hurry.

I stand on the hood of my car when I catch a glimpse of her hair in the last crowd of students spilling out the south exit. Dialing her number again, I hold my phone against my ear while waving my other hand in the air.

"Hello!" Logan, this jock asshole I have had way too many classes with, shouts, waving back while approaching me. He knows I'm not signaling for him, but the football players at this school like to think everything is about them. He sees it as an opening, which would be fine if his next move wasn't going to be something totally aggressive or demeaning. His dumb smile is way too eager, so I lower my hand as I glare at him and flip him off before he gets too close.

"*Pshh*, fine. Fuck off then, Hannah Banana." He has also called me that since fourth grade. He waves me off while his friends laugh and shove him off balance. I do my best to ignore the entire scene while they purposely slap the side of my car while they pass.

"Hey, what's up?" Bailey finally answers.

"Hurry. There's someplace I need to go." I wave again while I bounce on my toes.

"Are you on your car?" She's still walking slow, which is infuriating because beyond me telling her to hurry, clearly she can see I'm trying to rush her along.

"Yes, Bails, I'm on my car. I'm trying to get you to hurry!" I shout into the phone.

"Fine, geesh." She hangs up on me but breaks into a jog which is a fair trade for making her a little bit mad.

I hop down from my car's hood and get in, starting it

up and backing out of my spot so I'm primed to get into the exit line. I take off toward it before my friend has a chance to shut the passenger door.

"Jesus, Hannah!" Bailey whines, over-exaggerating her fall toward me while she tugs her door closed.

"Sorry. We're on a mission." I pull my sunglasses from the visor and slip them on while we roll our windows down. I don't have air conditioning in this thing, which is fine for half the year, but when the Arizona weather warms up, it's downright brutal. In March, the weather is still close to perfect, so the windows go down the second we go anywhere.

"Okay, I forgive you," my friend says. I swivel my head and meet her pursed lips and dimmed eyes. After a few seconds of silence, I bust out a laugh and squeeze her hand.

"I'm sorry. You're right," I admit. "I'm anxious, and I totally took that out on you."

Her mouth curves just enough to soften her eyes, and soon, she's laughing with me and squeezing my hand back.

"Okay, so what's this mission? Where are we headed?" she asks.

I hand her the receipt from Earl's.

"Oh, fun. An oil change place, *yay*." Her words drawl out to showcase her sarcasm.

"I need to buy something . . . for the boys," I say, stumbling on my words. I almost said "for Dustin."

"Can't they buy their own crap? I have to be home in an hour." She's already pulled the makeup wipes out from my backpack and is clearing her face of mascara and lipstick. She's just as pretty this way, but I wouldn't dare stop her from putting on my makeup every morning. It makes her so happy to have this tiny act of rebellion. Between this, borrowing some of my outfits, and crawling out her window on Friday nights, Bailey can survive all of the stern formalities that come along with life in her household.

"This one's a surprise," I say.

She flips the mirror closed on her visor then pushes it up to the roof.

"A surprise, huh?"

I can feel her eyes on me.

"Yep," I say, forcing my cheeks not to burn and my mouth to remain loose as I maintain a casual smile.

My friend snickers while I scan for traffic, pulling myself close to the steering wheel as I leave the student lot.

"Uh huh," she finally says.

"What?" I flash her a quick look, lifting my right shoulder.

I'm so busted.

"You're getting something for Dustin. Don't you lie to me, Hannah Lee Judge."

I cringe at the utterance of my middle name. She's broken out the secret warfare, and that tone, the one that's a little melodic. The one a smart-ass know-it-all would use.

I wrinkle my nose and squint my eyes, shaking my head to stretch out the lie. It's useless, though, because the moment my eyes meet hers, she cackles at my lame attempt.

"Girl, you are buying a present for a cute boy. There's nothing wrong with that, so quit trying to cover it up." She lightly pushes my shoulder.

I halt the car at the stoplight a block from campus and breathe out a heavy sigh. My shoulders sag. If Bailey can see through my façade, there's no way I'll be able to hide this from my brother.

"Okay, fine. But it's not like that. I swear."

I lie.

"I feel bad because Dustin's dad broke his windshield and he had to sell this part to pay for the replacement, and I know how important it was. I have the money, so . . ." I shrug.

"It's sweet," Bailey says.

"Yeah?" I lift a brow.

She nods.

I breathe in through my nose to ease the tightness in my chest. It has little effect. I have to ignore the feeling, though, and push on. It takes about ten minutes to get to Earl's, and I know the guys there are going to be a pain in my ass. I try to build up my pretend courage and arm myself with the bluster my dad and brother have taught me from years at the track. This scene—the shop, the track, the cars themselves—is very much a man's world. I fully expect the guys on shift today to try to take advantage of me and pocket the extra cash. I did not do two assignments and a test for Michael Bosa for nothing, though, and this one-seventy-five that I've saved up is the exact amount I need to reclaim that part for Dustin.

"You ready?" I turn to my friend.

Her eyes widen and she shakes her head.

"What? I'm not robbing the joint. I'm spending my money." I hold the wad of cash out as proof. I jacked one six-pack of beer from the corner market two months ago, and now Bailey thinks I'm a hardened criminal. I did it on a dare from my brother, and frankly, the way Dustin looked at me after made me wish I hadn't. I didn't even drink any of it at the party we went to.

Most of the guys in this place at least recognize me. I roll my shoulders back and punch my feet into the ground with my stride. I know how much Dustin got for the part. I dug the exchange receipt out of our dumpster. My lucky day, Earl seems to be off. The rest of the guys working for him are young and malleable. They have no idea I'm seventeen, and if I say things just right, they really don't care. I catch a faint whistle leaving someone's lips as I enter the bay.

"Hannah." Jim, the oldest one next to Earl at all of twenty-six, stops what he's doing under some Camaro hood and wipes his hands on a rag on his way to me.

"I'm here for the intake manifold my boys sold to Earl?" I've used the right words; the question at the end is an added dose of sweetness.

"What'd Dustin do, cheat a bunch of fools out of cash on the Straights to buy it back?" He turns his back to me and moves toward the counter. I pull my lips in tight and swallow the defensive comebacks I'd like to say. Jim's bent because he's lost to Dustin a dozen times. He's a shitty driver, but he refuses to see that.

"I'll be using my own money, thank you." I slap the cash on the counter as he turns around, unraveling the part from the plastic bag Dustin brought it in with. He sets the part down close to him and pulls my money into his permanently oil-accented hands.

"You're short fifty."

Bailey swallows hard enough that I can hear it over my shoulder. She's not a fan of conflict. I'm impressed that Jim's actually trying to pull one over on me like he does all the other clueless people who come into this joint.

"Yeah? You wanna sell me a new air filter while you're at it, Jim?" I level him with the same straight-mouthed glare he's giving me, and after a five-second stand-off he breaks our connection and shakes his head.

"Shit, fine. Take it," he mutters, cashing out the drawer. "Earl's gonna have my ass for being soft."

"Again," I mutter under my breath. I raise my voice as I edge out the door with my prize. "Yeah, but you're a good person and Earl's a real asshole, Jim!"

I bless the boys with my swaying hips as I march back out of the garage, Bailey rushing along in my footsteps. We break into a major case of giggles when I leave the lot.

"That Jim guy really likes you, and yet really hates you," Bailey observes, pulling her mirror back down to make sure she's completely free of any signs that she's a typical teenager.

"He hates the three of us—me, Tommy, and Dustin. Next time he's there on a Friday, I'll point his car out to you," I say, noticing the familiar Toyota grill reflect back at me in my rearview mirror. My grin inches up.

"Hey, look behind us," I say to my friend.

Bailey twists in her seat to confirm Dustin and Tommy are behind us. She waves and Dustin responds by flashing his headlights a few times and racing up dangerously close to my bumper. One touch of my brakes would really piss him off, but I would never do that to him. He must know I wouldn't.

Bailey unbuckles her belt when we reach the neighborhood, crawling through the open window and hanging out enough to let her arms wave and hair blow in the wind as she howls. My brother does the same thing as the four of us cruise by the senior center on the corner of our street, catching more than a few sideways glances from the social club letting out.

I speed away from my brother and Dustin and continue down the road to drop Bailey off, helping her to comb out her hair before she exits the passenger seat. Her parents won't let her drive yet, and part of me thinks she'll have to move out before she gets her license.

By the time I get back to my driveway, Dustin's car is already pulled in reverse with the hood popped open for the boys' daily tune-up session. Sometimes, I think they just like to walk around the car and stare at it.

I pull up right next to the car and reach into the back seat to grab the part I can't wait to give to Dustin.

"What's that?" Tommy asks before I'm fully out of the car. He's alone.

"A surprise," I respond.

He nods at it, rubbing his hands together as his eyes squint and focus the block-like part I'm trying to conceal behind my back.

"That our intake?" Tommy asks.

I don't know why the way he asks pricks the hairs on the back of my neck so much, but I'm instantly defensive.

"You mean Dustin's part?" I retort. It's not like my brother paid for it. My brother quit paying for things on that car months ago.

"Hannah." The scolding, condescending way he says my name really puts me off, and I slam my door closed now that I'm fully out of the car and take a huge step backward, away from him.

"Tommy." I echo his tone.

He reaches in at me and I twist to avoid his grabby hands, which only makes his immaturity tick up. Lunging at me twice, I flinch each time until he finally catches me turning the wrong way. He pries the piece from my hands and strides around the back end of the car while I practically chase him.

"Tommy! Give it!" I sound like such a child, but I'm

pissed. I helped a real douchebag cheat on a test so I could buy that part.

"This is too much, Hannah. I don't know what you think—or what you're hoping this will mean—but you have to stop. Okay, Hannah?" He points his long finger at me, along with the final utterance of my name, and I'm tempted to reach forward and snap it off.

"I'm not *doing* anything, Tommy! I was being nice! To . . . our . . . friend!" I shout, my hands flailing desperately. I can feel the fire tickling my cheeks. I always glow red when I'm angry.

My brother's eyes shift over my shoulder and he clears his throat. Out of habit, I guess, I obey. Maybe my body is trained to react and follow his lead, to keep my mouth shut when he hints that I should. It's the curse of being the younger sibling, automatic subservience. Whatever it is, it shuts me up.

Dustin pops out our front door with one of my mom's sugar cookies in his hand.

"What's that?" He nods toward Tommy, but his eyes flash to me for a moment. My stomach bubbles up with aching pride as the heat drains from my cheeks, anger replaced by an overwhelming joy because I'm about to give something nice to someone special.

"Surprise, dude! Had my dad pick it up today. Didn't say anything in case it was gone when he went in," my brother says, literally stealing my thunder.

What the . . .

I'm stupefied, my feet glued to the ground beside Dustin's car, my fingers curling into themselves until they practically lose feeling. It's not that my brother lied; Tommy lies all the time. It's that he lied to Dustin about me, in a way. That he stole a moment from me, and why? Because he's jealous.

"That's amazing, man! Thank you so much! I mean . . . *wow!*" Dustin slings an arm around my brother's neck, an arm that's meant for me. All that's left for me to do is nod while I smile through gritted teeth as Dustin pulls away and points to the part in his hands.

"Amazing." I can't imagine the resentment in my clipped response and tight smile doesn't beam through the seam between my lips. It's so obvious to me, but Dustin doesn't appear thrown by it. He's already under his hood, already calling out for tools that my brother scurries to find. The two of them are fast at work within seconds, and I'm still glued to the concrete beside a passenger door I've never even gotten to pass through for a ride.

Not even once.

6

The biggest perk of being a senior, other than almost being done with this school bullshit, is getting out early. I like the chance to make those last few tweaks to my car before the Straights, not that we ever change anything major. Normally, at least. I *need* those extra hours today. Tonight's races are going to have higher stakes.

Tommy has no clue what's going on. I didn't mention the boys from Vegas to him. I don't think he likes the side bets anymore, so it doesn't really matter. He used to love the money, and he still makes bets sometimes, but not as often. For me, the side hustle is life.

Literal. Life.

I can usually pull down a solid two or three hundred bucks on a good Friday night, and that's only off the locals and the people who come from the cities to race. You don't find back roads like we have in the metro. And those Scottsdale kids are easy money with their daddy's cars and engines they don't understand. You can't buy a car that wins. You build it. Fine by me, though; I like taking their money.

I've been trying to get the Vegas drivers I met last year out here for months. They worked me up pretty good on the track out in Henderson, but that was under strict rules —rules that I think played to their strengths. There aren't rules out here in the high desert. I'm looking for a little revenge, but mostly I want their cash.

"We should head out there early, open this baby up a few times and see how the intake holds," I say as I drop the hood and wipe my hands clean from my tinkering. I meet Tommy's hard stare, and it takes me a couple seconds to decipher it. Hannah's home early.

"Hey, can I come along for the test rides?" she asks, stepping closer to my car.

"We've got work to do. It's not a joy ride," Tommy says, clearly cutting her off to be an asshole.

I let my head fall to my shoulder and breathe out my nose before mouthing "sorry" to Hannah behind Tommy's back. Normally, I'd stick up for her. Sometimes he gets his big brother pants up his ass. But today I can't afford extra drama rattling around in my head. If I don't win my races tonight, I'm losing my car. I don't have the cash to stake, and I know the rules: if a driver bets a grand or more, loses and can't pay, winner gets the keys.

I won't lose.

That's the thing about me—when my back is against the wall, an acute awareness takes over my body. It's like muscle memory, formed from years of taking Colt's bull-shit and abuse. I don't take punches because I foresee them coming, and I don't get into situations I won't dominate. Tommy doesn't understand it, and he thinks I take too many risks, both behind the wheel and with my cash. I know what I can handle though, and I drive myself right up to that line. I'll never veer over it.

"Let's go," Tommy says, snapping me out of my head with a fat palm against the hood.

"Gentle with her," I tease.

He grimaces and laughs out of the side of his mouth.

"Yeah, like you're ever gentle with her," he says.

I roll my eyes as I climb into the driver's seat. I catch a glimpse of Hannah as I do. She's moved back to her car and is sitting on the hood, her ankles crossed. She'll be out at the track by the time the sun goes down, and maybe when Tommy is distracted with all the celebration—*after I win*—I can take her for a ride at top speed. Just once. As someone who has been in my corner for most of my life, that's the least I can do to show her how grateful I am for her support.

It takes us about ten minutes to clear the town limits, and the moment we do I open it up to get a feel for the road and adjust to the slight shift in speeds.

"It jumps," Tommy says as I drop into the next gear. I feel the jerk too so I downshift to make the climb again. We burn a few extra miles going back and forth until I find the perfect sweet spots to punch it into the next gear, and by the time we're ready for the Straights, I have this thing flying on the pavement.

I catch the grin on Tommy's face as we round the corner onto the old highway where cars are already lined up, boys leaning on hoods with cash in their hands.

"What you smiling about over there, Tommy Judge?" I throw an elbow at him in jest.

He shakes his head with a short laugh.

"Nothin', man. I just like going fast."

I turn my head to meet his eyes and our wide smiles

reflect one another. This has always been our space, where the bullshit falls to the sides and Tommy and I get to be two kids who like to race cars. When he smiles like that, I remember all the reasons we became friends in the first place. I hold out my fist and he drops his on top.

"Kick some ass tonight, brotha," he says, unbuckling as I slow and pull to the side of the road to join the other gearheads out here to tear up the desert.

"Always," I answer. My eyes lock on my friend's frame as the passenger door closes behind him with a heavy clunk. He's going to be so pissed when he realizes who's here tonight. A few of the girls from town have already gathered in the back of a pickup truck though, and that's where my friend is headed. He's a grumpy asshole most of the time, but he's also a ladies' man.

I rev the engine lightly, just enough to feel the rumble vibrate around me and under the pad of my foot. The power makes its way around the nerves in my body. I coast my way a little deeper through the rows of cars until I find a good spot in the middle of the action to get out and size up the competition.

Keys clutched in my hand, I cross my arms over my chest and lean against the side of my car, taking in the scene before the last of the sunlight goes away in the next thirty minutes. I spot the Vegas guys fairly easily—typical Subaru next to a dropped Tahoe the rest of them probably rode here in. I nod at the familiar face in the crowd. His name's Alex Offerman, and he's never without the four guys—who are at least double my size—standing nearby. I have a pretty good hunch that Alex's family is one of those that deals behind the scenes in Vegas, but I'd rather not confirm my suspicion. I don't know why I feel plausible deniability is a good thing with him, but I do.

"Hey, Dustin, my man!" Alex crosses the street to meet me halfway. His blond hair is slicked back and his white long-sleeve shirt is tight enough to show off his nipples. It's creepy. I smell his cologne from several feet away. I'm wearing my old black Thrasher skate shirt with a hole at the bottom, my lucky black jeans, and new Vans. I like the way they grip the pedal and I always get a new pair before a big race.

"Finally made it to my street. How was the trip?" I reach out and clasp his hand, noting the way he twists his wrist to make sure his is slightly on top. Headlight beams from the parked cars glint off his gold ring.

"The strip? Or the trip?" he jokes.

I give him a courtesy laugh for his dumb joke. Least I can do since I'm about to take his money.

"So this is the famous Straights you were telling me about, huh?" He spins slowly to take in the long strip of road that stretches far in both directions. Soon, it will lead to black nothingness to the north, away from town.

"This is my home turf, yeah." I shove my hands back in my pockets and press the ridges of my key into my thumb to keep myself alert and sharp.

Alex spends a few more seconds glaring out onto the road before turning his focus back to me. I'm not sure whether he's the one I'm racing tonight, or one of his guys. Doesn't matter. I see the car they brought.

"So what are you thinking? Five hundred? Thousand?" He doesn't mince words; straight to the money. That's good because I need to make a serious profit here tonight. I need seed money to get a basic truck if I plan on moving into truck racing for the circuit.

I swallow and hope he doesn't see it. I'm glad Tommy isn't here for this. He'd kill me for what I'm about to say.

"I was thinking more like two." I cock my head to the side and squint, acting nonchalant about an amount of money that makes me both tingle and want to pass out in my own vomit.

"Ha, two hunny? That's hardly worth the drive here."

He's wrong. I correct him.

"K. I mean two large." I open my eyes a little more to meet his serious glare. He's sizing up my pupils, making sure I'm serious and that I plan to back up the bet we're about to shake on.

"Two grand. You got that?" His brow arches.

"I got that." I thumb the key fob over my shoulder and flash the lights on my dusty blue Supra.

I can tell by the smirk that crawls up his lip and into his cheek that he's sold. He'd love to race my car as his own. My ride is the envy of a lot of guys out here. His hand stretches out for me to take again a second later, and Tommy walks up as we're shaking.

"Oh fuck, what did you do?" My friend already has a beer in his hand and he spits out his recent sip.

"You remember Alex," I say, completely ignoring Tommy's question.

"Yeah. Hey, man." Tommy nods. He's not a big fan of the Vegas crew.

"So, am I racing you or . . ." I lean to my right to take in the guys hanging out around the front of the Tahoe. Alex turns to look over his group of friends and I catch him gnawing at his lip. I've upped the stakes, and he's not sure any of these guys are good enough.

"Yeah, you know what? I think I'd like to try out this stretch you've been bragging about. But what if we make it interesting?" His grin is etched into his lips again as he turns back to face me. It feels like a sack of rocks just sank my gut.

Tommy grabs the sleeve of my shirt and urges me a few steps to the side. I hold up a finger, my face burning with heat that my friend is making me look weak.

"Dude, what the fuck are you doing?" Tommy's beer breath floats across my face, and the hairs on my neck stand. I roll my shoulders and shirk his hand off my shirt.

"I'm paying for my future the only way I can. If you wanna go home, go home." I hold his cold stare for several seconds before his focus flits just beyond me to the crew waiting for me to fail out here tonight. He breathes out a short laugh when his focus comes back to me.

"What, and let you burn out without me here to fix shit?" He takes another swig of his beer, which he knows annoys me, but I give in to the cocky sneer he lets linger afterward. While Tommy might not like the risks I take, he sure as shit likes to win.

I step back to Alex and shake his hand with a firm grip.

"I'm in." I tilt my head back enough to hold my jaw set and dim my eyes while I anticipate whatever "interesting" addition he's planning on throwing into our bet.

"We both have passengers. You pick mine, I pick yours," he says, and I sniff a laugh. I don't give a shit who's in my passenger seat. I drive how I drive.

"Yeah, okay." I glance over his shoulder looking for the right fit, and when I don't see his brother, I turn to the crowd around us, looking for the most annoying passenger I can find. My mouth snaps shut and curves into a wide grin the second my eyes land on Lawrence.

"Hey, Lawrence! Come here!" The six-foot-five, three-hundred pound lineman and only talent on our high school football team drops his empty beer can on the ground just after crushing it against his hip.

"Aw, hell," Alex laughs out, moving his feet nervously. He knows I've got him trapped with this one. Not only does Lawrence add some seriously dense muscle weight to his car, but the dude is wide as a Cadillac all on his own. Won't be easy to shift with his left arm encroaching on Alex's space.

"What's up?" Lawrence and I tap fists. I point my thumb to my side and Lawrence scans Alex with suspicion.

"Up for riding shotgun tonight with this guy?" I know he is. Lawrence loves speed and danger. I honestly think he'd prefer to chase down quarterbacks without pads and a helmet if the league would let him.

"Oh, hell yeah. In that thing? Sweet!" Lawrence makes his way over to the car, dwarfing it from a dozen feet away.

I cross my arms over my chest and return my gaze to Alex, knowing I've got him. I can practically feel the cash in my pocket. All it takes is the delicate brush of a few fingers on the back of my neck to snap me right out of my imaginary victory lap.

"Hey, you forgot these. I know it's a thing for you," Hannah says, her breath finding the exposed skin along my neck. I turn to face her and feel the color drain from my face. Alex is already chuckling as Hannah hands me the worn leather gloves. I like to wear them when I drive, not because I need them but they're just lucky. She bought them for me the first time I drove stock.

"Looks like I found your passenger. Oh, and my cousin Teddy is planning on parking our ride somewhere, oh say about a mile ahead. Just to make it interesting." Alex pats my shoulder but I don't bother to turn to face him.

"Nah, this isn't happening." Tommy steps in. I grab my

friend's wrist and jerk him back from starting a war we don't need.

"It's fine," I say, meeting my friend's fiery glare.

"It's my sister," he seethes back.

And he's right. *Hannah is family.* She's my weakness. And she showed up right in time for Alex to exploit it.

"I don't understand," Hannah interjects, her eyes working between me and her brother.

"No, you don't." Tommy's hostility makes Hannah flinch so I step into the tight space between them. Her hand instinctively falls on my shoulder, and I'm aware how this looks, not only to Tommy, but to everyone around me.

"She'll be fine. If it comes down to it, I'll lose," I say, not certain I really can do that. It's what Tommy needs to hear, though.

He holds my gaze for several seconds, his back teeth gnashing as his jaw works. His mind is playing out all of the scenarios—especially the gory ones where I don't see the black SUV in the dark in time and swerve the wrong way. His nostrils flare with a few sharp breaths and he steps in close enough to whisper at my ear.

"If you lose, you'll *lose*." He steps back and flattens his palm against the center of my chest with a thud that knocks some of the air from my lungs.

"So I won't lose. It won't even be close." I steel myself. Any other scenario and there wouldn't be a single ounce of doubt in that statement. But Hannah is the one percent.

"I'll fucking kill you," Tommy grits out. His voice is loud enough that I'm sure Hannah heard him. Her fingers curl against my shoulder and her nails dig into my skin.

Tommy staggers back a few steps and spits to the side, his beer still dangling from his left hand. He takes one more swig then tosses the bottle into the open brush. He's making a show of it to spite me. I don't drink. Don't smoke shit, either. Figure you can grow up one of two ways when you come from a house like mine—just like the parents who made you, or as opposite from them as humanly possible.

"What's going on?" Hannah asks. I drop my head and pinch the bridge of my nose.

"Nothing. You're getting your ride, is all," I say. I only glance at her before walking away with nothing but the feel of her hand skimming down my arm as I leave.

I squeeze my eyes shut and head straight for the car, glad to see Tommy already under the hood when I reopen them. He's thorough, but he'll be more systematic now that his sister is going to top one-sixty with me.

Shit.

I figured Hannah wouldn't drop the subject. It only takes her seconds to step between Tommy and me. I'm clutching the gloves she gave me, coating them in my sweat. I never sweat.

"What do you mean I'm going for a ride?" she asks.

"You're racing?" Hannah's friend Bailey's voice is full of giddy jealousy. She's clueless about this world.

"No, she's not racing. And if I had my way . . ." Tommy stops his words but stands and meets my gaze. He wipes his hands on his work towel then tucks it in his back pocket before grabbing the keys from me and moving on to the work we just finished last night.

"Dustin, what's going on?" Hannah's hand brushes my arm again, and I jerk in response as if she burned me with a match. My heart instantly races. *This is so not the state I need to be in!*

"It's fine. I promise you'll be safe. It's a bet I made with a guy I know, and he likes to race with passengers.

It's . . . a mental game for him. He's trying to get in my head." I'm right; that's totally what it is. And I bet it works against most racers. If it weren't for Hannah, it would be meaningless against me. Hell, I'd drive the same with Lawrence eating a steak in the seat next to me as I would racing solo. Nothing can distract me when I'm in my zone.

But Hannah is different.

Without warning, a hand fires across my right cheek, knocking my head off its axis in a whiplash. I cup the sting and stare at Hannah's Doc Martin-wearing feet on the ground before me.

"What the fu—" I flit my eyes up as she cocks her arm to take another swing at me, and I step back.

"Do you need more?"

I blink twice because how the hell do I answer that? *What does she even mean?*

"Are you pissed?" she asks.

"Kinda. Yeah." I work my jaw under my hand. I'm one-hundred percent positive there's an imprint of her palm on the side of my face.

"Good. Think about that then and drive fucking fast." She shoves her tiny backpack into Bailey's chest and rounds my car, flinging open the passenger door to get in. My mouth hangs open, mostly because I'm making sure it still works, but also because damn, I can't believe she did that.

Rumbling vibrates in my belly and I turn to catch the first duo about to go at it behind us. Two of the older guys from town with hot rods they only bring out here to show off line up as a crowd gathers around. It's a respect thing, one of those things people in this town do as this rite of passage moves from one generation to the next. Tommy drops my hood and moves to stand next to me. He chuckles at my side.

"You saw that slap, huh?" I say.

"Sure did." He rubs his palms together, loving that his sister smacked me.

"Make you feel better?" I give him a sideways glance as two classic Fords fire up a few hundred feet away and peel down the dark strip of roadway.

"Only for a second," Tommy says with a hardened stare. His eyes are like glass, cold and piercing.

"Well, don't worry. It worked," I say, rubbing my face one final time before slipping my hands into my lucky gloves. My thumb pokes out on the right one and Tommy laughs at it as he hands me my keys.

"When are you going to spend some of your gambling winnings on a new pair of gloves?" he jokes.

I shake my head.

"Nope, these stay. Superstitious bastard that I am. And it isn't gambling."

"No?"

"That would mean there's a chance I lose. And there's no way in hell." I don't bother meeting his gaze again. I don't want him to chip away at my swagger.

I get in the car and do my best to forget about the citrus-scented girl sitting next to me. I focus on my mirrors, my flexing forearm as I reach for the gear shift, the trip of the knob under my hand. I flex my fingers and feel the stretch of the glove, the way it crackles where it's most worn as I squeeze then stretch.

"You do this every race?"

I stare at the numbers imprinted on the metal knob and imagine myself shifting from second to third to fourth, then . . .

"Sorry," she whispers.

My eyes close. This is impossible.

"It's fine. Please try to not talk. I'm in my head." *I'm in my head more than I should be.*

"Zipped. Got it," she says.

I'm a sucker because I know she'll do it if I look, so I give in to a quick glance as she runs her pinched fingers along the line of her lips and fakes a lock before tossing the invisible key out the passenger window.

"Great, now we're going to have to go find that in the dark," I joke. She smirks but waggles a finger, reminding me that she's no longer talking.

My eyes roam back to my dash, but I caught enough of her bare knee to scorch the back of my mind with the temptation to look even more. I use it as a reward, only looking to my far right after I've gone through my mental checklist and adjusted my mirrors one last time. I swear Hannah has owned those shorts for years, but for whatever reason, the way her body fits in them now is entirely different. The fringe from the cut-off denim tickles against her upper thigh, rips exposing the pockets and a flash of her pink skin even higher up her leg—higher than any guy should ever see. She's tall enough that her knees poke up in my bucket seats, which means there's more of her bare leg to see, and my eyes make the trip up and over the hill of her knee then down her calf. She's wearing a pair of Tommy's old socks, the blue and yellow stripes bunched up where the length sticks out above the tops of her combat boots. She has a belly ring, and I indulge in looking for it while her focus is on the crowd outside our window. She's wearing this thin white shirt that falls off one shoulder, but it's cut short enough that when she lifts her arm, her midriff is exposed. All it takes is one small stretch and the silver stud she put in six months ago makes a quick appearance.

I look back at my wheel just before I sense her turning my way. My hands grip the wheel and run along the curves, feeling every ridge. The turn is going to be tough, especially if I hit the two-mile mark at the same time Alex does. I already decided that if it's too tight I'll give him the extra yards and take my turn after the mile marker, just to be safe. I know I can catch him.

The next set of cars is ready to sprint down the road, but nobody's looking at them. Eyes have started to wander over to me. The sun has dipped below the line of mountains to the west, and the faint purple in the sky is quickly fading. The stars out here are spectacular. I'm tempted to say that to Hannah, but she knows. She grew up out here too, and she's on this road every night I am. It's just that we never sit next to each other.

My attention turns to Tommy as he pats the hood and moves toward my window. I lower it and lean close as he kneels to talk.

"Okay, he's got the rules. The second mile marker and back. I don't like this whole Tahoe thing, but I trust you can handle it."

"Not even a worry," I lie.

"All right. Well, we're up next. And I put a hundred on us, so if you lose that's two things you owe me." He points at me, and I know he's being both funny and serious.

"Start counting your winnings now," I say, rolling up my window.

Hannah's knees are locked tight, and tiny bumps cover her skin, lit up by the LED glow of my interior lights. She's nervous, and I wish I could say something to calm her. But I'm in character now; I have a job to do, and easing her discomfort can't be part of the description. Besides, she's a big girl. She can handle this.

I pull my seat belt out from my chest and let it fall snug against my skin as Hannah does the same. We've both seen enough go wrong when people don't wear them. I give the Supra gas and it sings under my feet. God, that sound is sweet.

Spectators peel away as I crawl from the side of the road to the pavement. The lights from the last two racers glow in the distance. They'll be back in seconds. Nobody cares. Money flashes around me. I catch rolls of it exchanging hands in my periphery. I knew Vegas would bring in the money. I only hope the cops keep their unspoken promise and stay away tonight. We have a no-harm-no-foul agreement that's never been uttered out loud but is understood, mostly because the chief's son has been racing out here for years.

The cars in the race before ours hit their brakes several hundred feet away, and the one on the right smokes and fishtails from his inexperience. It takes a few minutes for the driver and his friends to get it to the side of the road and crack open the hood. While we wait, I glance over to my competitor, amused as he's smooshed against his door in an effort to give his right side the room it needs to work. I lean forward a little more and wave to Lawrence, who gives me a thumbs up as he rocks back and forth to what-ever music he's pumping through his earbuds.

"What are you doing after this, sweetheart?" Alex shouts. His voice permeates my entire body. My eyes narrow on him after I see Hannah squeeze her legs together tight.

My hand reaches to the right, gripping the shaft with enough force that I may yank off the metal ball.

"Letting Dustin take me shopping with all his winnings," she hollers back without pause.

Alex rolls his eyes and shakes with laughter I know is an act. He doesn't like being disrespected like that. The one thing I know for certain from the short time we spent together in Vegas is that Alex has zero problems getting women to fall at his feet. That cologne of his must stop working past the state line.

She rolls up her window before Alex can think of a good comeback, and her eyes lock on the road ahead. She's stoic, like me. Learned behavior from miles and miles of watching me do the same thing.

Atta girl.

Ava Cruz strides between our cars, her long nails dragging along the chrome and glass as she passes through and continues several feet until she's far enough in front of us that she's clear to see. Looking at her, you would never know she's a mom of five and in her forties. Earl's her father, and Ava's been known to drag on this road a time or two. I've heard stories from Tommy's dad about the hell she raised back in high school. She's royalty on the Straights, and if it's a race that matters, she still comes out to start it.

I nod at her through the windshield and tighten my grip before relaxing into my zone. For the next four minutes, nothing else matters. I breathe in the mix of warm desert air and cooled AC that's trapped in here with me—with us.

No. I have to remember that I am here alone, even if I'm not.

Alex's engine revs and I allow one last glance to my right. He's locked in, and it seems he convinced Lawrence to chill out and sit still in the tight space next to him. My eyes scan along the dash and I will myself to forget the passenger in my car. *I am all that matters.* I breathe out, the air spilling slowly through my slightly parted lips. One blink. Two.

Ava holds her arms high in the air, the bright yellow scarf wrapped around her wrist as the tail flaps in the breeze above her. My hand caresses the knob of the shifter, my touch light and seductive. You can't punch a car into driving past its limit; you have to coax it. And faster than the other guy.

I rev.

Alex revs.

The scent of burnt oil and toxic gas fills the air, permeating through the vents and filling my lungs with my secret serum. When I feel like this, I am unbeatable.

I count the sways of Ava's hips. I'm too far away to see the smirk on her bright red lips, but I know it's there. This is my home court advantage, and I know it's the reason she's here. Six sways and the yellow will fall. My muscle twitch is ready, the rhythm in my lungs as calm as an early morning lake prime for fishing. Nobody is here—no Tommy; no crowd. It's just me and a yellow scarf that will drop in three . . . two . . .

My foot takes over and my hand follows. My limbs dance together, each knowing what to do independent of the other yet coming together when they should. The wheel feels good, ride smooth despite the roar hugging me through the leather seats. I don't need to look to my right; I already see Alex's lights. The desert dust catches everything, and it tells me all I need to know. I only have him by inches, but I have him.

The next series happens fast. The climb from third to fifth is effortless, and I push to sixth sooner than I should because I'm feeling it. The drag isn't there, and I blow out a hard breath because I took a risk and it paid off.

"Come on, baby," I mutter, glancing down then up over and over as my speed climbs over a hundred, one-oh-five, one-ten. Dust particles, insects, and the glimmer of desert brush lit by my headlights whir by and the light to my right dims. I have him by feet now. Not many, but I have him.

I lock my arms and hold the line, feeling the road, knowing the posts we're blowing past by heart. The flip is coming, and it'll come fast, but I think I've got the edge. I won't need to give up my lead. Alex doesn't deserve to feel comfortable.

The familiar stretch in my lips inches up and my breath steadies in and out of my nose. My chest barely moves. My muscles are locked, holding their position for thirty seconds, for twenty, for ten. My hand knows exactly where to go, gripping the shifter while my legs work the clutch, the brakes, the gas. The spin to double back happens so fast I barely remember going through it, the only proof I ever spun at all the stench of burnt rubber and the faint trail of smoke illuminated by the red of my taillights.

I don't know where Alex is, but he's close behind. His headlights light up the road to my left now, the specks on the pavement too bright. *He's too close.* I lean forward ever so slightly, wanting to be ready for the unknown. The Tahoe's coming up ahead. I don't know whether it's heading right at us or if it's parked, but I know it's there, and I know the lights are off. It's going to be a matter of seeing it first and gaining the position. Only one of us will be able to pass. Whoever gets there last will have to slam the brakes.

My palm instinctively pounds the wheel, willing my baby to go faster. My jaw clenches as relaxation loses out to grit. I don't like this, not knowing. I grip the shifter on a gut feeling, and the glow to my left gets brighter.

"No fuckin' way," I fume, my foot heavy on the pedal. My body rocks forward and back as my eyes scan the road, the mirrors, the road, my left, the road—the Tahoe. It's just a hint of the bumper, a faint reflection that most people wouldn't notice, but I see it. It's there, and it's directly in front of me. I'm either going to have to beat him outright or give up my position to get behind him and pass to the left.

If I do that, I lose. And I don't lose. Not ever.

I inch closer to the line between us, my tires warning me of the action, the constant drumming of reflectors being ripped from the ground under my tread. I move in closer, sensing the nearness of my back tire to Alex's front. He's holding his position, and there's time, but not a lot. My mind races through the calculations as I lean back and let feel take over. Tommy wasn't completely wrong. This is a gamble. And this is the moment it all comes to a head. What I do and what Alex does, both independently and in response to one another, shatters into a dozen possible outcomes: he hits my tail and I spin out; he hits my tail and rolls into the desert; I hit the brakes and he sails by, which is *not* an option; or he chickens out and I beat him outright.

What kind of man are you, Offerman?

I commit to my choice before the next beat of my pulse. I veer left, and nothing about my movement is subtle. It's a decision, and it will either hold or not. The Tahoe is growing closer. I could slow down and try to push Alex out right now, but he's too good. He'll take advantage of that and swerve into me. I won't have a choice. The only option is to hope he gives in. Even if he doesn't, I'm not changing my plan.

We're nearly touching, and the thought of jacking up my right side to prove how crazy I am flashes across my mind. Lots of details pass in a flash. The road so rough, vibrating my hands on the wheel and my thighs in my seat. My leg jack-knifed, knee locked as I press the pedal through the floor to take the lead. My engine roaring so loudly that the sound makes my ears feel full of cotton. Tires swerving and the stench of brakes working hard. The Tahoe in my headlights, then gone—in my taillights.

I roar the rest of the mile in a trance, blowing past the crowd honking horns as headlights light up the road where everything ends. I keep going, everything numb, the joy still behind held at bay. My mind has gone where it goes, a level that's almost insanity but one that ensures I never lose. The rush is coming; it gurgles in the depths of my belly. The burn hits my chest.

Fists pound against the top of my steering wheel, and I press on the brakes as I let out the air in my lungs.

"Yes!" I shout, my hands letting go of the wheel as I fish-tail. I grip the wheel to whip around and jerk to a stop. The smoke from my tires colors the road.

"Fuck yes!" I shout again, pounding the wheel a few more times as my eyes gloss over from adrenaline. The road ahead is a blur, the lights from the cars like one of the Impressionist paintings.

Tommy is running down the center of the street and I kick open my door, ready to join him in celebration when everything from the outside comes soaring in.

Hannah.

My head swivels to the side and I briefly catch Hannah's form, her eyes forward, hands on her knees, gripping them tightly, blood drawn on her skin where her nails dug in. She's rigid, and I don't get to stare long enough to tell whether or not she's breathing before I'm yanked the rest of the way out of my car and pounded in the face not once, but twice. My nose is bleeding and I stumble backward several steps as my head jerks to the side. The cut on my lip tastes like metal. *What's with the Judge kids hitting me in the face?* I deserve this one, though. I know I do, and it's the only reason I leave my hands out to my sides and stand my ground, preparing for more pummeling.

Tommy runs his sleeve across his nose while I do the same. Mine leaves behind a streak of crimson. His eyes are wide with fury, his hair is wild, and sweat soaks his T-shirt. Beads of sweat dot his forehead too. It's warm out but not *that* warm. He's hot from nerves and anger.

"Fucking careless! You could have killed her!" His voice curdles with anger.

He's right. I could have.

"I'm sorry." I shake my head, more reality seeping in. *What the hell was I thinking?*

Tommy turns and stalks away, his hands threaded behind his head and elbows splayed. He makes it a dozen feet before spinning and pointing at me again.

"You drop this thing you have, whatever it is. With my sister? That's a hard no, Dustin. You understand? N. O. Hannah never gets in that car again." He charges a few steps closer and our eyes lock. My mouth is heavy on the corners, the weight of my risk sinking me into the ground. I've never felt the sting of having something to lose. Tonight . . . I could have lost Hannah. Not my car, or my pride.

Hannah.

"I understand," I say to my friend. My arms dangle limp at my sides and I hold the stare that is meant to imprint every word on my soul. Those words were threats and rules—they were law when it comes to his sister.

I didn't only cross the line.

I obliterated the line.

"Alex's cousin has your cash," Tommy barks out. He pinches the bridge of his nose and glares down at the pavement between us. "Nice fucking race."

He turns and marches away, back into the lights to the kegs and weed that he will no doubt get lost in both to forget me and to spite me. I'll wait and drive his ass home. Sick as it is, I can't help the tiny smile that itches the right side of my mouth. My chest puffs with a single laugh, part exhale of stress and part appreciation. As pissed as Tommy is, he's still in my corner when it comes to my gift.

Nobody beats me. Nobody. And one day, nobody in the world will.

I kick at the road a few times and breathe out all that's left in my chest before rolling my head to my right. Hannah's eyes are waiting for me. She hasn't moved much, but she watched all that go down. Hard not to, I suppose.

I climb back into the driver's seat and drape my hand over the wheel, as if we're out for a Sunday drive. My body is poised the exact opposite of how it was only minutes ago. All of that aggression has passed. It's like sex, driving like I do. I'm satiated. And as wrong as it was to put her through that, it also felt right.

"Hannah—"

"That was the single most amazing feeling I have ever had," she glees, cutting me off. "Ever."

My grin returns, bigger this time, and I jerk with another short laugh.

"I almost got us killed."

Turning slightly in her seat, her hands release their grip

on her legs. Her eyes square with mine and her gaze locks on mine for several wordless and breathless seconds. Reaching to her side, she clicks the safety belt free and lets it coil away from her body before leaning over the center console and pressing both of her hands on my burning hot cheeks.

"You would never hurt me, Dustin Bridges. I know it. I trust you with my life—every . . . single . . . time."

I barely have time to unravel the mystery of her words when her lashes sweep down and kiss her cheeks as she leans in and presses her cool pink lips to mine. It's the faintest touch, a taste of heaven and all its angels that sends a chill down my body and through every inch of my veins. She pulls back slowly, our lips almost clinging to stay connected.

"I'll walk back," she says in a hushed tone, the smirk on her lips just enough to seal the mystery in place.

Hannah Judge is all grown up, and she thinks I'm all grown up too. I see a woman and she sees a man. And we are doing a lot of things we promised Tommy we wouldn't do. I don't think I can let the taboo stop here. I'm already buzzed on her kiss.

7

I don't know why I was so calm.

I should have been screaming, begging to be let out of the car.

Instead I sat there, eyes locked on the lines in the road, the distance shrinking, the milliseconds remaining for Dustin to make a move all flying through my mind in calculations. My body felt the same way it always does when I watch Dustin race. Or at least, I thought it did.

When my brother punched Dustin in the face, I peeled my hands from my legs and realized how hard I had been holding on. I don't think it was fear of dying, though. I meant what I said. I do trust Dustin with my life, probably more than I trust Tommy. It would hurt my brother to hear that, but it's the truth.

No, I wasn't afraid for me. I was afraid for Dustin. I knew he wouldn't lose, but I was willing him to win just the same. I was anticipating the big cheat, waiting for one of Alex's guys to break the rules. I was waiting for fate to steal this from him with a blown tire or gasket. That's what gripped my chest and held on tight. That's why I cut my fingers deep into my skin. I didn't want anything to take this from Dustin. I wanted him to get what he earned, what he deserved.

I always do.

I always have.

I knew he'd come to my house tonight, even if he didn't have to. Bailey and I watched a few more races and I filled her head with what I thought she wanted to hear about: what it was like in that car, the intensity, and how close we were to losing it all. The entire time, though, my thoughts were on that kiss. And I knew Dustin's mind was there too. I saw it in the glances he gave me from across the road where he leaned against the side of his car, hands deep in his pockets, relaxed. The only time he is ever relaxed, at least fully, is after a big win.

His headlights illuminate our driveway from down the street, the familiar growl of his engine music to my ears. I draw my legs in and hug them as I wait, barefoot, on the hood of my car. The air is a mix of warmth and the cool that drifts up from the river. It feels like summer.

Dustin isn't in a hurry. It may be because my brother is on the verge of vomiting in his passenger seat and he doesn't want to push him over the edge. Or maybe he's thinking about what comes next, after he gets my brother inside, when we talk about the night.

The Supra's lights dim as the car crawls into the driveway, and Dustin flicks them off before killing the engine. I stay where I am, coiled on my car, chin balanced on my right knee and gaze locked on Dustin's through the windshield. I see him so clearly, even through the blur of reflected stars.

When Tommy pushes against the passenger door,

Dustin leaps from his, jogging around to finish opening it before my brother gets sick inside. Tommy rolls out onto his hands and knees, heaving the cocktail mixed in his system onto the pavement. I roll my eyes and let go of my legs, sliding down the car to help. I move to Dustin's open door first and reach in to grab his keys before closing it. By the time I get to the passenger side, Dustin's managed to get my brother to his feet. I tuck myself under Tommy's right arm to help keep him steady.

"Sorry about this," I say, knowing how much Dustin hates this kind of stuff. My brother usually doesn't get shit-faced. He has a good time, but that's as far as partying goes. He did this to be a jerk.

"This isn't your fault," Dustin says, glancing at me as he leans forward and kicks the passenger door closed. I press the lock button on his key fob then stuff the keys into my pocket.

Thankfully, Tommy isn't out enough to not be able to walk. He isn't steady on his feet, but he's at least able to prop up most of his own weight as we help him amble toward the front door. It's two, maybe three in the morning by now, and our parents will be up by six for an event my mom is hosting at Town Hall. Thank God my mom quit trying to make Tommy and me volunteer for her craft fairs and bake sales. It's mostly older ladies who help out, and they always want to teach us lessons. I don't know that the good word can be heard when you're seventeen and eighteen in a small town. Temptation comes in the form of nothing better to do out here, as my brother is so gracefully proving right now.

Dustin and I manage to get Tommy through the door and up the stairs before he nods off, his head slumped forward and body instantly a thousand pounds heavier.

"I got it from here," Dustin says, sweeping my brother up in his arms. I pull my phone from my back pocket and snap a quick photo in case I need to hold this image over Tommy's head sometime, then pull the comforter back on his bed before Dustin sets him down.

"Think we should take his shoes off?" He steps back to stare at his friend, my brother, as he inchworms into the covers and instantly begins to snore.

"I don't think he cares," I say, flipping the cover over half of his body. "I say we leave him."

I move to the door and flick the switch for the ceiling fan. Tommy's always liked the noise it makes; helps him sleep like a baby. Maybe he'll make it late into the morning and avoid the massive hangover waiting to move in. Dustin stares at his bed for a few seconds before pushing his hands into his hair and blowing out. He rocks on his feet and spins to face me, our eyes meeting automatically.

"Come on," I call to him, urging him out of my brother's room. Frozen in place, he stares at me for a few breaths, probably considering the hidden meaning in my request. Where will he go when he leaves this room?

I step into the hallway and a second later, Dustin follows. I close my brother's door and turn to find Dustin near. His body looms over and around me, my face at his chest. I reach up and run my finger along the center of it, drawing a line in the cotton of his T-shirt. I lift my chin to find his dipped, his eyes locked on my face, waiting for me to tell him what to do. I tilt my head to my right, toward my bedroom, then let my finger trace down to the bottom of his shirt, hooking the hem briefly as I turn away.

He doesn't follow immediately, but by the time I reach my door, he's only a few paces behind me. I hold the door wide for him to enter, breathing in his scent as he passes.

He is all the things I love—oil, leather, a hard day's work, his coconut shampoo, spearmint.

I push my door gently until it clicks at my back as Dustin moves slowly through my room. He's been in here a thousand times, yet everything feels intimate now. My things feel on display, as if everything I own is a representation of who I am, and I'm suddenly worried he won't like the story they tell. But Dustin, he's one of those things too. He's perhaps the biggest piece of my story, owning more than even my own family.

"I heard you won two grand from tonight," I say, my voice low so I don't wake anyone.

Dustin's shoulders lift and he glances at me over his left shoulder, his lips ticked up with pride. "I did, yeah."

Our eyes flirt, and eventually I have to blink away. My gaze falls to my feet, but I can tell he's still looking at me. I feel it.

"Han . . . I'm real sorry. Tonight, what I did to you—that was too dangerous." There's an ache in his hushed tone, and I hate that he feels guilt over the best night of my life.

"No, it wasn't." I lift my head to find his eyes waiting, as I knew they would be.

His head briefly falls to the side then he shakes it.

"It was stupid. Careless," he continues as he backs up to sit on the edge of my bed. The space around him feels so childish—my wall covered in band posters and dumb drawings of hearts and flowers I made with Bailey. The giant pink teddy bear my mom bought me for Easter is propped in the corner of my bed, and my comforter is woven with pink and gold glitter thread. It's hard to make someone see you as a woman when everything about your space screams baby sister.

"I wasn't scared," I croak out.

Dustin laughs out quietly before looking up at me from under his golden lashes. The faint smile tugs on one side of his mouth more than the other, that same sloppy grin he wore when we were kids and Mom gave us ice cream. I think I've loved him my entire life, but it took seeing that face—the mix of innocence and sheer elation that colors his features when he's happy—to make me realize how long my heart has been tied to his.

"I mean it. I wasn't scared," I insist, ungluing my feet from the hole they've dug in my carpet. I step toward him, noting the way his hands move to his knees and his shoulders roll as he straightens his spine.

"No?" he whispers, lifting his chin as I come closer.

"Uh uh," I say, shaking my head.

My heart is racing, the beats so fierce I'm sure my skin is pulsing. I can't breathe, yet the air is coming in and out so fast. Hours ago, I flew through the desert at a hundred and sixty miles per hour yet the five feet I just slowly crossed were far more terrifying.

I reach toward Dustin's right hand just as he lifts it from his knee and our fingers twine, our touch soft and timid. So many times he's held my hand through things—through haunted houses and rushing across highways. This touch, though, it's different.

Palm to palm, our fingers fold together as we stare at the way we fit. His bronzed skin marred by grease, my pale pink fingers ringed with twists of gold. *Lady and the Tramp.* I step in closer, raising my left hand to his cheek and skimming along the roughness of his whiskers. He leans into my touch as my fingertips dive into his hair. The curls wrap around me, soft and cool.

As Dustin's eyes close, his free hand moves from his other knee to the belt loop on my shorts. Hooking two of his fingers through the denim, he tugs me close. I straddle his legs instinctually, and when I feel the slight pull at my waist followed by the gentle tickle of his fingernails along my bare midriff, I take his lead and lower myself until I'm sitting on his lap, my knees bent on my bed.

Our hands untether and as mine roam along his neck, his drift up my body to my shoulders, then eventually push into my hair, twining the strands around his knuckles with a forceful grip that echoes the feeling in my chest—the feeling of wanting something so badly yet holding it out of reach because you know you shouldn't. *We shouldn't.*

His eyes bore into the divot at the base of my throat. I let my head fall forward until it rests against his, my view of his lashes, the sharp angles of his cheeks, and the line formed by his jawline—a line that wasn't there a year ago. Everything about Dustin is grown up and ready for the world. I'm convinced he's going to leave a massive mark on this life—on anything he touches. *On me.*

"Hannah." He breathes out my name.

I close my eyes at the feel of his chin lifting, our heads rolling against each other. His nose drags against my cheek as his mouth lifts to meet mine, and I let a tiny gasp slip through my lips as I pant and wait.

"We shouldn't," he says. His breath dances against my cheek, crawling around my neck and filling the slight space between us with his own intoxicating drug.

"I know," I agree, both of us doing little to stop.

He takes a careful nip at my upper lip, and a small whimper slips from my mouth in response. The sound drives him in for more, this time his lips clamping around mine, sucking in with a gentle pressure that completely melts me into his body. The more I sink into him, the stronger his grip is in my hair until one hand trails down my spine, lower and lower still until it sinks into the back pocket of my shorts and pulls me into him.

There's nothing subtle about his lips on mine now, and I hold nothing back either. We're holding each other as close as we can without literally becoming one. His tongue works inside my mouth, tasting me and filling my mouth with his sweet spearmint aftertaste. All of this—his scent, his body, his mouth, his skin—is as I've imagined when I lie awake at night and fantasize about a world where I'm not his best friend's little sister. And right this moment, that's the *last* thing I am to him.

His fingers curl in my pocket, nails scratching against the denim as he grips my ass and holds me tight against his hard body. Hard everywhere. I find myself wanting to nudge him farther back into my bed so I can press into him even more. I roll my hips against him to release the pressure, but the only thing it does is make me crave more. I do it again, and Dustin tugs my hair gently to tip my chin up and release our kiss. His teeth grit as hooded eyes meet mine. He's lost to this as much as I am. We passed the option to turn back long ago. The only choice now is to wring every last pleasure out of this forbidden indiscretion.

Dustin bites at my chin, his lips softening the cut of his teeth with a kiss that he trails along my neck. His tongue finds the tip of my ear and he tastes me there too, sucking in then gently biting. I tilt my head back to expose my neck, urging him to enjoy more of me, and he does, kissing down my neck and along the collar of my shirt. His hands have crawled to the small of my back and are slowly gliding up my bare skin, finding shoulder blades and a spine free of bra straps. I took it off when I got home. I did that on purpose, because I hoped.

Dustin notices.

His hands flirt along my sides, his thumbs edging closer to my front until they finally meet the curves of my breasts. I arch out of need and peel away from our kiss, wishing . . . *hoping.*

The familiar double beep of a car alarm outside my window forces us to freeze. I clamp my lips shut and drop my forehead to Dustin's shoulder as we hold our breath and listen. The heavy clunk of my dad's truck door comes next, followed by the click of the front door shutting, the deadbolt locking into place.

Footsteps pound against the wood stairs, my dad's inability to be quiet the only thing that saved us from perhaps getting carried away.

Saved. *Spoiled.*

My parents' bedroom door creaks open then shuts and we exhale. Neither of us moves for several seconds, though we both know that whatever this was—what was happening tonight—it's finished, at least for now.

"I better sleep on Tommy's floor," Dustin says, his voice a gravelly whisper.

"He might throw up." I'm only half joking.

Dustin breathes out a quiet laugh that dances against my skin, firing goose bumps at the back of my neck and down my arms and legs.

"I'd deserve it," he says.

I nod, my cheek rubbing against his. We peel apart with a reluctant sort of guilt, and our eyes barely meet. My skin warms every tiny second they do. I'm not sure whether I'm embarrassed or still reeling from wanting him so bad.

It's clear Dustin is still feeling the effects of our massive make-out session. His jeans bulge at his crotch, and I'm deviously satisfied that I made his dick so hard. I wonder if he touches himself thinking about me the way I do about him?

I twist to sit on the corner of my bed he just abandoned, the blankets still warm from his body. I smile at the sight of his twisted up hair, knotted in the back from my hands. His frame takes so much space, his chest wide, shoulders broad, and back muscular. I've admired his body so many times, so many ways, but now having felt it . . .

He pauses at my door, his forehead pressed against the jamb, one palm flat against the wood, the other wrapped around the knob.

He glances at me over his shoulder, his eyes drawn in, almost afraid . . . until he sees the coy smile breaking through on my lips. The moment his gaze dips, a smile of his own takes hold.

"Good night, Hannah Banana."

I blink slowly, top teeth clamping down on my bottom lip before letting go.

"Good night, Dustin Bridges."

He reaches to his left and flips the light switch, cloaking my room in darkness. In another breath, he's gone.

He's gone. But he's also everywhere. And I don't think I'll ever be able to shake him.

8

I'm in trouble. And not, like, just a little trouble. I can't fight my way out of this trouble, or run. I'm tangled in it, a mess of my own goddamn making. And I have no idea what to do.

I crept into Tommy's room like a dog caught in the rain. No, in a mudslide, fur matted, belly hungry, paws raw, and eyes weary. One taste of Hannah and every drop of self-control was zapped from my body. I thought putting a pair of closed doors between us would help me rebuild, but damn if I don't want to rush into her bedroom and pick things up where we left off.

Sleep is not an option. It hasn't been for the last four hours. The sun is up now, and Hannah and Tommy's parents have left to set up for the spring fest at town hall. I probably should have gotten up and gone with them to volunteer, or even better, headed straight for Bailey's house and insisted on joining her family for Bible study. But man, would that have raised a flag or two. I've been to church twice, and both times were with the Judges. Once for the fall fest when we were nine and they gave out free pumpkins, and once my freshman year when Hannah's mom thought we might like the youth group because she heard a band was playing. That band consisted of six people from our high school, and one of them played the clarinet.

All that aside, it would probably do to repent right about now. Maybe wash my soul out a bit and examine my priorities in life. *I can't be doing this.*

I slap my hand on my face and splay my fingers wide, muffling my groan. I rub life back into my skin and then run my hand through my hair a few times before sitting up from the rollout mat on the floor. Tommy hasn't stopped snoring since I dropped him in his bed hours ago. He smells of tequila. That's where it all went wrong. You don't mix beer and tequila if you can help it. But Tommy was sticking it to me. *Who's suffering now?*

The slight creak in the hallway catches my attention and I study the space under Tommy's door while I hold my breath. Hannah's door is open. I can tell by the way light pours in through her window that faces east and reflects off the floorboards. The shadows of her bare feet tiptoe by, pausing for a few seconds at Tommy's door. She's probably listening to see if either of us are awake—*if I'm awake.*

I don't move until the shadow of her feet disappears and the water turns on in the bathroom a few feet away. Where she's undressing. And getting into the shower. And my God, do I want to join her.

Clearing my throat, I rock myself to a stand and roll the mat with my feet before nudging it under Tommy's bedframe. He still hasn't moved. Part of me wants him to wake up and accuse me of hitting on his sister so I can get this over with. The other part of me? He's already gliding stealthily down the hallway in an attempt to get out of here without being noticed.

My efforts fail the second the bathroom door flies open and Hannah steps out wrapped in a towel, steam from the hot shower billowing behind her and cascading around her amazing skin.

She startles and clutches at the place where her towel is knotted above her breasts. I shove my fists in my pockets and will my cock to remain chill.

"Sorry. I was just . . ." I take one hand out and grab at the back of my neck, laughing lightly as I avert my eyes and stare at the floor.

"You want to go with me to help at the spring fest?" she asks.

I glance up and am shocked at her nonchalant expression. Her head leans to the side, and her hip is jutted out enough that her thigh peeks through the edges of the towel.

"Sure," I croak out, my voice cracking like a thirteen-year-old boy. She calls me on it with a tight smile and laugh. She steps forward and touches her fingertip on my nose. I literally cross my eyes to stare at it as she taps a few times.

"I'll be right out," she says. And so I'm not tempted to follow her or watch that towel fall before the door closes completely, I excuse myself downstairs where I take the world's fastest, coldest shower.

Hannah is already dressed and buzzing around the kitchen by the time I exit the small bathroom behind their laundry room. Her wet hair is glued to her back, soaking her pale yellow T-shirt, the fabric clinging to her skin and showing off the lines of her shoulder blades, the slope of her back, and the band of lace that crosses the middle. *So much for the benefits of a cold shower.* I lean forward and rest my palms on the counter while she drinks milk straight from the container.

"You're such a dude," I tease. She turns and wipes the milk mustache from her upper lip with the back of her hand before putting the lid back on the container.

"It was always hard keeping up with you and Tommy. It was either fit in and join the ranks or fall behind." She laughs lightly then turns to put the milk away.

Me and Tommy. Me, *Hannah,* and Tommy.

Before she turns to face me and disarm me with her ice-blue eyes, I let all the thoughts battling it out in my head come running out my mouth.

"About last night. I was . . . Tommy was . . ." Clearly, I don't get far. Thankfully, Hannah takes over for me.

"It was a mistake. We were both tired. The race was intense, and you don't want to hurt our friendship and the friendship you have with my brother." She pulls her lips into a tight smile that pinches the sides of her mouth as she blinks at me slowly.

"Basically, uh, yeah." I swallow because her tone doesn't sound as though she's on the same page. Hell, I'm not even on the same page with myself.

She holds my stare for a few seconds then laughs before rolling her eyes in the direction of her purse that's tucked in the corner of the kitchen counter.

"Fine, whatever," she says, moving straight to the door without glancing my way again.

"Hannah, don't be like that." Deep down she has every right to be that way. Because everything she just quoted for me is bullshit. I couldn't even get it out of my own mouth; she had to spout it for me.

"So, are you still coming with me or not?" She pauses at

the door, back still to me, T-shirt still wet from her twists of hair.

"Yeah," I say, because she's like a drug. I don't know if I can make it through withdrawals.

I don't think I've ever been a passenger in Hannah's car. The fit is strange, and I find myself fumbling with the seat belt and shifting my feet around the floor as she backs out of her driveway. She shifts her eyes to me a few times and laughs under her breath.

"You always have to drive, don't you?"

I glance up to catch her eyes, and I can tell she's still ticked. One brow is higher than the other and her mouth is a straight line.

"I might be a bit of a control freak about being behind the wheel, yeah. It's your dad's fault." I pull the chest strap out and hold it with a stiff arm, elbow in my gut. It feels like it's choking me.

"My dad didn't make you a control freak. He showed you how to work a manual and time the clutch. Your control issues are of your own making." She slaps my arm aside and sends the safety belt back to its original snug position across my chest and neck. *Why does it cut in there?*

I give her a polite laugh as I twist and inspect the harness buckle along the door frame. It doesn't adjust. Great.

I cough out a cat-like noise and turn back to face the front as Hannah stops at the intersection. She laughs at me one more time and mumbles something under her breath. I can't say for sure, but I think she called me a child. Fair enough.

The drive to town hall is quiet, and she doesn't even make a move to turn her radio on, which for her is extra weird. She's obsessed with that thing. I think she's trying to punish me with the silence, and the lack of music makes things that much more uncomfortable. I pat my palms against my knees a few times, playing along with the music in my head. Hannah drives on, unfazed, and definitely unimpressed. She pulls into a parking spot between her dad's truck and her mom's van, and she's barely stopped the car by the time I unlatch the safety belt and crack open the door.

I race out of the tight shared space, reveling in the lingering smell of her shampoo. I take long strides, glad I know my way around this area so I don't depend on following Hannah for directions. The faster I walk, though, the quicker her stride becomes, and by the time we hit the main park square, we're in a stupid speed walking race like children competing to tattle. When our feet hit the sidewalk leading to the booth her mom is running for the day, Hannah shoves my side and knocks me into the rock garden that lines the walkway. She begins a full-on sprint.

"Oh, hell no," I say, finding myself caught up in her all over again. She looks over her shoulder, smile wide and cheeks blushed as her purse swings from her shoulder, bouncing off her hip as she speeds away from me. I'm caught up to her in seconds, first grabbing her purse strap that she manages to spin free of before my other arm wraps around her waist and swings her around in circles.

Her laughter booms and draws the eyes of almost everyone setting up at the festival. Her hands form fists that pound gently at my back as I sling her over my shoulder and continue to run toward her mom. I don't let her down until we're in front of a table of craft supplies. Her wet strands of hair encircle my neck and slide free from my skin, leaving the cold trail of their presence behind.

Our eyes lock as our laughter fades, and I can't help but hold on to her gaze when it stops completely. I'm suddenly aware of how we appear to the dozens of eyes on us. We look like two young people doing a shit job at pretending not to like each other. We look exactly like what we are.

"Who wants to paint faces?" Hannah's mom interrupts our truth stare by shoving a paint set and two brushes into view.

"I'm not a very good artist," I say as Hannah takes the supplies from her mom.

"Then you can be in charge of taking the tickets and helping people pick out their designs." Mrs. Judge shoves a binder into my chest and I hug it as she walks away, already on to the next task she needs to get handled for the day.

"Your mom seems stressed," I say, flipping through the pages of the folder she gave me. There are butterflies and flowers and superhero designs all sketched out in colored pencil.

"She's *always* stressed out," Hannah jokes.

I follow her down the series of canopies to a booth right next to the park Hannah and I ran off to whenever we played hide-and-seek with Tommy. She catches me staring at the swings and waves a hand to get my attention.

"Tommy hated it when we did that," she says, drawing from the same memory.

"He totally did. Served him right, though. He cheated. Fucker always looked while he was counting."

Hannah sets out the paint supplies and fills a few water cups at the nearby drinking fountain. By the time she gets back, I've already taken six tickets and formed a line for her to start painting. I'm flipping through the book with her first customer as she calls him over to take the seat in front of her.

"That one," the kid says, pointing to the page that shows a football player throwing a ball. The drawing seems kind of intricate.

"You got it," Hannah says, swirling her brush in the water before dipping it into one of the colors.

"You sure you can do all the things in here?" I ask, flipping through the remaining designs that only seem to get fancier.

"I mean, I drew them in there, so not sure there's much of a difference," she says.

I flash my eyes to her then back to the book a few times and she laughs.

"What?" she says.

"I didn't know you were an artist." I mean, I knew Hannah could draw decently, well enough to make posters for school and stuff like that, but the images in this book are pretty spectacular. At least, compared to the stick people I can manage.

"There's a lot of things you don't know about me, Dustin Bridges." She gives me a sideways glance, her lips puckered slightly as a sinister smile plays at them. I don't argue with her, and I don't look away. Instead, I wait for her to return her focus to the wiggly boy sitting across from her. Then I watch her work.

Two hours fly by, at least for me. I'm not sure Hannah would agree. She ran out of black and white paint about twenty minutes ago, and she just finished an elaborate fairy design on a kindergartner's entire face. I notice that all of her water cups are muddied, and since nobody is stepping up with tickets to join her line, I make an executive decision and shut down our booth.

"I think the artist is done for the day. How about you?" I fold up the spare chair and dump the water cups into the grass.

"I agree," Hannah says, flexing her tired fingers out then shaking her hands. "I think I have carpal tunnel."

I tuck the binder under my arm and motion for her to give me one of her hands as she stands from her seat. I rub the meat of her palm with my thumbs, squeezing her fingers one at a time, and her eyes flutter shut.

"Dear God, I think you might put me to sleep if you keep this up," she says.

I take advantage of the moment, looking at her soft lashes as they brush the tops of her cheeks above the satisfied smile that stretches into them. As if under a spell, I lean down and gently press my lips to hers. The second our mouths touch, her hand tenses and she takes a quick step back.

"I thought this was too complicated," she says, her tone even, soft.

"It is. Incredibly so." I shrug and look over my shoulder, making note of the people still milling about. We might be out of view of her mom, but everyone at this thing knows the two of us on some level. That's the thing about a town like this, only two degrees of separation exist between anyone.

"What about our friendship?" she asks. There's a smugness to her tone, and I look back to her and quickly sink into the pools of blue staring back at me. I swim in her gaze, drown in it. I dive in and come out reborn.

I briefly drop her hand and move to the front of our booth, unlatching the flap meant to block out the sun, giving us privacy. I turn back to stare at this girl I've known all my life. Paint speckles dot her arms, a little of it in her hair too. I nod a few times, smiling, and give in. Really, I never had a choice. It was probably always going to play out like this—now, a year from now, someday.

"I think maybe our friendship is the reason *this* is happening," I say, reaching forward and taking the white and blue strips of hair between my fingers. I pinch the dried paint and slide it from her hair before dropping the strands and pressing my thumb lightly to her chin. She looks up at me and I can tell she agrees. Hannah has always enjoyed being right. She's always been the first to say "I told you so." She was right about us. And though she didn't say it with words, she said it loud and clear. She said it with her mouth on mine, with her body pressed against me, with the trust she willingly gave me out on that road last night, and in her bedroom when we were all alone.

"This is going to be messy," I say, closing the space between our lips an inch at a time.

"It already is," she responds.

I breathe out a laugh and nod again. My eyes dive to her mouth, hands slide along her jaw and into her hair just as she grips a fistful of my T-shirt, the same handful of cotton she gathered up last night. We're cursed to replay this scene over and over again it seems. If she weren't so delicious, I'd be able to stop. But she is. She's sweet like honey, and my body grows hungrier and more dependent on her every time we touch. We probably only have minutes before someone peeks inside or her mom comes to check on the booth.

Minutes.

I thrive in a world of seconds. Milliseconds. When I think about it that way, Hannah and I have all the time in the world. Long enough for me to memorize every sound she makes when I suck in her top lip, bite at the tender skin of her neck, and trace each curve of her back, following the arch all the way down to the inside of her jeans.

This secret, it won't last forever. Tommy will find out. And he will fucking kill me. But my God, will I die happy.

9

Having a secret like ours is a tantalizing burden. I get why Dustin was afraid. What we're doing—what we've done? It redraws lines. We will never go back to just being the three of us. "The kids," as my parents used to say. As much as Tommy thinks of Dustin as such, he's not like a brother to us. At least, not to me. He's like a fire, a dare that has tempted me since the day I let him cry in my arms when we were kids and his dad showed up to further ruin his life.

Dustin and I will never go back to merely being friends. We simply can't. More than the fact I don't want to, I don't think I could stand having him in our house without the knowledge that we could slip away somewhere or outwait the rest of the house at night to be together. As it is, this simple act of watching a movie with Tommy and my dad on a Sunday afternoon is torture.

My brother sits between us, which is nothing new. But somehow now it feels purposeful, as if he knows he has to chaperone. Dustin must feel it too because he's extra cautious reaching in the popcorn bowl propped on Tommy's knees, careful never to dive in for a handful when my hand is there so our fingers never touch. Our chemistry is too rich. I'm convinced any interaction in front of my brother would be sniffed out in an instant.

Tommy picked the movie, one of those heist films with an ensemble cast of actors he says I should know but I don't. My brother is way more into movies than I am. Even now, I'm sure this movie is good, but it's not as good as the thoughts running through my head about the guy sitting to my brother's left.

My brother leans forward, rests the half-eaten bowl of popcorn on the coffee table, and hits the pause button on the remote before standing.

"I have to piss," he says, and my dad tosses a throw pillow at him from the other sofa.

"Language. Your sister is still a lady," Dad chastises. My mom's been on Tommy's ass about his words lately, which is the only reason my dad is reinforcing it. I don't care how my brother talks in front of me.

"Sure she is," Tommy chides, picking the pillow up from the floor and stuffing it into my face.

I laugh it off but there was an edge to the way he spoke. Or at least, I think there was. Maybe it's my heightened paranoia. The second my brother leaves the room, my dad stands and stretches his arms above his head with a big yawn.

"I'm brewing coffee. Anyone want in on it?" My dad points a finger to me first then to Dustin.

"Actually, I've got to run to my house soon and check on my mom. She wasn't doing so good when I left this morning." Dustin plops his hands on his knees and tenses his shoulders as my dad offers a sympathetic nod and smile. Last night was one of the rare nights he spent at his own home, and only because his mom seemed genuinely sick. I can tell he's worried, but we haven't been alone enough to ask many questions.

"Let me know if I can do anything for you, Dustin. We're always here. You know that, right?" my dad offers.

The two of them share a silent stare that softens both of their eyes. Dustin looks away first, probably before he feels too much from my dad's genuine love for him. He nods as he stands.

"I do. Yeah, thanks," he says.

"I can come with you." I stand about half a second after he does, a move that would probably jack up my brother's suspicion but to my dad seems utterly normal.

"You don't have to," Dustin says, but his eyes connect with mine and relay the exact opposite.

"I'll let your brother know it's an extended pause. Maybe he'll spend the time wisely and clean out the garage like I asked him to a week ago," my dad mutters on his way to the kitchen.

"You sure?" Dustin mouths. As much as he wants to spend time with me, he doesn't like exposing me to his house. As much as he's over being embarrassed by his family, he's never quite gotten past being ashamed.

I nod and glance over his shoulder then behind me to make sure our coast is clear. I turn back to him and lean into his chest, pressing my palm over his heart while I rise up on the tips of my toes to dust his lips with a soft kiss.

"Positive," I whisper.

He leans down to let his forehead rest on mine, our noses touching as his eyes shut and he exhales.

"If I mess this up, promise me you'll kick my ass," he says.

I chuckle as I step away before we're caught then cross my heart with my finger and wink.

"I promise."

"You're a little too enthused about kicking my ass," he jokes as he fishes out the keys from his pocket and heads to our door. We've almost escaped to the front porch before my brother pulls the door wide open behind us.

"Where you guys goin'?" Tommy's eyes shift from Dustin to me.

He knows.

"I have to check on my mom. Hannah was gonna come, be a witness or whatever," Dustin says with a shrug. He plays it off so naturally, I'm impressed. I wonder if he's calculating every word he says in front of my brother as much as I am.

"Oh, hang on. I'll come too," Tommy says, dashing back inside to grab his shoes.

Dustin lets out a full breath in my brother's absence as his gaze falls to mine.

"Sorry," he says.

I shrug.

"It's fine. Just means I can't hold your hand in the car and call you my boyfriend is all," I say, lifting a shoulder. His eyes flare a little at the *boyfriend* part.

My brother busts through the door before we have a chance to delve further into that topic. Probably for the best. What we are is a lengthier conversation, one shrouded in pinky promises and covert intimacy. Even if we can't publicly declare it, I still want to know exactly where we stand—where I stand, with him. I know exactly what Dustin is to me.

When it's three of us, we never ride together in Dustin's

car. It has nothing to do with my brother wanting to keep me safe. In this case, it's a matter of logistics. Three people of average size fitting in a Supra is, well, fucking impossible. As limber as I am, I don't want to fold my knees up to my neck just to drive a few miles to the north. We all pile into my brother's car, and I slip into the back seat, letting Dustin have the passenger side. It all seems so normal, as if we're making a run to the convenience store for snacks, only I'm acutely aware of the remaining scent of Dustin's cologne, and the way the back of his hair curls at the base of his neck because it's in need of a cut I secretly don't want him to get.

My brother pulls out of our driveway and I turn my attention to the stream of photos on my social media apps on my phone, lurking on the ones people took at the Straights Friday night. Someone caught a shot of Dustin and me sitting in his car. We're wordless, staring at one another. This is just before my brother tore Dustin a new asshole. This moment was true bliss. I capture a screenshot of it.

"Hey, so . . . about Friday night," my brother begins. His forehead is wrinkled. I sit up tall to catch his eyes in the rearview mirror, instantly panicked that he's bringing up Friday.

"Forget about it," Dustin says, leaning forward and turning up the music. I smirk to myself. He's not going to give my brother a chance to rehash me being involved in the race, their ensuing fight about it, or my brother getting shitfaced and leaving us with his messy-ass self to get home.

Tommy continues on for the next mile, seeming to drop it as Dustin asked, but when we get to a stoplight he turns the music down and rests his hand over the stereo controls, almost as if guarding them from Dustin turning the music back up.

"Just . . . let me say this," he grits out, frustrated and maybe a little embarrassed. My brother likes to talk with his hands when he's uncomfortable, and right now, he's pretty much *all* hands.

Dustin sighs.

"Fine."

My brother's jaw works, a trait he exhibits when he's trying to spit out something he doesn't want to say. He's going to apologize; I can feel it. It won't be obvious, like an "I'm sorry." Tommy Judge doesn't put words out there that might be used against him in the future. But he'll be frank enough.

"I was a dick," my brother says.

Yeah, that's spot on.

"Like I said, forget—" Dustin begins, getting cut off by one of my brother's gesticulations.

"I got piss-ass drunk because I knew you would resent it. To hurt you, really, because I don't like my sister being put at risk. That wasn't cool. And thank you for cleaning up my vomit," my brother says, never making full eye contact with Dustin. His eyes shift over his shoulder to me and dim when he catches my smirk.

It's sweet that he worries about me. But I was never in danger. I knew I wasn't. Now's not the time for me to say that to him, though. Now's the time for his sorry-less apology to be accepted.

Dustin reaches over with a fist, holding it out for my brother to land his own on top of. He does with a breathy laugh of relief.

"We're cool," Dustin says, and my brother relaxes back in his seat. "I didn't clean up your vomit, though."

Tommy's head slingshots to the side. He definitely vomited. A few times.

"Yeah, saved it for you. Not gonna tell you where, either," Dustin deadpans. My brother deserves this.

"Shit," Tommy mutters under his breath.

We all bust out laughing about it after a few seconds, and for a moment, we're those three kids we always were. Maybe this can work after all. Maybe, eventually, my brother will accept what my heart needs.

Any morsel of comfort is swept away the second we pull in front of Dustin's family's trailer. Flashing lights glare brightly, even under the harsh noon sun. The back of an ambulance is wide open, doors slung out on either side.

Dustin flings his door open and takes off in a sprint before we're fully stopped, his voice breaking as he yells out, "Mom!" Tommy abruptly halts the car, choking us with our safety belts before we're thrown back into our seats.

"This isn't good," my brother says.

I unbuckle and pull the handle of my door, but before I get out, my brother spins in his seat and holds up a palm.

"Just wait. Let him deal with this. It might be bad in there." The crease in my brother's forehead is deep. I meet his worried eyes with what I'm sure are terrified ones of my own.

"That's exactly *why* I need to go in there, Tommy!" I shake my head and continue my way out the door. My brother gives in, following me as we take cautious steps around the side of the trailer to the oil-stained driveway. It's littered with abandoned car parts and pans from work Dustin's done here, and things Colt left behind. At least six cats huddle underneath the home, their eyes glowing from the daylight while they hide in the shadows. I wonder if Dustin's mom has been feeding them.

"County, we've got a nine-oh-one N coming in, code three," a voice says from just inside the door. Dustin and I remain at the bottom of the small set of porch steps, and I wrap my right hand around my throat out of fear for what's happening inside.

"Can I go with you? Or do I need to drive myself? What do I do?" Dustin's voice displays rare panic. It breaks me, and tears well in my eyes. Tommy's mouth is a hard line, and his chest stopped moving. He's holding his breath.

"Do you know what your mom took, son? Anything you can get us will help. Anything," someone says to him.

Unable to let Dustin navigate this conversation alone, I pass by my brother and jog up the steps to enter the messy living room that I've never been allowed to see before. It smells of burnt plastic, chemicals, and cat piss. How Dustin ever survived a night in this place is lost on me. This is the kind of place people cultivate to slip away from the living, which seems is exactly what his mother has done.

Dustin is standing over his mom as she lays on a rolling stretcher that paramedics are about to carry through the door. His hands fist his hair and his eyes dart around the floor as if the answers he needs are written on the matted carpet and vinyl.

"It could be anything. Fentanyl, oxy . . . I don't know. I —" Dustin's gaze meets mine and his skin turns gray. I move to him and reach for his hand, not giving a shit about anyone seeing it or what Tommy will think when he does. I grip his hand tightly and force him to look at me.

"It's okay," I say, my voice low at his side. He squeezes my hand with enough strength that my fingers grow numb. I let him.

I don't have to ask. His uncertain words are more than panic over finding his mom limp on her side, body twitching while medics hook up her IV and monitor her oxygen. Sadly, this isn't the first time Dustin has walked in to find his mom overdosed on the floor. What has him truly worried is that Colt isn't home, but he has been—recently. The half-drank bottle of beer on the coffee table is still cold, the glass beaded with sweat. The living room TV is on, though muted, and it's showing basketball. Dustin's mom is not the kind of woman who gives a shit about sports. To be fair, she doesn't give a shit about much.

But the biggest sign? That's coming from the vent swinging above the bathroom door, held on by a single screw. No, Colt isn't here right now. But he was. And he left with something he didn't want anybody to find. Something he kept behind that vent. Something more important than the woman who birthed his only son, who's lying on the floor, seconds from death.

10

"Your mom got lucky this time."

I didn't have the heart to tell the emergency room doc that my mom got lucky last time too. And the time before that. Seemed like bragging. Too much luck for one woman to have in a lifetime. Instead, I gave him a response straight from my heart.

"Yeah, she's real fuckin' lucky," I said.

He wasn't impressed with my honesty. Or my tone.

This is the third time I've driven my mom home after a near-deadly overdose. The first time I drove her was without a license. I was eleven. Seemed like a no-brainer to talk my way out of trouble if a cop pulled us over.

Sorry, sir. My mom overdosed.

No cop's going to punish a kid in that situation. Besides, it's a small enough town that most people around here know my story. *Colt Bridge's kid.*

So far this time, I've been able to ignore my mom's promises. It's the same string of words it always is—lies about getting clean, about this being the last time, and about telling Colt to get out and stay out. Nothing will change, and this drive? It will happen again. Only, I swear to God, I won't be the one making it. I'm making that promise, and I'll keep it. This happens again and I'm around, I'm slamming the door shut behind me and driving away for good.

When we arrive home, I'm not shocked to find Colt's El Camino pulled up nice and tight to the front door. I wonder how much shit he had to get rid of after he called 9-1-1? I bet he parked nearby to watch it all play out so he knew when it was safe to come back. He's not a big-time drug dealer, but busy enough that if authorities opened their eyes and saw the evidence, they'd have to do something about him. He's small time enough to fly under the "who gives a shit" radar.

"Alright. Home. Go on, get out. Put yourself in bed for the next week or whatever it is you do after this," I say. If I could reach across my mom and push her door open, I would. As it is, she moans and rolls to her side in the passenger seat. I wish I had a single memory of this woman being sweet to me so I could muster enough empathy to actually want to help her.

"Don't be like that, Dusty." She reaches for me, her shaking hand and dirty fingernails coming at the side of my face. I flinch and scowl.

"Uh, no. This is not that moment. Time to get out. Go on," I say, pushing myself against my door to gain as much distance as I can. I actually felt sorry for her last night. She seemed lucid and flu-like. We conversed, and she asked for soup. I heated up a can on the stove. She wasn't sick like that, though. She was withdrawing. Probably from something new. It's hard to keep up with her highs.

Her shoulders shake as she fumbles with the safety belt.

She's going to fucking cry. This is usually what breaks me, but I'm numb to it this time. Annoyed more than sad or sympathetic. I can't keep doing this. I've been her caregiver my entire life, only she has no desire to get well.

"Dusty . . ." she mumbles through spit and tears.

"Gah!" I push open my door and rush around the car, not because I'm in a hurry to help her but because I need her out of my car. I need to get out of here.

She's unable to work the handle to open her door, so I yank it open wide and grab her arm, propping her up against me. She's strong enough to walk inside. If I weren't here, she'd do it on her own just fine, probably make herself a snack and turn on her soap operas. She's putting on this show for me. She likes to play invalid, which is shameful and a punch in the face to people who really need to be cared for.

"Come on. Let's just get this over with," I hope she at least takes the stairs without going limp. We slam into Colt's chest at the doorway, and I grit my teeth and look down at his feet because if I look him in the eyes right now, I'm going to lose it.

"Oh, ho ho! Look who's got time to help out now, huh?" His breath smells of stale cigarettes, and his unwashed body reeks.

"You should be saying that shit to yourself," I say, pushing past him. He steps in front of us again before I get my mom fully inside. She slips from my grip, collapsing to her knees with one hand on each of our legs as she starts to cry.

"Don't do this. No, no, no . . ." she moans. I pinch the bridge of my nose and pull my foot away. I'm pushed into the trailer with a hard thrust to the center of my chest the second I do.

"Don't kick your mother!" Colt comes at me, his hand cupped and out to the side. He swings it at me and I flinch, preparing to be hit. He stops before contact though, his belly rumbling with an amused laugh that gurgles out of him. I hate that I give him this power.

I move so the recliner my mom practically lives in is between us. My pulse steadies just having some sort of barrier. It's not that Colt is bigger than me. He isn't anymore. Hasn't been for at least two years. It's that he's so wild and unpredictable. I'm never sure whether a fist is going to land on my face or a knife at my side. He's made threats, flashed metal, and even shown off his gun a time or two. That threat keeps me in check, and the fact he has this hold over me makes me hate myself sometimes.

"Look, let me get her to bed. You can go back to . . . whatever you're doing." I hold out my palms and glance around the shithole they call home. A few duffle bags are piled in the corner of the kitchen. Probably the cash he took off with, maybe his supply too. It doesn't smell like burnt acid in here, so I don't think he's cooked anything yet. That's Colt's thing—he melts down shit he buys at the border and mixes it with over-the-counter crap to increase his profit. I know guys at school who use his stuff. They call him the Candy Man. Hell, he probably melts down Jolly Ranchers with that shit.

Colt's upper lip raises into a cocky smile on one side that shows off his discolored teeth. He takes a few steps back, gripping the door jamb as he leans out and looks into the driveway.

"You got that windshield fixed, huh? How you pay for that?" He pulls himself back inside and his demon eyes land on mine.

"I sold something," I say, instantly regretting answering him at all.

He snickers and steps back outside, lifting my mom. She's shaking, a little because she's scared of him, but more because she's lost control of the act she was putting on.

"Why don't you go on to bed. I'll go get us some burgers later," Colt says, nuzzling his chin in the crook of her neck. She nods slowly and turns into him, croaking out an "okay."

I step to the side, flattening against the far wall as she passes through the living room and levels me with her pitiful gaze. I used to fall for this, feel sorry for her and tell her I loved her. I haven't said that to her in so long. Haven't said it to anyone. I'm not sure my lips know how to form the words anymore.

My mom drags her fingers along the wood-paneled hallway and I watch her in my periphery until her door clicks shut. My attention snaps back to Colt the second we're alone.

"You didn't sell anything of mine, did you?" He knows I didn't. He's fishing, pushing me.

I laugh out a breath and grip my lip with my teeth, lifting my chin as I stare him down.

"I don't need to make money the way you do."

His eyes dim and his mouth ticks.

"You sure about that?" He holds up a handful of cash. *My* cash.

"That's mine!" I lunge at him, no longer caring about the bulky piece of furniture between us, stepping over it as if I'm going to leap at him with a fist like some character in a video game. He strong-arms me, grabbing my forearm with his other hand, holding my money out of reach. I take wild swings at him but his grip tightens, his nails digging into my skin.

"Now, you know I had to check out that ride of yours last night. I haven't gotten a good look at that engine in years, and you were sleeping so peaceful on the couch."

I lunge again, knowing I can overpower him. It's the first time I've ever actually tried, and the move catches him off guard, his grip on me slipping, his hand falling away.

"You son of a—"

The cut is swift and stops my words. It stings at first, and I back up several steps in shock, my mouth hung open as I lift my sliced T-shirt to get a good look at the slit across half of my stomach and side. I'm too stunned to speak actual words, and instead, this awful sound escapes my throat, like a wounded animal. I flatten my palm across my skin to test the amount of blood, my hand covered in a matching crimson strip. I lift my chin in time to see Colt tuck his blade into his back pocket, stuffing my money in the other one.

"It's about time you get on out of here, don't you think? Maybe stay at that little girlfriend of yours' house for a while. Hell, stay there forever for all I care. That pretty family you like to pretend is your real family, you think they'll get sick of you being around too much? You think they'll love you? Shit, all you ever was to me was a mouth I had to feed. Until, ya know, you started leaving cash around and bringing me things I could sell. Look around at this palace, son. You helped me build some of it, you know. You think you're the only one who knows about your little races out on the Straights? I've made some nice cash off of you. Even better sales. You could have been something with me. You have no idea what I am—*who I am*. But maybe that'll scar up nice and pretty so you'll always remember who your daddy is."

Undeterred by the pain, I growl and lunge at him again, but he whips the blade from his back pocket again and points it at me, a sinister laugh vibrating his lips, the volume growing in his chest, crackling in the shell of his drunken, drug-fueled body.

"Ah, don't get sloppy, Dusty. You know better."

I hate when he calls me that. Same with my mom. It's not like the way Hannah says it. It isn't kind. When they use Dusty, it's childlike, and it pulls me back to the depths of my youth, when Colt knocked me around simply because it was a Sunday and the liquor store was closed.

Dusty, don't upset your father. That's what my mom would say. As if my mere presence and being alive and breathing wasn't what upset him most.

I'm broken and helpless, still, even outweighing him by twenty pounds or more. I growl, my back molars pressing together so hard they might crack. I feel the burn on my face as the blood rushes to my forehead, my nose, my cheeks. I'm bursting with anger and so much self-hatred. I might hate myself more than I hate this man, and that makes me feel charred and empty inside. Who am I? I'm still the twelve-year-old boy who can't stand up for himself and who stuck around way too long.

Colt ambles down the hallway, coughing out a laugh that's the equivalent of spitting in my face. The moment the bedroom door creaks open and closed again, I rush toward the junked up kitchen counter and knock every last thing to the floor with a sweep of my arm. Dirty pans clang across the vinyl floor, pancake mix that's probably so old it's crawling with weevils puffs up in a cloud as it tumbles after it. My mom's bong cracks into pieces, the glass burnt from too much use. I'm suffocating in here, my chest heaving with the need to breathe, my heart raging to leap from my body.

I rush through the door, shoving it with enough force that the wall cracks behind it. I don't stop and I don't care. I march to my car and fire up my engine, peeling out of this hell that clings to me, my tires kicking up gravel as I spin out. I don't bother to peer in the mirror as I race away. I don't need one last look. I don't need to ever come here again. If this is how my mom wants to die, under the pathetic control of a madman bent on taking away anyone's glimmer of hope or happiness just to get a fix or buy his way into small time, trailer park, drug kingpin status, then they can have each other.

They deserve each other!

I race to the only place that has ever felt like home. I rush through the Judge's front door without knocking, taking the stairs two at a time, passing the worried faces of Hannah and Tommy's parents as they stare at me, instantly alerted by my manic speed and streaming, hot tears. I push through Hannah's door, collapse on her lap where she sits on her bed, and bleed on her pretty pink quilt as my arms wrap around her so tight.

Tommy rushes in. I don't know what's next, and I know this won't last—it can't. But I do know that this family is all I need. It's the only thing that has ever seen me through to the next day. And right now, Hannah is the one piece holding me together.

11

I've never been good at lying to Tommy's face. I've been lucky with my feelings for Dustin. So far, they've been one-sided. Lines have bled together though; Dustin needs me. I *want* him to need me. Rather than attempt to lie to Tommy about the scene he witnessed when Dustin crawled into my lap looking for home, I've decided to avoid him.

I've kept my door shut and my light dimmed, not stepping foot in the hallway since our mom set Dustin up on the pullout sofa downstairs. When Tommy knocked to see if I wanted part of the pizza Mom and Dad ordered, I said I was full even though my stomach was grumbling. And the last text my brother sent to see if I was awake, I completely ignored, hoping he'd give up and give me time to conjure something to say in the morning. If not a better lie, at least an undeniable truth he won't rip to shreds.

Midnight seems late enough.

It isn't.

"Do you really want to eat that pizza cold or are you

trying not to make noise with the microwave?" Tommy asks.

His observation is pretty spot on.

I set down the paper plate holding the slice I just surgically removed from the pizza box in the fridge. For some reason, I cling to the idea that if I don't lift my head and actually look him in the eyes I can still get out of this unscathed.

"I woke up hungry," I say. My gaze darts near him but never lands on him directly.

"Uh huh," he says, sliding the paper plate across the counter then taking a seat on one of the stools at the kitchen island. He folds the piece of pizza in half and takes a huge bite.

"I guess I'll get another piece." I sigh, opening the fridge door and fishing out the entire box this time. My brother snaps behind me and I glance in his direction, still not fully looking.

"I want another slice after this one," he says.

I set the box down and flip the lid over, pushing it his direction so he can get his own slice. After he does, I hook my finger in the corner of the box to drag it back to me, but he slaps his palm on the open lid and holds it in place—holds it hostage—until I look at him. *In the eyes.*

The shivers come first, slithering down my spine and followed by a rush of heat and instant sweat that tackles my palms.

"Hannah."

I hate when my brother says my name like that, in that tone. He's not my parent, and being sixteen months older doesn't give him authority. He still thinks babysitting me when he was nine and I was seven counts for something, but it doesn't. In many ways, I'm more mature than he is.

I'm not the one who gets drunk and high on Friday nights because I suck at fending off peer pressure.

"Thomas," I throw back at him.

He sneers at the formal version of his name. If he's going to act like Dad, I'm going to use his name.

My brother lifts his hand in the air as some grand gesture of surrender and I pull the box back into my possession, tearing out another slice of pizza to heat in the microwave. I roll my eyes at my brother's smirk.

"Fine. I did want to heat it up. I didn't want to wake our guest." My voice is defiant, a child caught fudging her F grade to a B with a felt marker.

I push the pizza box back into the fridge and flop my slice on another paper plate before sticking it in the micro for thirty seconds. I'm tempted to stare at it as it spins on the turntable, cheese bubbling.

"What are you doing?"

I close my eyes at Tommy's question. I know he isn't asking about my microwaving method. Still, I don't answer right away. I let my pizza finish, stopping it just before the timer beeps. I pull the plate out and test the cheese with a touch of my finger.

"*Ow!*" I poke my finger in my mouth to ease the burn.

I can feel Tommy's eyes boring into the side of my face. I won't be able to put this off forever, but do we really need to have this conversation with the boy it revolves around sleeping two dozen feet away on our couch?

"It's better warm. You should heat yours up too," I say, blinking to meet his gaze. I hold my bluff in place as I blow on the edge of my slice. My act won't hold up much longer.

I nibble on the end of the pizza, no longer hungry, and eventually I give up, tossing the plate and piece on the counter between us.

"He's going to hurt you. You know that, right? He can't help it, Han. And I don't blame him for it. It's not his fault that he was born to two of the worst people on the planet. Colt? He's not his fault. You don't get to pick your father. But that stuff, Hannah? It still matters. Dustin is like my brother—he's *our* brother—"

I hold up my hand and wave it at Tommy's face, stopping him before he tries to convince me that his relationship with Dustin is anything like mine.

"Just don't. Not with that 'we're family' shit, okay? I know we're like family. I know we all grew up together. But damn it, Tommy, I can't help how I feel!" Even whisper-shouting, my voice cracks. My brother's head falls to his shoulder at my confession. I ache at the disappointment I see pulling down the corners of his mouth and drooping his eyes.

"You could date literally anyone, Hannah. You'll be a senior next year and, hell, who knows where the fuck Dustin will be!" My brother waves a hand over his shoulder toward our sleeping friend—*our brother.*

"He'll be with you!" I growl.

My eyes lock with Tommy's in an intense stare as we lean toward one another. That's when I see it—the secret my brother has been hiding from me.

"Tommy?" My face falls as I say his name.

My brother's gaze falls to the counter, guilt taking over every little movement he makes. He shoves his half-eaten crust and plate away before resting his forehead in his fingertips, letting them sink into his temples.

"I don't know, Han. I don't know. That's always been the plan, but that's *his* plan. I'm starting college in the fall—"

"You can do both, Tommy! It's just the weekends, and

it's not every weekend," I argue, trying to convince my brother to stay on board with the plan he and Dustin hatched when they were eight.

It's one thing being the King of the Straights, but that's not where the road ends for Dustin. Anyone who has seen him drive knows that. He's meant for greatness. Sponsorships, titles, leaderboards, and so much money—money he earned the right way, legit, with his own two hands, a heavy right foot, and a daredevil in his heart. My brother has always been at his side. There's trust between them. My brother understands how engines work, and his presence gives Dustin the edge he needs on the road. An engine that's been blessed by Tommy Judge is one that can be pushed to the brink. Anything less is faking it, waiting to blow up in someone's face.

"It's not like I won't try, Hannah. I will. It's just—"

"You want different things," I answer for him.

His eyes meet mine and the truth sits heavy in the quiet between us. He shrugs and leans back, threading his hands behind his neck and eventually letting his head fall so he's staring at our ceiling, the dim light my mom leaves on so we can see down here glowing above us.

"Not really different. I mean, I love engineering, and that stuff comes easily to me. I don't know that I want to spend the rest of my life on a track somewhere, hauling a beat-up car around the country waiting for a break." My brother rolls his head, and this time he's the one avoiding my waiting eyes.

"You really think that's what it's going to be like? Years of dirt tracks and drag races? Drifts and pay-to-plays? Side bets and small towns?" I know my brother can't think that. He might not like Dustin's family tree, but he believes in the guy who has been his best friend for more than a decade. Doesn't he?

"I don't know. Is Dustin good? I mean, yeah. He's the best we've seen. But really, what have we seen, Hannah? Dad driving us around the Southwest to kart races? Some small-game races in Phoenix and Vegas? The odds of breaking in are so thin. I don't want to look back on my college years and wish I'd actually *lived* them, ya know?" My brother's gaze lifts, his pained expression cutting into my chest.

"Odds are for the other guys," I say back to him. His lip turns up, but only briefly. That's one of Dustin's favorite sayings. It's cocky as fuck, but it's always been true when it comes to any race he's in. Whatever wheels are being driven by Dustin Bridges are the ones crossing the finish line first. Everyone else fights for second.

"Whatever," Tommy says abruptly, standing and circling the stool he abandoned. He positions his hands on the back of it, fingers wrapping around the ornate metal design. My eyes focus on his hands, the way they seem to be stuck on pause, anchoring him here with me.

"Just see how it goes," I spit out. My words sound desperate, even whispered. Tommy can't abandon Dustin, though. He just can't. My insides burn at the mere thought of what that would do to Dustin.

"Yeah, I guess that's really the plan. I'm kind of doing that. But"—he pauses, letting go of the chair and flexing his fingers, curling them into fists that he holds in front of his chest, head down as he stares at his knuckles. His head starts to shake—"you don't need to see how this goes, this *you and Dustin* thing. It doesn't go anywhere. You understand?" My brother lifts his head, his muscles flexed and jaw clenched like a father putting his foot down. He's not even giving our father a chance at the role.

"What happens in my life and who I decide to share parts of it with isn't up to you." I fold my arms around my stomach and tip my chin up to let him know I'm not afraid of his pseudo-authority.

"It's not. It's up to you, but . . . *this?*" He gestures over his shoulder. "Getting involved with Dustin won't end well, Hannah. Hell, it won't even start well. I don't want you to get hurt, and he's a whirlwind. No, he's a fucking tornado. His life, his family—it's one giant black hole. It will suck you in, sink you. I want more for you than that."

"That why you lied about the car part I bought for him?" It's an odd thing to throw back at him, but I've been harboring resentment over the credit he stole from me. And maybe I'm a bit of a petulant child. Sure, Tommy thinks he's coming from a good place with all of this "advice," but it's preachy bullshit. He doesn't see Dustin the way I do. He can't.

"Tell him. I'll tell him. You want me to wake him up right now and let him know my sister has a crush on him and bought him a present so he'll pay attention to her?" He rolls his eyes as he dishes out the insults, and I shift my feet, offended.

"Are you serious with this?" My molars grind together while I bite my tongue—literally—to hold back from saying more.

Tommy moves close to me, dipping his hands in the pockets of his sweatpants as he steps close enough to show off his height advantage. He loves looking down on me when he's trying to win an argument. It's a power play for him.

"I'm dead serious. This crush of yours means a lot more

to you than him. I guarantee it does. He's clinging to you because he's hurting, and you're familiar. But Hannah, you've gotta know that if it ever comes down to you or the race, he'll choose the race. Always. Every single time. You'll never be more than a girl who gets him and his history, and that might feel all warm and fuzzy and full of butterflies and shit right now, but a month from now? Or when he's graduated and you're still a high schooler? Consider the optics of that for a second."

"*Pfft*," I retort, turning my head to the side so my brother can't see the sting that left in my eyes.

He clears his throat, probably baiting me into looking back in his direction. I don't, especially as I feel him step back.

"You do what you want. But don't say I didn't warn you. When this hurts—and it will—don't expect me to listen to your broken-heart sob story."

Tommy slaps the wall where the light switch is as he leaves the kitchen space, killing the soft light and leaving me standing alone in the dark. I give in to the burn in my eyes for a few seconds, squeezing my lids shut tight so the tears welling up release down my cheeks. I run my palm over my face almost instantly, erasing their existence before breathing in deep. My attention shifts to cleaning up our mess, tossing the half-eaten pieces in the trash, along with the paper plates. I follow the same path my brother took, but instead of rounding the corner, I halt in the space that leads to the stairs and the direction of the couch, where Dustin is breathing softly.

Holding my breath, I listen for pops and creaks in the house, testing to see who else might be awake. Tommy won't come back down here. He's thrown all his moves, and he loves having the last word. My eyes adjust to the darkness as I scan the familiar things in my living room, the extra blanket still folded on the back of the sofa. I move toward it, taking the soft knitted throw in my hands and unfurling it as I round the couch arms and rest a knee on the mattress.

Dustin's back is to me, one leg bent, the other straight as an arrow, his foot poking out from the sheet he's sleeping under. I start covering him there, draping the throw over his body until it runs out at his chest. I'm slow and gentle with my movements, not wanting to wake him. I want to lie with him a little while, to hear his heart beat and smell the faint trace of oil on his T-shirt. I nestle in behind him, touching my nose to his spine before rolling my head so my ear rests flat against his warm back, the steady thump taking over all other sounds. I bring my palm up to his bicep and shoulder, and hold on softly, wishing I could reach around his chest and cling to him harder.

My eyes close and I draw in his scent, the mix of my mom's fabric softener cutting through all things Dustin. I promise myself I won't stay for more than a minute, but those plans change the moment his hand reaches around and covers mine where it rests on his arm. Our fingers naturally twine together, loosely at first, then our grasp grows tighter as his body shifts and his back is soon replaced with his chest.

"I didn't mean to wake you," I say.

He breathes out a whisper of a laugh.

"Hard to sleep through a creepy stalker smelling your clothes," he says. I blush and press my face into his chest as I playfully slap at his arm.

"I didn't say I wasn't glad you woke up." I lift my chin to peer up at his dark eyes. Even in the darkness, I know exactly how his features look—the sharp cut of his jaw, the flex of his neck muscles, the split in his eyebrow from the stitches he got when he was eleven and his father threw a wrench at his head. I move my hand up his body to his face, my finger tracing the familiar scar.

"You really got the intake back for me, huh?" He heard. *How much did he hear?*

"Mmm, yeah. I mean, technically, Michael Bosa bought it for you."

Dustin's body shakes with a silent laugh.

"You raise your prices on that douchebag?"

"I sure did," I say, smiling proudly. Dustin's thumb lands on my lips as they curve, and I close my eyes again at the feel of it tracing along my mouth. My lips part, kissing his thumb first then his wrist as his hand snakes its way into my hair. His warm lips find my forehead a second later.

"Thanks, Hannah. That's the nicest thing anyone's ever done for me," he says, and sadly, I know he means it.

I grip a handful of his T-shirt and slink my way up a few inches so our lips meet.

"Didn't even let the guys at the shop take advantage of me," I say against his lips. His quiver with a proud, quiet laugh in return.

"Thatta girl."

He sucks in my top lip, tracing the tender skin with his tongue. I open my mouth for more, and he gives me what I crave, cradling my head in his palm as our mouths collide into a hungrier kiss this time. Nothing is rushed; our movements are soft and silent. There's something taboo about us, though Tommy seems to see what's happening despite our efforts to hide it from him.

I nudge his frame as our kiss deepens, wanting to push him to his back so I can hold myself on top of him, feel him under me. *Feel what I do to him.* With every push I give, though, he pushes back. I know it's not because of the cut on his stomach. Mom and I cleaned him up and it wasn't as deep as he thought. Of course, my mom also thinks he snagged his skin on barbed wire while leaving his house, not that his father tried to gut him.

After one more failed attempt to move things further, I grow frustrated and suck his bottom lip hard, letting my teeth graze against his skin as I let go.

"Nobody is coming down here," I say, more forward and obvious than I want to be, but I have a growing need boiling in my body.

"Maybe," he says, his hands cupping my face, thumbs sweeping my hair from my eyes. He brings our foreheads together and I can tell by the way the air slowly escapes through his nose while his shoulders remain tense that he heard Tommy's warning.

"My brother doesn't understand," I say. Long seconds pass without a response, and I regret saying anything at all. Eventually, though, Dustin's lips brush against mine, peppering me with soft kisses while he seems to think.

"He's just being Tommy," he finally settles on. I shift to put space between our faces, to adjust my sight enough to stare into his eyes. His long lashes tap his cheeks with a few slow blinks before I catch the slight gleam of his pupils from the room's dim light.

"I know. But Tommy isn't *us*. And I can't go back to pretending, Dustin. I've wanted this—*you*—for a really long time, and I'm tired of pretending I don't." My breath stops with the last word and my throat burns from honesty.

More slow blinks mark the face of this boy I crave, nearly a man but so far from grown up. He needs someone to care for him so badly, and I need him to let me.

His eyes close and he brings our foreheads together

again, several breaths passing between us before he finally speaks.

"I feel exactly the same, Hannah. And we won't go back. We'll never go back."

I'm somehow both settled and terrified at his words. I choose to hold them close and think of them as precious, and I choose to hold on to him for a few minutes longer, at least until he's fallen asleep.

12

Sometimes it feels as though I'm watching the Judge family through a pane of glass. As if I'm stuck on the outside, always forced to look in. Though they've never made me feel I don't belong here, I still very much do —often.

It's hard knowing you're a charity case. Hearing those words from Tommy's own mouth last night really settled things for me, too. In the back of my mind, I've had this hunch that for Tommy, things were temporary. Our dream was really *my* dream, and the steps we were taking to reach a goal were, for him, pretend.

I felt Hannah leave my arms last night. I didn't want her to but I was glad she did. I meant what I said when I agreed with her. She and I? We can't go back to only being friends. But I don't see how we can move forward together either, at least not in the way I want us to. Tommy wasn't completely wrong. Her being with me—*around me?* It puts her in danger. But not for the reasons Tommy thinks. I know who I am. I would never intentionally hurt any of them. They're my family, more real to me than my actual blood. But sometimes I get in a place, in my head, and forget about the casualties of my actions. Like Colt, I can be driven by rage and determination. Combine that with my need to always win, and I'm not sure what cost I'm willing to pay.

Never intentionally; I fear it's just in my nature. And more than anything, I'm afraid of the emotional damage that comes with being with me.

The Judge family rushes around the kitchen, their dad popping bread in the toaster as their mom fills coffee cups. They slide one on the center island for me, and Tommy takes it for himself before I can get myself up from this couch. I'm much happier watching them than actually participating anyhow.

It doesn't take long for my eyes to land on Hannah. She glances my direction as she rounds the hallway and enters the kitchen. She's wearing an enormous sweatshirt that covers the length of her shorts. Somehow, over time, her legs went from these gangly sticks covered in bruises and scratches from climbing trees and trying to keep up with us on our dirt bikes to smooth, golden, tempting curves that beckon my hands to travel from the backs of her thighs up under that sweatshirt and the way-too-short shorts she's wearing underneath.

She kisses her mom's cheek and snags a piece of toast from her dad's plate, the one with more peanut butter. Her favorite.

"Hey!" He pretends he doesn't always make two just to share with her.

Tommy stands from pulling out two energy drinks from the bottom drawer of the fridge. He tosses one to me and I catch it as I stand, letting the blanket that Hannah put over me pool at my feet.

I twist the cap and turn my chin to my shoulder for a quick smell test. I wasn't much in the mood for getting up early this morning to shower. Not that I wasn't awake. I was pinned to the sofa, staring at the family portrait on the bookcase directly across from me. One more reminder that as far as they let me inside, the Judges can't give me everything I need. I don't think anybody can. That would require a trip to my past—a miracle.

No. I'm meant to grow up and become something despite my family. That's my lot.

I gather my school bag and hover by the door, taking sips from the energy drink while Hannah and Tommy finish pulling their things together. I cringe when Tommy's mom stops him and tugs on his backpack, exposing the bright orange packet filled with graduation information.

"Dustin, I expect you'll leave your folder for me to take care of?" She's using her business voice, which is hard to say no to.

"Yeah, of course. I think it's in my car. I'll bring it in tonight. It's not due for a week yet," I say, knowing full well that I plan to dodge her offer to buy my cap and gown and be my surrogate parent at some stupid ceremony on our football field later next month.

She points at me, her nonverbal way of putting me to task. I nod and cross my heart. I've gotten used to lying to myself, but I don't ever lie to Tommy's mom. I figured I would be out of here by the time all that pomp and circumstance time came around. Now that I'm two grand short and possibly going out on my own, well, maybe a cap and gown isn't the worst thing to indulge.

I manage to slip out the door before Hannah does, so I nudge Tommy's shoulder in the driveway.

"Hey, can I get a ride with you? Supra's got a funny sound. I don't wanna mess with it, ya know?" It's a lie, and I have an inkling that Tommy knows it is because he glances behind us to Hannah.

"Yeah, sure," he says, his tone clipped.

I climb in the passenger side and scan the driveway in the mirror when I shut the door. Hannah pauses halfway between her car and mine as she realizes I've already gotten into her brother's car, and my gut sours seeing the way her shoulders drop. Her eyes meet mine for a blip. We're too far apart to really see her expression, but I swear to God I can read the hurt in her eyes.

"This is exactly what I'm talking about," Tommy mumbles, climbing in and starting his engine. His lips are set in a smug line.

"Exactly *what* are you talking about?" I ask but really, I know. He means drama between me and Hannah, him in the middle. Still, though, I'd like to hear him say the things I overheard last night. I'd appreciate getting the tough talk right to my face.

Instead, Tommy shakes his head, pushing his sunglasses on as he cranks the wheel to back out of the driveway. He peels out, a little aggressive for him, and all I can do is chuckle. I should have gotten in the car with Hannah or offered her a ride in mine, pushed the doubts and worries out of my head.

We get to school minutes before Hannah, who probably stopped to pick up Bailey. I'm sure she's not in a hurry to see me now that I basically ran away. The front of the school is covered in balloons and posters about prom. As if the cap and gown speech wasn't a reminder of how little I feel I fit in, this scene I'm walking into nails it. A girl squeals to my right, her boyfriend's shoulder bumping into mine as he stands up from kneeling. Kneeling, for a prom ask. An ask for a girl he's already dating. But everyone at this school is all about the show and the big gesture and standing out and getting attention, and prom is like one big attention celebration.

I'm about to gripe about it to Tommy when I realize he's disappeared about a dozen feet to my left and is pulling some bullshit rolled-up poster out of his backpack to show to some girl I swear he's hooked up with twice and dumped as many times. She should slap him for assuming she'd go to prom with him, but no. She's covering her mouth. And here come the fake tears. And . . . she's hugging him.

"Wow," I mutter to myself.

"You know, doing the *in* thing isn't necessarily a bad thing," Hannah says at my shoulder. A shiver runs over my skin, wrapping around my neck and choking me a little. It's a mixture of guilt and schoolboy delight. I turn to respond but she's already moved on, up the steps to the main doors. Bailey glances at me over her shoulder, her eyes drooping with pity.

I didn't even get a chance to get myself out of the hole I made. Serves me right, I guess.

My morning is a blur, and I've run my phone down fifty percent by obsessing over underground races north of the city that I might be able to get to in the next few weeks. I don't like racing in the city. Empty streets are never truly abandoned, and it's barely worth the gas it costs me to get there just to pull in a win or two. But I'm out serious cash now, and my shifts at the yard have basically dried up. People won't be betting big at the Straights for the next few weeks, not after last weekend's race. If I can find a race or two that have a little buzz, maybe I can turn them into something worth my time—and rubber.

My attention is completely consumed with social media chatter when I feel the soft tickle of paper flutter across my arms. Mrs. Collins, my history teacher, taps the screen of my phone with her long, glossy, coffee-colored fingernail, and between the quick glance at the F on the paper she just dropped in my lap and the scowl waiting on her face when I look up, I'm feeling pretty screwed.

"Sorry," I say, leaning to one side to push my phone into my pocket. I pull my paper to the top of my desk and trace the bright red F with my finger. Why do they have to use such a glaring color? Couldn't this information have been delivered by, say, faint pencil markings?

"See me after class," she says, pushing my paper down flat with the same shiny fingernail. Those suckers are like weapons, honestly. It doesn't seem right that girls have to turn nail files in to the office because they could be used as knives but Wolverine claws are fine.

I nod and sink back in my chair. I don't even remember taking this test. It's my handwriting, though, so I must have. I read over the first few answers and my lip ticks up, amused. I'm a dumbass, sure, but I'm a funny one.

The question: What ended in 1933.

My answer: 1932.

I fold the test in half and flatten my palms on top while I fake engage with the last few minutes of class. My eyes are on my teacher's face, and I think there's a hint of a smile on my lips, but I don't hear a word. I'm calculating how quickly I can get to south Phoenix and back on Friday before the Straights, maybe squeeze in two races and make a little headway toward earning back my cash.

The bell dings and the entire classroom erupts with shuffling papers, feet, and backpacks. Zippers go one way then back as serious students take their tests home to study for the final. I'll be lucky to find mine an hour from now.

I lean forward in my desk, pulling my feet under as I fidget with the folded edges of my test. My heart is pounding, which is such a foreign sensation. I'm not the kind of guy who gets nervous, but something about school zeroes in on all my insecurities. Years of missed parent-teacher conferences, detentions and threats of expulsion for fighting, or worse—*home visits*. When it comes to life, I feel prepared, probably more than most. I know how to handle myself in the real world. I'm ready for all things cruel and unfair. But at school, in situations that are academic, I have always felt stupid. The heat from everyone's eyes on me when Mrs. Collins asked to talk to me after class still burns hot at my neck even though everyone's gone. I brace myself for the worst as Mrs. Collins turns the desk in front of me around and takes a seat.

"Dustin, I'm not going to dance around this topic. You're not going to pass this class. You won't graduate with the rest of your class. It's a mathematical impossibility." She actually looks sympathetic, which helps tamp down my instinct to become defensive.

"Oh," I say instead. The word comes out quiet and I study the blank side of my test as I spin it on my desk in slow circles.

I glance up with an arched brow.

"Are there, like, retakes or something?" I lift a shoulder and am encouraged by her soft smile, but I can tell by the way her eyes still and hold their lock on mine that there aren't.

"There's summer school, and with just one class, you

147

could have your credit done in four weeks. If we get you enrolled, maybe I can talk to the principal about letting you walk the graduation line with your friends. You won't get an actual diploma, though."

I chuckle at the thought.

"So, like, what? I'll get a prop?" I imagine a blank piece of construction paper with a gold ribbon tied around the middle.

"Something like that," she says, flattening my amusement with the hard truth. Yeah, I'll get a fake diploma. I fucked up getting the real one. Tommy and Hannah's mom's conversation with me this morning replays through my head, and my thoughts bounce between breaking her heart, and how very little a high school diploma really means to me.

"What if . . ." I suck in my lips as I hold in my thought. My eyes blink rapidly, eventually opening on Mrs. Collins'. Her hands are clasped together on the desk, and if I hold my breath, I swear I can hear the tick of the second hand on her gold watch. I wonder how much that thing is worth.

"What if I just didn't finish. Like, I end up one credit short, and maybe later I finish or get a GED or something? Is that an option?"

Her mouth falls at the corners and her eyes become flat with disappointment.

"Dropping out is always an option, but I think it's a coward's way out."

Wow. She's not exactly warm and fuzzy. Kinda makes me respect her a little more. I don't know much about Mrs. Collins, or any of the teachers at this school. She lives in town, though. She knows about life here, she knows my story, and she has spent a few years at the very least in this environment.

"I understand," I say, and she breathes out a sigh as her shoulders relax. She thinks she's gotten through to me, and I feel bad because she has, but not in the way she thinks.

"It's just, I'm not going to college. My skill set isn't something that comes from schooling, and four weeks of my summer is four more weeks in a place that has done nothing for me since the day I was born. I don't think it's for me, is all. No offense."

I step up from my desk and tuck my test in the small hole in the top of my backpack. It's the last I'll see of it. I sling a strap over my right shoulder and hold out my hand to thank Mrs. Collins for at least caring enough to talk to me in private. Most teachers would have embarrassed me and dished about my sucky grades in front of everyone else.

She blinks twice as she stares at my hand, but eventually takes it as she stands, covering the top with her other palm. It's a caring gesture that immediately pricks the hairs on the back of my neck. When people do this, it has to be a trick. I feel trapped. My jaw tightens in response, my muscles rigid and ready for someone to knock me down.

"Think about it, Dustin. And don't sell yourself short. There are people here who want to see you succeed. Just because this is a small town doesn't mean we can't have big dreams."

I have big dreams, and I want to shout that at her, but suddenly, I have a hard time meeting her gaze. I force my eyes up for one quick glance, long enough to gauge how genuine all of this is. Her grip on my hand is firm enough to hold me in place, and her lips don't wear a fake smile. My heartbeat picks up again, and I hate the vulnerable feeling that seems to be snaking its way into my body. I feel powerless. Clearing my throat, I jostle my hand free and give her a quick nod.

"Yeah, sure. I can think about it." I say. My body thrums with anxiety.

I head straight for the door and don't look back, but I know she is staring at me, waiting for one more chance to zap my nerves. I'm buzzing as I walk the hallway, and the last thing I want to do is sit through my math class where I'm sure I'll be told the same thing. I can't fathom that I'm passing that class either. I haven't done a damn thing all semester. I'm so out of it that when I round the corner, I slam into another body and send papers flying in all directions. Hannah's bright white Vans instantly trigger recognition, and I lower myself to the floor to help her gather the copies of some flyer she was probably carrying to a teacher as a favor.

"Damn, I'm sorry Han," I stutter out.

"It's fine." She sniffles, and I stop grabbing papers at the sound of her broken voice.

Shit.

This is about this morning, and the way I just left. I'm still not sure Tommy isn't right. Me and Hannah aren't a good fit. I'll ruin her, or at least take her down while I'm consumed with my own *big dream*. My baggage is so heavy and so endless. I don't even know how to process what went down with my mom and Colt. Hannah says she understands, but she's never actually seen what's been done to me. Sure, she's helped me clean up the aftermath—bandages, ice packs, and my occasional need to shout the hate from my body. But I've lived through hell, and it follows me around like a sickness. How do I know that Colt's blood in my veins — the damn DNA that makes me a living, breathing human

—won't one day turn me as ugly as him? That my mom's genetic need to drink and float through life barely living won't become my fate too? Hannah might be able to clean out a cut from taking a punch to the face, but I'm not so sure she can fix how fucked up I am on the inside.

If I listen to the onslaught of negativity that streams through my mind twenty-four-seven, it's an easy choice. I walk away and let Hannah hate me, think I was merely playing into hormones and using her for a distraction. She'll get over it and fall for someone else in a couple of years, maybe some college guy who has solid plans for a real job and can give her the kind of life her parents have.

Most of me knows letting her go is what's best for her. But then . . . she looks at me. And I know nothing.

"Hey," I croak out, reaching out to her arm, my fingers grazing her skin. She freezes and drops the few papers she's gathered before falling back on her ass and looking up at the bright florescent hallway lights. Her eyes glisten as she fights off tears—tears I put there.

"Hannah," I say, scooting in close and taking her hand. She jerks it away and runs her fingers under her eyes with another big sniffle. Her eyeliner's smudging into her temples. I reach forward to fix it, but she scoots back a little more.

"It's nothing. I'm fine." She returns her focus to the papers, leaning to the right and sweeping them into the space between her legs then doing the same to her left. I crawl a few feet away to grab the strays that slid down the hall and then hand them to her, noticing the bold PROM written on the top.

Her hands tremble as they straighten out the stack I destroyed. When she gets them semi-sorted, she pulls her bag around to the side of her body and stuffs them inside, almost as if hiding them from me.

"I'll totally go, if that's something you want to do. Prom? I could go to prom," I say. She laughs almost instantly, a quiet one at first that gets louder and messier as she stands. I get to my feet, my hands not sure whether they should hide in my pockets or reach for the girl of my dreams whom I don't deserve and somehow keep pushing away. She tugs her sweatshirt back down over her shorts, and my eyes drift down her legs—legs that are mine to touch if I want them, if I would only earn them. I pinch the bridge of my nose as I replay my words.

"Gee, Dustin. That's exactly how a girl wants to be asked. Especially one whose mouth was all over yours last night. Thanks, but I think I'll pass," She tugs the straps of her backpack tight around her shoulders. Her chest lifts with a cleansing breath, one that seems to dry the leftover tears from her eyes. The redness lingers, though. I made those eyes sad like that. I made them cry and I'm the reason they're red.

This is what I do.

"Han," I say in a hushed tone as she turns and walks away. I should fight for her, rush ahead and spin on my knees, my hands clasped in the begging position, but that wouldn't be right either. She'd laugh me off and have every right to do so.

I didn't think. Of course prom is important to her. She probably always had plans to go her junior year. I remember her watching movies downstairs with Bailey when Tommy and I got dressed for junior prom last year and his mom gave us corsages to give to our dates. She watched us get to do this stupid rite of passage and when it's finally her turn to participate, I make a joke of it.

Like I've made of my life.

My phone buzzes in the middle of my self-pity session, and though I'm walking toward the math class I swore I wasn't going to, my mind is lost elsewhere. It's not on the dollar signs in the text from Alex about a race up in Henderson in three weeks, either. Nothing can penetrate my thoughts, not until I erase the picture of Hannah's sad eyes now imprinted in my mind and the lifetime of disappointment that awaits her with me.

13

Bailey thinks I'm nuts. Maybe I am. I've been an emotional wreck since my birthday, since Dustin gave me that stupid chime and I got this idea that maybe we're some great destined couple, like the fantasy that plays out in my head. It's only gotten worse as I've let my guard down and allowed him to completely consume me. I thought I was doing the same to him, but I guess that was just me being a silly girl.

The chime isn't stupid. I take that thought back, Universe.

I thought I would be okay with the secrecy. It felt necessary to protect what was so new, and my brother has this way of spoiling things for me. But this isn't new at all. The way I feel about Dustin is something that's aged within me, grown to be a part of me. I don't think I would even know how to look at another guy and get the same tingles across my skin. Michael Bosa, for all his frustrating jock-headedness, is a really good-looking guy. He's hot in that all-American boy way—the typical way that most of the other girls at our school and in this town seem to go nuts over. Tall with muscular arms he puts on display with his ripped-up T-shirts. He's had the same buzzed haircut since he was eleven, and he's grown into the military vibe of it, chiseled where chisels are supposed to be and tanned skin fit for a male model. And though he depends on me to be his academic lifeline, I know in my gut that all I'd have to do is flirt *just a little.* I could have Michael Bosa. Become Mrs. Bosa. Have little Bosa babies.

But that's not who my stupid heart beats for!

I thought Dustin was starting to see me differently, the way I see him. But that's only in private. I get that we were hiding our relationship from Tommy, but that's over now. My brother knows; Dustin heard him last night. There's nothing to hide, and I thought maybe today we could wake up and show the rest of the world the little bit of wonderful we found. But how practical is that? I can't pretend my parents aren't going to have the same cautionary advice.

I pace across my room and rip the biggest purple heart from my wall, tearing it in half, leaving an ugly ball of tape and half a heart in its wake.

"Okay, that's a bit dramatic," Bailey teases, glancing at me in the mirror as she works to pull her hair back into the strict fashion her mother prefers. From what she knows, this is all about prom and my brother having a date and me not.

"What do you know?" I throw back. Her brows lower, and I feel bad the moment my words hit her ears.

"I'm sorry," I say, and she waves me off, turning her attention back to her hair. I know she's hurt, though, so I step in behind her and take over brushing her hair.

"One day, you should let me cut your hair to your chin. You'd look really cute with one of those blunt bobs," I say, relaxing my hold on her hair and folding it at the base of her neck to mimic the way a bob would look.

Her mouth curves at the look and she turns her head slightly to the right, her eyes flitting to meet mine in the reflection.

"I could so rock that look, huh?" she says.

I nod and lean forward a little to hug her around the shoulders. She grabs my hand as I do and squeezes.

"I'm sorry," I whisper.

"I know," she responds, patting the back of my hand.

We both admire the look on her for a few more seconds before making plans to actually follow through with the cut when we go away to college. When it's too late for her mom to stop us, and when she's already had her first semester of tuition paid for.

With all things bland and proper recreated on my best friend, we head downstairs so I can walk her home. We're halfway down the driveway when my brother's car rolls up toward us, Dustin in the same seat he left in this morning. Tommy pretends to swerve to hit us and Bailey flips him off.

"That's probably the one untoward thing your mom would be okay with you doing," I laugh out.

"Oh, when it comes to your brother, I don't think she has any rules as long as I'm clothed head-to-toe. She's still not over the fact I wore a swimsuit in front of him last summer." Bailey rolls her eyes as my brother parks in the side garage.

"It wasn't even a two piece," I add.

My friend busts out a snorting laugh.

"Oh, my God, could you imagine me in a bikini?"

I step to the side and glance up and down Bailey's frame. Truth is, she would own every man in this town if she put on a two piece and took a dip in the town pool. I'm about to shower her in compliments, partly to bait her into trying it sometime, when my attention gets completely sucked away by Dustin's gaze. Tommy's already slammed the driver's door and is busy with something in the back of the garage, but Dustin is lingering, one hand resting on top of the door, the other flat on the roof while his eyes rake over me. His mouth hangs open, as if he's trying to push out words that will meet my expectations—something sweet or affectionate. Hell, I'd even take an apology for being clueless earlier. Eventually, his mouth snaps shut and my brother makes a noise that draws his eyes the other way. He doesn't look back again as he shuts the passenger door, and the whole thing pushes me to the most extreme measures.

"Hey, Dusty!" I use that name to scratch at his insides. His relationship with it is part love, part hate, and now I've gone and thrown myself into the mixture.

As expected, his shoulders bristle before his head jerks my direction.

"Don't worry about prom!" I yell. I feel Bailey's eyes on me, questioning. She's not subtle sometimes, and I can see her hands out at her sides. "I got a date already!"

Pulse racing from the lie I just uttered, I flex my fingers to signal to my friend that I've got this handled. I need her to keep her mouth shut until we're out of here.

Dustin's turned to face me completely and he's moving toward the back of Tommy's car. His hand drags along the trunk, and everything about his movement reads *territorial*. This is the single best lie I've ever told, and it's about to get better.

"Someone make you a cute poster board you just couldn't resist?" His words are touched with humor, but the way he nods at me, his mouth a hard line, teeth clenched so hard I see the movement in his jaw, I know that nothing about this is funny to him.

"Nah, he just asked. I said yes. Simple." I shrug.

Dustin takes a few steps away from the car and toward me, glancing over his shoulder to where my brother has popped the hood and is distracted. I'm sure Tommy's listening to all of this. I couldn't care less.

"I said I'd go," Dustin says in a loud whisper, leaning toward me.

I lift a brow.

"Again with the romance," I chide.

His chest deflates a bit as his shoulders slump and he sighs, weight shifting to his heels.

I shrug again.

"You can still go. Just . . . not with me." I shift my weight so my hip pops out. He wants to ask, but Tommy's bound to hear us eventually. I'm sure my brother will interject and applaud the idea of me going with anyone else, even though I made it up. I know that's not what Dustin wants. He's just afraid. Yeah, maybe some of it's warranted. He hasn't had a lot of people in his life actually care about him. But I've never wavered. Not when we were friends, and not now that we're more. He needs to believe that it's worth it, that Tommy will come around, and that my parents will, too. That it's not a choice between having a family or having me; he can have it all.

His tongue is pushed to the roof of his mouth, his smile showing a hint of his teeth, one dimple deeper than the other. He nods, and I brace myself for the question, ready to make this lie massive.

"I bet you'll look real pretty in your dress."

His eyes settle on mine and there's a brief flare in them

that fills me with a fire so hot and angry that it rages up my throat. I'm not sure what it means. Is he trying to be cruel? Or just taking my brother's advice, ending us before we get in too deep. Tommy, who has never had feelings for anyone other than himself.

"Huh," I eek out in a whisper-type pout. I grip my bottom lip with my teeth and shake my head. He's really going to listen to my brother . . . over me.

My gaze falls to the ground as my head stills, and after a few seconds, I glance up to my friend, whose eyes aren't burrowing into me anymore with shock but instead are tilted and heavy with pity. Pretty sure Bailey knows more about what's going on than I give her credit for.

"Let's go," she says quietly, leaning her head in the direction of her house.

I manage to pull my lips into a tight smile, one that I'll leave plastered there until we're safe in her room and I can tell her everything, from the first kiss to the last one right before Dustin fell asleep last night. I fall in line with her footsteps, but in my periphery, I can still see Dustin standing there, watching me go.

Letting me go.

I spin to walk backward, not slowing, but giving him one last chance to choose differently. His expression is unchanged—almost void of feeling, eyes steely and jaw locked. It's as though he's trying to become an impenetrable wall all on his own. Why, though? For Tommy?

"I think Michael Bosa will love it." I don't smile when I utter the words, and I'm sure there's a part of Dustin that knows it's all bullshit, that I would never let that guy near me unless it's to hand over cash I'm owed. But I've sold it well enough to leave him unsettled. His façade cracks, just a little. His brow draws in, creasing briefly. It's almost a flinch, but it's there, and I catch it. I take some pleasure in him having to think about my lie while I'm gone. And I don't plan on coming home until well after midnight so he can suffer with it for a few hours.

A s suspected, Bailey knew more than I originally thought. I've been sneaking her out for parties, races, and meet-ups with cute boys long enough for her to shed most of that sheltered cocoon her parents raise her in. What I didn't expect was how much she understood my feelings for Dustin.

"I've been watching you two together for years. You've always had a *thing*," she said.

And we have. I just thought I was the only one aware of it.

Whatever that thing was, it's entirely different now. And the closer I get to the glow of solar lights that lead up the gravel pathway that cuts through my xeriscape front yard to my driveway, the less sure I am about any of it.

I shouldn't have turned this into a game. I should know better than to go against a guy who doesn't lose. Besides, the one true thing that makes my bond with Dustin special is our honesty, and instead of following the path we've forged our entire lives, I made a sharp turn. An immature one too. At this point, I'll be lucky to get Michael Bosa's baby brother to take me to prom.

My feet crunch against the pebbles that wind toward my house, and when the gurgle of the dripper system kicks on to water my mom's few flower beds, I startle, gripping my chest as I take a tiny leap backward.

"It's not a snake," Dustin's voice says. It's too dark to tell where he is exactly, but I sense he's near the garage.

"You told me that once before, and I seem to remember it was a snake," I say, recalling a family hike Dustin joined us on when we were younger that ended in me sprinting down the mountain when I discovered Dustin had been lying about the cricket sounds. My hand grips my T-shirt for a different reason as I inch forward. My eyes scan the driveway, adjusting to the dim light as I search for him.

His legs come into view first as he kicks off from the back of Tommy's car and flips on the light by the garage entry. His hair is a disheveled mess. He's wearing a pair of my dad's extra-large sweatpants that hang from his hips enough to expose the red band of his boxer briefs, and a gray racing T-shirt that he's worn several holes in over the last few years. Sloppy, like a kid wandering out from a sleepover, and still the most attractive guy my eyes have ever seen.

His feet shuffle toward me in Tommy's too-small slides, and I smile at the sight of his white socks, heels hanging off the back of the shoes.

"In my defense," he says, drawing my eyes back to his face. His head is cocked, and his smile is crooked as he bites on the tip of his tongue. "I was fourteen, and I didn't want you to freak out. We were on a canyon trail and you were inches from the edge."

"What's the worst that could have happened, I'd slip and fall to my death? I mean . . . snake versus plunging death. Tough one, really," I joke. One look in Dustin's eyes, though, and I can tell he isn't amused.

"That's pretty much the worst that could happen, yeah," he says, no more humor in his voice. His response weighs heavy in my chest, smothering my heart and muffling the beat. Gone is the daring look from earlier, too. He's dropped the charade, and it's time for me to as well.

"You wait up for me?" My hand lets go of my shirt long enough to slide across my body and weave under my other arm. It's warm out tonight, no reason to be cold. Yet I can't seem to hug myself tight enough.

"You really going to prom with Michael Bosa?"

He knows I'm not.

I hold his gaze through a full breath, and eventually shake my head and look down at our feet. We're still too far from each other to touch. A small cricket cuts through the space between us, and I take a quick step back, my jumpiness amusing Dustin enough to pull a breathy laugh from his mouth.

"What? You have me thinking about snakes," I say, kicking gravel from the walkway onto the driveway at his feet. He leans back, thumbs hooked in the sweatpant pockets, and laughs for real. I guess I'm in the mood to blame him for everything.

"I'm sorry I made that a big deal. Prom is stupid," I say, glancing at him briefly before looking out at the dark roadway, stars spilling down from the sky. I swallow the rock in my throat.

"No, it isn't," he says, his voice nearer. I work my jaw, afraid to turn back and face him because he's right, it isn't stupid. For some reason, it's important to me. But it's more important to me that I go *with him*. That we show up together, for people to see—for Tommy to have to accept.

Giving in, I turn my head and find him close and waiting. He reaches for my arm, dragging his knuckles from my elbow to my wrist until I relent and let go of the vice grip I have on my chest. He takes my hand in his, weaving our fingers together, and my pulse races. I blink wildly, strangely overwhelmed, but then one touch of his other hand under my chin and my body calms.

"Prom isn't stupid. *I* was being stupid. And I don't want you going anywhere with that Bosa asshat," he says as the right side of his mouth lifts into a smirk.

"He'll be so disappointed," I say in a hushed tone.

Both of our chests lift with a short laugh.

Closing all space between us, he cups my face and moves so his toes touch mine. I look up from his shadow to find his eyes peering down at me while his thumbs draw tender circles on my cheeks.

"I'm going to talk to Tommy tomorrow and tell him how it is," he says.

My lips pull in for a tight smile, and I let out a soft laugh.

"Oh, yeah? And how is it, exactly?" I ask.

His hand moves into my hair as he coaxes my chin to tilt, making room for his mouth to cover mine, pausing right before our lips touch.

"It's me and you, and then Tommy. And if he has a problem with it, he'll have to sort it out on his own, or pout about it like a whiny little bitch."

His mouth stretches into a grin that I feel grow as it tickles against my lips. The sensation makes me smile, too. That's what Dustin used to say in junior high to make Tommy mad. When my brother didn't want to do something the rest of us did, Dustin basically shamed him with peer pressure. It's a bit mean, actually, but in this case, I think it's called for.

"Okay," I say, the last word I'm able to utter before Dustin's mouth collides with mine.

We turn, Dustin walking me backward as his hands hold my kiss to his until my back finds the wall of the garage. I reach to the side and flatten my palm along the wall until I feel the light switch along with the button to close the door. I return us to the shadows before the door completely shuts so we can keep doing this without catching unwanted attention.

My thumbs hook under the bottom of Dustin's shirt and I lift it up his chest, allowing myself to feel the hard ripples of his stomach and chest along the way. His body is warm to the touch, and he lets go of my face long enough to let me pull his shirt up over his head, freeing his arms on his own. He bends down and lifts me against him in a blink, and my legs wrap around his hips as he spins around and moves toward the hood of Tommy's car. He sets me down, but I keep my grip on him with my thighs. It's dark in the back of the garage, but my eyes have adjusted enough to see Dustin's form, and my God, is it straight from my dreams. The skinny kid who jumped from the high-dive platform with me when I was eight and he was nine has grown into something spectacular, with defined lines along his biceps and back, and tight muscles that arrow beyond the waist of his boxers.

Our lips break and I run my hands along the sides of his chest, leaning into him so I can kiss the skin over his beating heart. It's not long before he bends down enough to find the nape of my neck with his mouth and I lean back, exposing my throat as I arch and urge him to keep going. He does, his teeth gripping the center of my T-shirt, tugging it toward him like a hungry animal. A coy smile plays at his lips when he lets go, his hands taking over, gathering up the fabric of my shirt and pulling it over my head and from my arms in one smooth movement.

The roughness of his chin scratches the skin between my breasts and he soothes the light burn quickly by pressing kisses in his wake, his hand gliding up my side to my shoulder where he slides the straps of my bra down my arms. I arch again on instinct as the straps fall and the cups of lace loosen their grip on my breasts. Dustin's breath is hot on my skin, his mouth hovering at the edge of the lace as his hands come together to unhook the clasp at my back. When the material breaks free on my spine, I suck in a quick breath, ready for more of this moment I've imagined so many times.

His fingers hooked in both straps, I lay back completely as he drags the delicate material down the front of my body, slow enough that I think he's teasing himself, until I'm bare for him to see and admire.

"Fucking hell, Hannah," he utters, his mouth hung open, hungry.

My palms flatten against the hood at my sides and I lift my chin as my knees fall open, welcoming him closer. His hand flattens on my stomach, fingers splayed wide, and his touch firm as he trails up my stomach to the center of my ribs. Leaning down, he sweeps his other hand behind my back, supporting me as he presses lingering kisses on my stomach, following the same path his hand took.

I whimper as his fingertips tease along the curve of my breast, his thumb moving up one side while his fingers graze the other. I hold my breath while his mouth moves higher, his thumb inching closer to the hard tips of my breast, the ache from want so strong inside me that I feel as though I may pass out from it. When his thumb finally passes over the tender skin of my nipple, I cry out and clasp my legs around him.

Dustin's breath cools my skin as he samples my skin with his tongue, his mouth moving from the center of my chest toward his hand, growing closer to the sensitive hard bud of my left breast. I feel the sharp pinch as his thumb and finger bring my rosy peak to a painful head that is instantly consumed by his mouth, his tongue swirling around the hard tip while he sucks it raw. Unable to take it, my palms abandon the cool metal of the hood and grasp the band of Dustin's pants, tugging him closer to my center as my body slides along the hood into him. I hook my right leg around his waist and am rewarded with the sweet pleasure of his hard-on pressed between my legs.

"Hannah," he growls in a whisper against my nipple, letting go of his hold on it. The release knocks the wind out of me. His chin digs into my skin, his tongue and teeth dragging up my breast and neck until our mouths collide as he rocks into me, hard melding into soft, heat against heat. Dustin grinds into me while we kiss, his force so strong at one point I think we may dent my brother's hood. I'm lost to him, to his touch and taste, and to the pressure that both tempts and satisfies the need growing between my legs. We kiss through raw lips, our bodies covered in a sheen of sweat, and our eyes meet as he moves against me.

So many times I have imagined the feel of him. My hands curl against his skin, my nails scratching along his sides hard enough to leave red lines in their wake. I flirt with the top of his boxers while my heart hammers against my chest. One dip of my fingers under that elastic is all it would take. Dustin wouldn't stop me. I know he wouldn't. His control is gone, given over to me, and so much of me wants to take this all the way. It's what I have been waiting for. *He* is what I've been waiting for, what I saved myself for. To have it—taste it—and be this close and not go all the way feels like something I would regret. My mind made up, I suck in a deep breath for courage and run my thumbs inside his boxer waistband just as the piercing double honk of my dad's truck horn stops all blood from pumping through my body. The flash of his headlights accompanies the sound.

Dustin's mouth stills against mine, his lips open and desperate for the air we've been depriving ourselves of in exchange for kisses. Heavy work boots clap together just outside the garage and I bring my hand up to Dustin's mouth, pressing my finger against his lips as if he'd really make a sound right now. This is not the way we want anyone to find out about us, especially my father.

Long seconds pass as Dustin and I lie, pressed together, on top of my brother's car. Our shirts are somewhere on the other side of the garage, along with my bra. My dad hasn't gone hiking in months, and of all mornings for him to decide to get up early, he chooses now.

The heavy clunk of my dad's truck door is followed by the growl of his motor. A breath later, the line where the garage door meets the concrete lights up as his headlights pass on his way out of the driveway. We remain still, wordless and holding our breath while the familiar rumble of his truck grows fainter until we can't hear it at all.

Dustin's shoulders relax and his weight lifts from me as he turns his head, resting his brow against mine. We both let out a breathy laugh in relief. The mood is definitely different, and maybe my first time having sex shouldn't be on the hood of my brother's car. Still, if I ever doubted Dustin wanted me as much as I want him, that worry has been erased. Obliterated. Ground into nothing when his body pressed against mine.

14

All the cold showers in the world couldn't cure me last night. One of the curses of living in the desert means getting your shower cold enough can sometimes be impossible, especially in the warmer months. Last night? I needed ice cold water. I settled for lukewarm. I settled for struggling not to finish myself off in the Judge's downstairs shower while I thought of Hannah's body lying in bed one floor up.

The pent-up frustration led to zero sleep for the rest of the night. My restless mind took advantage of the time, dreaming up all the scenarios that could happen the minute Hannah and Tommy's parents learn that I'm *with* their daughter.

With.

That's the next thing I obsessed over. That word. The phrase. Which one is right? What are we? We're Hannah and Dustin, same as always yet nothing like we were. It seems too light to call what we have "dating," and we're not "seeing each other" or any of those other bullshit terms people use to describe high school relationships. That's not what this is. I won't belittle Hannah's and my connection with something so fleeting. We're an evolution. An inevitable result. Fated, I guess.

All that time to find a better way to break the news to her parents, yet all I came up with is what I'm about to do right now. My knee bobs nervously under the lip of the counter as I sit on the stool picking at the blueberry muffin her mom put on a small plate for me. I guzzled the glass of orange juice so fast she quirked a brow at me and automatically refilled the glass, then felt my forehead.

Shit. This woman takes care of me like a mom and I'm about to tell her I've fallen for her daughter, whom I sleep near every night.

Shit.

I dismiss her offer of coffee because fuck if coffee won't give me a heart attack right now. My palm is sweating so hard that the minute I see Hannah's face come around the corner from the stairs I feverishly wipe it along my jeans in an attempt to dry it off.

"Morning, sweetheart," her dad says, leaning forward to kiss her cheek as she puffs it out with air toward him.

He's going to hit me. Right in the face. I've been hit in the face. I can do this.

Her next move is to sit in the stool next to me, as I hoped, and maybe a little as I dreaded. I'm really going to do this.

Before I have a chance to change my mind—*to chicken out*—I slap my hand on top of hers where it rests on her knee and twine my fingers between hers so we make a joined fist. I lift both of our hands up and rest them on the counter on full display for every pair of eyes that isn't ours. It takes about four seconds for everyone to take note, and about five for Mr. Judge to spit a full mouth of coffee all over the kitchen.

"Oh." That's the only word uttered and it's from Mrs. Judge's lips. She slides the coffee pot back into its place and leans against the counter before fidgeting with the crystal hanging from a chain around her neck. That thing is only decorative but right now, I think she might be praying to it.

Tommy's laugh is the first thing to break the thick silence.

"Yeah, this is how I thought it would go down," he says, making a point to meet my eyes and point at me. His smirk isn't just smug, it's full of doubt and warning.

You won't make it out of this house intact. That's what he's saying with that look.

"You knew about this . . . this . . ." Mr. Judge waggles his finger in Hannah's and my direction, struggling to label us. *Welcome to the club, Mr. Judge.*

"Hey, I told them it was a bad idea," Tommy says, popping an apple in his mouth and gripping it with his teeth while holding both palms up as if he's totally innocent.

If they only knew how many times I dragged your drunk ass home.

Tommy hits me with one last glare as he pushes through the door with his back. I hold him hostage with my return stare and unlike the smile on his lips, my jaw has grown rigid and my mouth a tight, soured line. I look at the door he shuts behind him and replay the last minute, wondering if it could have gone any other way. It's hard not to be hurt by their reaction, even if I expected it. I'm good enough to be family, but not good enough to have the feelings I do for their daughter.

Mrs. Judge runs a paper towel across the counter in front of me, luring me back to the unpleasant scene in the kitchen. She's already turned all of her focus to cleaning up the coffee spray mess, and her husband—the man who is more father to me than anyone I've ever known—is leaning over the counter with both palms flattened on the surface with so much force I think he may be trying to sink into the granite.

"Dad—" Hannah starts, but her words are quickly cut off by her dad.

"Don't," he grunts, holding up one hand while keeping his stare on the counter between us. His rigid hand, fingers splayed, sits in the air like a stop sign for several seconds while he shakes his head before coming back down to the counter with a heavy slap that jolts both Hannah and me back in our seats.

My grip on her hand tightens and though I feel her squeezing me back, it doesn't do much to slow the rage building in my chest. My upper lip sneers as my mouth waters. Mr. Judge finally raises his head, his red, furious eyes meeting mine that aren't that far behind, though our anger has different motivating factors.

"She's my daughter, Dustin!" He grits the words through his teeth.

Somehow, I keep my words inside. I tighten my lips as my nostrils flair, and I shake my head to show my disappointment. My other hand comes up to the counter, curling into a fist that I fight not to pound in the same alpha-style Mr. Judge used. I'm huffing, my breath hitting my ears and sounding like a bull waiting for an opportunity.

"I love him, Daddy!"

Hannah breaks free of my grasp and stands from her

stool, her body now closer to me but both of her hands flat on the surface as she leans in to stare her father down. His fuming eyes widen and gloss over in a wild look that I recognize as fear. I made that same face the first time I found my mom unresponsive on the floor.

"No!" her father yells in return.

Hannah's mom sobs where she sits on the floor, no more coffee droplets to clean. She covers her face in her hands, and my stomach rolls with a feeling of betrayal I never thought I could feel.

"Am I really that awful?" I utter. My voice is half the volume of Hannah's and her father's, and seems to take everyone by surprise. My eyes wait to meet Mrs. Judge's, and she winces when our gazes tangle. There's a shift in her eyes, from wide orbs fueled by worry to an instant droop of sympathy. Her lips part, and I sense she's about to say my name, but I don't want pity. I got my answer. They won't be able to back away from this truth.

I'm not good enough.

A sad, breathy laugh quakes my chest as I stand, shifting to meet Mr. Judge's still hardened gaze. His jaw works back and forth and I can see the physical pain he's being caused by the conflict in his chest. He wants to love me like a son, but he just . . . doesn't.

"Yeah. I am," I say with a slow nod.

"Dustin," Hannah utters my name. She reaches for my arm, but I pull it away and turn my back to all of them before they see the tears welling in my eyes.

"I'll have my stuff out this afternoon. I'll leave the key in the pot by the garage," I announce on my way to the door. My steps are purposeful and quick. I open the door and slam it closed behind me, regretting that I did the moment it makes a cracking noise behind me. I shouldn't give them the satisfaction of seeing me so angry and upset. It only makes them right.

I fumble for my keys in my pocket and ignore Hannah's voice calling behind me. I get in my car and start the engine, peeling out backward with enough speed that I fishtail on my turn down their street, leaving more evidence of all the reasons Hannah shouldn't be with me.

I speed to the stop sign and slam on the brakes, burnt rubber leaving a billow of smoke outside my back window. I'm panting and my chest hurts, it squeezes so hard. My eyes catch movement in the rearview mirror and I tilt it enough to see Hannah's car speeding toward me.

"Fuck!" I shout, fist pounding the steering wheel. I shift gears and turn the opposite direction from school, to the Straights where I can go for miles as fast as I want, until the world catches up with my racing heart.

My eyes shift to the mirror as I pull away, and though I see Hannah turn to follow me, in a minute she'll be completely lost.

The speedometer reads one-ten by the time I hit the outskirts of town. It's flat enough around here to see the cops coming, so I give it more gas and get the Supra up to one-thirty, flying through the few stop signs out on the desert roads that nobody drives on. I downshift as I approach the empty two-lane highway and rumble to a stop at the junction, the vibration of my engine like a salve to my broken heart and soul.

I'm not good enough.

I want one thing in this world, and I'm not good enough for her.

The tears threaten to come again, so I run my thumb knuckle under my eyes and push everything that *feels* to the depths of my body. No heartbeat. No breathing.

Nothing but me and the tread of my tires. I shift fast, peeling out again with a hard left and I straddle the dotted yellow line down the center of the only place left I have to feel at home.

My eyes lock on the flat rocks of the mountains miles and miles ahead. My right hand works with my legs, every new gear upping my speed until I'm cruising as fast as I was the night I beat the Vegas guys with Hannah sitting next to me.

I love him.

My eyes flutter but I keep roaring forward. I heard the words she said, and for the tiniest of milliseconds, my heart swelled with such a foreign drug—I was high from hearing her use that word about me.

"Fuck!" I scream again, pushing the Supra to its max extremes. The ride isn't smooth, but I like it. It reminds me how fragile this balance is, how close to a dangerous line I can get and how much power there is to be gained in inches.

In seconds.

I love him.

A weight suddenly falls from my heart to the pit of my stomach and I let off the gas completely, gliding on the asphalt while my eyes blink at the road ahead.

I love him.

Nobody has ever said that to me before. My mom never told me she loved me. The only thing Colt loves is beating me and stealing anything I value. I've never had grandparents, or aunts or uncles. Even the Judges, through all these years, have never said they loved me.

Hannah Judge did. She announced it in defiance. She said it proudly. She uttered words right to her father's forbidding face. And I fucking left.

My eyes flicker to the mirror—nothing. I've gone too far to see whether Hannah is still behind me, chasing me. I pound the brake and flip around once I slow enough to turn the other way and race back to the intersection where I tried to leave it all behind. I pound the wheel with the butt of my palm while I will myself to somehow go faster, my eyes scanning and waiting for the heat waves to clear from the place where the road meets the air so I can see the horizon more clearly.

A figure forms. It's her. Her car is there. She's there.

I let up on the pedal and glide along the roadway again, this time dropping my hands to the bottom of the steering wheel while I sit back in my seat and let out a quaking breath.

Someone thinks I'm good enough.

Once I'm maybe a hundred yards away, I roll to the edge of the road and kick open my door. Hannah hugs herself at the side of her car, her eyes visibly red. My strides aren't fast enough so I run, my legs pushing me faster when I see the tears still running down her cheeks. She shakes her head as I near, but I don't give her time to speak.

"I'm so sorry," I plead, moving my hands into her hair and walking her backward until she falls against the side of her car. My lips are on hers before she can respond, and I lean into her body, kissing her so hard that she gasps for air in the only break I give us. Her chin lifts to meet my height and she clutches at the sides of my T-shirt, wadding it into her fists while our lips tangle between the whimpers of her cry and repeated whispers of apology from my mouth.

Her hands claw their way up to my face and she tangles her fingers into my hair, holding on as if I might run away again. I can't promise I won't. But I will never doubt her.

She loves me. She said she loves me. The only person who ever has.

We kiss in the middle of the desert under the scorching morning sun, not a cloud for miles. I'm breathless and so is she, but neither of us wants to break. Our kiss is hungry, and I hope mine tells her the things I can't yet say, things I don't know how to say. I love her, too. I want to scream that I've always loved her. That she is the one person I can confide in, the person I run to, and the only thing that keeps me from following in Colt's dark footsteps. But saying that—laying all of my baggage and bullshit on her heart like that when I'm nothing—isn't enough. I need to be worthy, to be the man she sees in me.

So instead I say I'm sorry again, and again.

It seems to be enough, or she seems to understand the deeper meaning, the truth beneath the surface, because she accepts me.

"It's okay. We can do this," she utters, her lips clinging to mine even through words.

I don't have the heart to tell her I don't think it is and I'm not sure we can. The way her parents reacted, her brother's warnings? Those aren't without reason. They love her, just as she loves me. *Just as I love her.* They see the risk that comes with my future. If it were only my dream, my need to push myself to the edge of danger for a taste of victory, they'd learn to live with it. But that's not what made her father pound his hand on the counter. It's because of who I am and what I'm made of; or rather, who made me. I come from nothing and know little about affection. I've never had it, other than the small strands the Judges have given me. I'm the son of a drug addict and a drug dealer. The offspring of a man so vile that people around our town know him simply by his first name. Businesses tell him to leave before he speaks. Criminals point at him and shoot invisible pistols at his head with threats to do it for real. One day, they might. They've tried.

My genetic code is written with so many flaws, it's a miracle Hannah sees anything in me worth loving at all. But she does. And for that, I'll try.

"I'm gonna need a tux for prom."

She breaks away, her head rolling against mine, and I feel the stretch of her smile along with her breathy laugh.

"You sure?" Her lashes flutter against my skin and I can tell she's glancing up at me. I pull away enough to lock our gazes.

Her hair is a mess from my hands twisting it into knots and the slight, warm breeze blowing in from the south. I sweep the wild strands from her face with both of my thumbs, then rest my palms on her cheeks. My eyes study her pink skin, the raw puffiness of her lips. I move my thumb to her mouth and brush it against her pout. Her lips quiver against my touch.

"I'm sure," I say, lifting my gaze back to hers. I don't have to look at her lips again to see her smile. This one reaches her eyes. And as pointless as I thought something like a formal dance was a few days ago, now something has never seemed so important.

I love you, too. Mean it.

One day, I'll tell you all the reasons why.

15

I get to school late, and Dustin doesn't even bother to come. I think it's more about avoiding my brother than anything else. If I could have gotten away with skipping today, I would have too. But me ditching would only fuel my family's case about Dustin leading me astray.

My best friend's reaction to the news is the exact opposite of my parents'. True, she's partly glad to not have to deal with me whining anymore about my unrequited crush and prom, but I can also tell she's genuinely happy for me. That doesn't mean she isn't guarding my heart, though. I wish she wouldn't plant worries in my head so soon.

"You're sure he's not running away, right? That he didn't send you here so he could skirt off guilt-free?" She leaves me with this new fear on our way to last hour, dismissing it with a wave of her hand and an added "I'm sure it's fine." *But is it?*

I wander into my last hour dazed by her theory. What if Dustin kept driving after we parted? I nibble on my fingernails, one at a time, while my lit teacher drones on about terrible fathers in Thomas Hardy novels. I pay attention to that part, laughing quietly to myself at the striking resemblance some of his characters have to Colt. I bet he would have sold his wife and son for cash like the main character in *The Mayor of Casterbridge*.

I'm lost in that thought when Tara, the quiet girl who sits next to me, nudges my elbow with her pen then points toward the window when I glance up. I turn and my eyes meet Dustin's almost immediately. He lifts a hand and I check to see whether my teacher is looking before holding mine up in response. Soon, I'm biting my lip and remembering how his feel.

He's like a dream. The wavy locks of his hair blow in the window, crossing his forehead that he wrinkles by furrowing his brow in response to the bright afternoon sun. He's wearing all my favorites, though I doubt he knows that—black jeans, the black Vans, and the long-sleeved gray shirt that hugs his chest and smells like every dirt track we've ever visited. Last time he was resting on our couch with his feet up on one side, I drew hearts on the bottoms of his shoes. The ink bled deep into the rubber, making it hard to wear off.

The final minutes of my class are spent with my eyes glued to him, though he only looks my way once or twice. I love the way he reads his phone, the way he slides his hand into his back pocket when he's done, and how he gnaws at the inside of his cheek while he's thinking. So much to think about, and I'm sure he dreads walking back into my house, but I'm determined to change everyone's minds when it comes to Dustin Bridges.

He is not his father. If anything, he is *better* than all of us *because* of his father.

When the bell rings, I waste little time, gathering my

things and scrambling out the door and through the hallways to the curb of the parking lot and the boy I've been staring at for what's felt like hours.

There's no hesitation in my steps, and I march right up to him until my chest is pressed against his and our lips meet. His hands slip from his pockets and hover at my sides for a second, stunned by my boldness. But he comes to quickly, dipping them into the back pockets of my denim shorts and squeezing my ass enough to lift me into him more.

"I guess we're letting everyone know what's what then?" he says against my lips as we part. I fall back and his hands slip from my pockets but linger on my hips. His brow is arched on the same side as his raised lip and dimple. It's perfectly adorable and I take a mental picture to dream about later.

"Just Michael Bosa," I tease, knowing the jock will walk through the school gates to his Mustang any second now. I doubt he even glances our way, but the chord of jealousy I strike does its job.

"Oh, well, in that case," Dustin says, moving his hands into my hair and dipping me back for a possessive kiss that instantly leaves my lips raw and satisfied.

"Hey! Get a room!"

I laugh mid-kiss at the sound of my best friend's voice. Dustin pulls away enough to make eye contact but still holds me with my back arched.

"I'd love to get a room . . . and do *so many things*," he says loud enough just for me. My cheeks burn at his offer, followed by a swollen ache between my legs. I'm wet just from his suggestion.

"You following me home?" I ask as he lifts me back to a standing position.

He sucks his lips in and looks off to the side, the dent in his forehead putting me off ease.

"Dustin," I say, my voice quiet and pleading.

His head swivels back to face me and our gazes lock. His throat moves with a hard swallow.

"Don't let them run you off so easily," I say, reaching up and grabbing hold of his shirt at the center of his chest. He laughs and covers my hands with his, leaning forward to drop a kiss on my forehead.

"Han, I want this to work. And if I'm going to win over your parents, I don't think I should be living under your roof. I'll be fine. I should probably check on my mom anyway," he says, his voice strained.

I shake my hands against his chest, pounding lightly while he holds on to me. He laughs lightly. I glance to my right to where my car is parked, Bailey sitting on the bumper.

"I have to take her home," I say, nodding toward my friend.

"Good. You should do that," he says, walking me backward a few steps. He moves his hands to my cheeks, cupping them before dusting my lips with a chaste kiss that leaves me buzzing for more. I grab his wrists as we stare into each other's eyes.

"I grabbed my clothes and stuff already, not that I have much. I'm gonna drop the box at home and then I've got a race I wanna check out in the Valley tonight. Maybe I'll cruise by after and we can meet up in the garage again?" His teeth snag his bottom lip as he raises his brows, which makes me laugh.

"I don't want you to go." I sigh, knowing he's right and that he's going to respect my father as much as he can.

"And that makes me feel amazing," he says.

My heart pounds, its strength growing and pushing against my insides harder and harder the longer Dustin and I stare at each other in complete silence. I told him I loved him. I told *everyone* I loved him. I know he feels the same, and I'm patient, but the truth of what I said lingers in the air between us right now. I feel it, taste it.

"I'm holding you to that promise. I'll see you tonight," I say, slipping from his fragile hold while wishing he'd reach for me, hold on and never let go.

"Tonight," he repeats, tugging open his door and leaning on the window frame to watch me walk away. I sway my hips a little more knowing his eyes are on them.

"You two are seriously hot together," Bailey says.

I smile and say thanks before getting in the car, my inner voice saying "I know." Bailey has no idea how fucking combustible we are.

I drop Bailey off and decide to start the hard work of moving my parents over to my side. My dad's the harder sell, and I get that he's conflicted given how close he and Dustin are and what we've all been through together. We were, on many weekends, "his kids." I'm sure his head is a little screwed up over the idea of us as a couple.

My mom, however? She's soft. She's the reason we took Dustin in when he couldn't be at home. She's seen the bruises, and I heard her and dad fight about calling Protective Services when we were younger. For a while, I thought she was going to push to adopt Dustin. *Fuck, what a mess that would have created now!*

I pull into the small parking lot behind city hall and dial

her office on my phone. She picks up in the middle of the second ring.

"Hannah? Are you all right? Is everything okay?" I can almost visualize her cupping her phone and pacing her office with worry by the way her voice sounds.

"I'm fine," I say, killing the engine and getting out of my car. My brow pinches so much I feel the fold of skin between my eyes. "Why are you so worried? I call you all the time."

"I know. I wasn't . . . I just . . . I'm glad you're okay." She coughs down her overreaction.

It hits me suddenly. I stop midway to her office, just outside her window.

"Is this about Dustin?" I ask pointedly. I turn so I'm square with her window, looking at my own reflection as it outlines her behind the glass. She twists in her chair and our eyes meet. "What, did you think he kidnapped me? Took me off to start a meth lab and make babies out of wedlock?"

She recoils at my hyperbolic questioning.

"Hannah." Now her tone is condescending.

"No. Don't *Hannah* me. Mom, even if you don't like the idea of me dating a boy—"

"It's Dustin, Hannah. *It's Dustin.*" As if this makes it all okay.

"Yeah, Mom. It's Dustin. And even if you don't trust him, you trust me. You do trust me, don't you?"

There's a pause that lasts just long enough to dry out my throat. I punch out an offended laugh.

"Are you kidding me?" I turn my back to her and head toward my car, sorry I ever tried to make any of this okay. Maybe I should run away with him. I'd be the one kidnapping him, but that's not how anyone would see it. Their minds are so made up, and they are so wrong.

"Hannah!" My mom's voice comes from behind me, not through the phone. I unlock my door and toss my phone to the passenger seat, then stop to stare at her over the roof of my car.

"Shame on you," I grit out.

Her eyes start to tear right away. Imagine how this must look to anyone in their offices looking out on this tiny parking lot. The mayor's daughter is making the mayor cry. Hell, in this fucking small-ass town, this outburst might make the news.

"He's been through so much, he doesn't even know what his life experience has done to him yet. And I worry. Can't I worry?" She's begging me.

I look down at my palm as I grip the keys in my hand, the teeth digging into my skin, and I chuckle to myself.

"Sure, Mom. You can worry. But you should also have some faith. A life like his might just make someone resilient." I lift my head until our gazes meet and I hold hers through the slight flinch she makes just before the corners of her eyes soften.

"I'll see you at dinner, Mom," I say, not waiting for her to respond.

I climb in my car and pull away, only glancing in the rearview mirror once as I pull out of the city hall lot. She's still standing where I left her.

16

Deep down, I knew I'd come back to this place; I just didn't want it to be so soon. The familiar smell of dirty clothes and piled up garbage assaults my nostrils as soon as I step out of my car. Colt's ride is nowhere in sight, which is comforting. Mom is home alone.

I grab my box of belongings from the trunk and carry it to the back door, knowing it will be unlocked. My mom always leaves the back door open; that's one of the things that sends Colt into a rage. He's convinced she's working with ATF or the FBI to grant access for a raid. I hate to break it to him, but I'm pretty sure toddlers could punch their way through one of the walls and make their way inside if they wanted to. An open back door is the least of his security worries.

The theme music from her favorite soap opera echoes from the shitty TV speakers as I enter, and I can see the top of her head peeking out from the recliner as I walk in.

"Hey, Mom," I announce. She leaps to her knees in her

chair and spins so our eyes meet. Her right eye is ringed in black, no doubt a gift from Colt.

"Dusty!" She wiggles her way to a stand, a half-spent cigarette dangling from her fingers, the ash so long I'm not sure how it hasn't fallen to the floor. She grinds out the butt in a cereal bowl on the small table next to the chair.

Ah, home.

"Do you want some eggs? You must be hungry. Let me make you some eggs." She stumbles her way into the kitchen, her arms swinging wildly for balance. She knocks over a few stacked pots but somehow manages to catch one of them mid-air before it clanks on the floor. She glances up at me and grins, proud of herself.

"Look at that," she says, winking.

She's high. I'm guessing opiates, probably prescription. It's sad that I can identify the difference.

"I'm just dropping off some stuff for my closet, Ma. You don't have to make me anything." It's three in the afternoon. Not that you can't eat breakfast whenever, but I don't think she has a clue what time it is.

I kick a few empty snack cake boxes out of my way as I amble down the narrow hallway and try like hell to keep the visual of my mom passed out on the floor out of my head. I haven't really had a bedroom for years. There's a room and there's a bed in it, but it's covered with boxes filled with shit my mom thinks is too important to throw away. I think it's probably where Colt hides money, too. I never touch those boxes. I'm better off not knowing. The closet, though—that I got to keep.

I slide the door open and wedge my foot between a few bins, sliding them apart enough to drop my box to the floor. I pop the top open and hang a few of my old shirts. These aren't things I wear much. I keep those in my trunk.

But I was so freaked out when I left the first time, I just grabbed random things and took off.

The smell of burnt egg drifts into the room, so I close the box and swear under my breath. The last thing I want to do is hang around this place, but if my mom is actually going to make an effort, I may as well indulge her and try to eat them. I'm sure they're dry as fuck.

I grab the edge of the sliding door and begin to move it when something glaring hits my frame of focus. I let go of the door and reach up, holding my hand a few inches from the bundled brick of cash before convincing myself to go ahead and touch it. A second stack rests below it, both bundles wrapped in Saran Wrap, but the second one is clearly drugs.

Fuck.

The cash is heavy in my palm. I can see enough through the layers of plastic to get that they're all hundreds. *Hundreds* of hundreds.

Fuck.

"Dusty? Eggs are ready!"

My heart pounds heavy in my chest, pulse ratcheting up at the sound of my mom's voice, and I drop the bundle to my feet.

"Coming!" I yell, scrambling to pick up the money. I tug one of my T-shirts free and wipe away my prints, not that I even know if that's a thing. I just know if it *is* a thing, I don't want my prints on this shit. Holding the cash with my shirt for a glove, I slide it back into place and finish closing the door.

My heart thunders against my chest cavity and the rhythm of my pulse drowns out the sound of Mom's TV when I walk back into the living room. There aren't any chairs in the kitchen, so I stand at the clear spot on the counter that my mom made by shoving crap out of the way with her arm. She drops the plate of steaming and slightly browned eggs in front of me and I commence shoveling them in my mouth as fast as I can.

"Aww, you were hungry. My sweet boy," she says.

She's super sentimental when she's high on opioids.

"Thanks, Mom," I say through a full mouth. The eggs are fucking awful, but I power through them, my mind calculating how much cash fits in an eight-inch-by-four-inch brick. Thousands. *Fucking thousands!*

By the time I finish my plate, my arms and legs buzz with nervous energy. I have to get out of here, make sense of what I just saw. Colt's always had drugs and cash around the house. Hell, he cooked his own meth a few times. But the things I found in my closet? That's another level. That's cartel kinda shit. That's dealing for real, not passing around baggies of weed and watered down blow at the truck stop.

"Do you want more? I can make more . . ." My mom is already moving toward the carton of eggs still on the counter. I think that's the only edible thing in this house.

"No, I gotta go. I got a race to get to, but thanks. That was great," I lie, dumping the plate on top of the dozens of dirty ones piled in the sink. At some point, my mom will clean a few of those. That's how it works around here, a constant state of washing what you need when you need it . . . sometimes.

"Okay, baby. Momma loves you!" she chants as I race out the door. I cringe at her syrupy banter. I'm not sure what version of her I'd rather have—the angry rage-a-holic in detox, the depressed, doped-up zombie, or this woman who's manic and full of way too much energy.

I get in my car and roar out of the gravel driveway,

backing into the street, racing away from my house as fast as I can. I hit eighty by the time I reach the end of my street and peel around the corner, smoke spilling from the back of my car so heavily it's almost impossible to see out the back window.

So much money.

My head is dizzy with all of the thoughts running through it, some I'm not so proud of, like the fact I left behind so much money! I could just take it. Take it and run. But run where? And without Hannah?

Sometimes, I think God has a wicked sense of humor. Now is one of those times as Hannah's car passes mine heading the other direction. I spin around and chase her, glad to see her pull to the side of the road because she saw me. She was probably headed to my house, and that's the last place she should ever go. I can't fathom what Colt would say or his friends would do if she showed up there alone.

I rumble to a stop behind her, my fingers still teeming with guilty energy. I actually considered stealing that cash. For more than a few seconds, that thought sat in my head and I could have convinced myself.

She opens her door and swings her legs out but remains sitting so I get out and walk over to kneel in front of her. I grab her hands in mine and hold them on her lap.

"Where you running to?" I glare up at her with a squint because of the bright sun above.

"To find you," she says through a smirk that I can tell is pasted on. I hold her stare long enough for it to slip into a frown.

I nod.

"What happened?" I ask.

Her eyes fall, her lashes kissing her freckle-dusted cheeks. Goddamn, is she the sweetest angel on earth.

"Had a not-so-great talk with my mom at her office. It's fine, really. She's just being overprotective." She pulls her hands free and makes air quotes around that last word. It makes me laugh. I grab them again and thread my fingers between hers before leaning in to press my lips softly on hers.

"I assume the subject of *me* came up." I sigh. I'm not upset. It actually feels nice that she wants to fight for us so badly, enough to barge into her mom's office. I picture her pointing and telling her mom how it is. Hannah has a bossy streak.

"Why are you smiling?" Her head tilts. I slide my hands along her hips, up the bottoms of her shorts until they cup her ass. I squeeze and she blushes.

"You make me smile, is all," I say. One eye squints as I look up, and this time because I might be blushing a little. I want to tell her how I feel—*how she makes me feel.*

"*Ooof.*" I blow out, shaking my head and squeezing my eyes shut. The weight of our quiet moment has ticked up my pulse, a different type of racing than the one that accompanied the idea of ripping off Colt's drug money. I bury my head in her lap, my lips kissing the skin of her thighs. Her hands fall into my hair and she weaves her fingers around, massaging my scalp while I sink into her and relax for the first time in, well, maybe ever.

"Where is this race?" she finally asks.

"It's in the Valley. It might be nothing, but I could use the cash," I say, lifting up enough to meet her gaze. I can tell the instant our eyes meet that she wants to come. My mouth parts but before I speak, a short laugh escapes.

"Your entire family will kill me if you come," I say, dragging my hands back down her thighs as I stand. I grab her hand on the way and tug her to her feet. I hug her the minute she's standing, and my mouth goes to its now-natural spot in the crook of her neck, peppering it with kisses. She smells like summer—like coconut and pineapple and sunscreen.

"So we'll take Tommy," she says, and I laugh harder.

"What, are we going to throw him in my trunk? Race off with him bound and gagged?" I can't imagine Tommy is in a hurry to go anywhere with me.

"Hmmm, tempting, but no. We'll ask. I know my brother. He might be pissed, but he also loves you like a brother. And if I say I'm going with or without him, well . . "

I roll my eyes at her idea and back away, shaking my head. I stumble back a few steps and point at her, still smiling.

"This is a bad idea, but who am I to tell you not to do something.".

She lifts her chin and rolls her shoulders, emboldened.

"Good boy," she says, and everything about those two words reaches into my body and stirs up memories of her bare breasts and how they felt in my mouth.

"Oh, I'm no good boy, Hannah," I say, eyes hazing a little as I back away and let my lip curl. I like the way she crosses her legs at my flirtatious words. Damn, did she grow up pretty.

17

I t helps knowing my dad isn't home and my mom will probably be avoiding me for awhile. She's sent three texts, all half-assed apologies, minus the one that went on and on about how I'll understand one day when I have a daughter. To spite her, I'm only having boys.

Tommy is messing under the hood of his car when I pull into the driveway. Dustin pulls in behind me. My brother walks around his car and through the garage and I chuckle to myself, knowing what I did in there last night. I wonder if he noticed smudges on his hood.

"Mom's looking for you," he says, his focus shifting from me to Dustin mid-sentence. "Not you," he adds, just to be a dick.

Rather than engage, Dustin tips his head back with a short but condescending laugh. His eyes roll to meet mine, and I can tell he's silently telling me this is a bad idea that won't work. He should know better, though. I get my way.

"You got plans?" I ask.

My brother's eyes linger on Dustin for a few seconds, a

hint of a smile playing at his lips, but eventually he returns his attention to me.

"Maybe. Why?"

He's a liar. He doesn't have shit to do. It's a Wednesday.

"We're driving into the city. Dustin's got a race." Tommy's eyelids raise, just a tick, but I notice. He likes the scene, as much as he thinks he'll outgrow it. And any excuse to go into the Valley, where the towns aren't so small and stifling, he leaps at it.

"Big one?" He looks back to Dustin; I turn to take in their exchange. Dustin is leaning against his front bumper, arms crossed over his chest, shirt lifted enough that I see a peek of his stomach and the deep red line of his boxers.

"Big enough," Dustin says. "Mostly a money grab."

"Scottsdale boys?" Tommy asks, mostly confirming. Dustin nods.

"I mean, we can go without you, but—" I start, dropping my proverbial fishing line in the water. It takes half a breath for Tommy to bite.

"*We*? Oh, no. Hell, no. *We*, yes," he says, waggling his finger between him and Dustin. I step close enough to my brother to grab his hand mid-air and move his gesturing finger in my direction.

"The only we is the three of us," I say, my other hand crossing fingers behind my back. I'll go without my brother, even if I have to slip into Dustin's trunk and sneak my way in.

My brother's stare drills into my eyes, searching for cracks in my resolve, but when he realizes he won't find any, he backs away with breathy laughter.

"Fucking hell, Hannah. Fine. *Fine!*" He pulls a work rag from his back pocket and wipes away some oil from his hands, then tosses the cloth into the garage and points to me. "You're driving me."

"Figured," I say, my eyes fluttering at how dramatic he is. He doesn't want to be *in* the car with Dustin because he's still mad at him. It's like when they were kids and my brother got butt-hurt over something, like Dustin beating him in a game of Sorry. He would pout and refuse to share the sofa during movies or eat at the same table for pizza. Tommy may be older than me, but maturity he is definitely lacking.

"San Tan?" Tommy asks Dustin. He nods to confirm where we're going. It's the only civilized conversation I expect them to have for the next several hours. Maybe days.

I won't be so lucky. It's about two and a half hours from our house to San Tan, so after a quick stop at the gas station to load up on fuel and drinks, we hit the road. Dustin purposely cruises behind me as we make our way into town, and it makes me smile when I catch his reflection in the rearview mirror. My brother is quick to call me out on it.

"You're like a puppy dog," he bites out.

"Am not," I shoot back. I work to keep my eyes on the road, but after only a mile I catch myself checking my mirror again. My brother chuckles and I swing my arm in his direction to slap him against the chest.

"Ow, haha! Asshole," he says, shoving me back. I swerve a little but immediately right the car. I'm sure that made Dustin nervous. I've never thought about things making him nervous before, but I like the fantasy that he worries about me. I don't think it's much of a fantasy anymore.

The playful moment lightens the mood a little, and I'm grateful. My brother turns up the radio and we join together, singing along with one of our favorite songs. I catch myself relaxing for the first time since we began the drive, my shoulders leaving the high perch they've been on near my ears. As one song shifts into the next, we both settle in, my brother's gaze drifting off to the side, toward the rolling desert hills that become covered in pink-tiled rooftops as we get closer to town.

He chews on his thumbnail for a while, and his brow grows heavy as time passes without us talking. I brush my fingers against his arm to snap him from his daze and bring him back.

"Oh, sorry. I was just thinking," he says.

Tension climbs back into my neck and shoulders.

"What about?" I'm sure I already know, but it's a long trip. I'm making the best of it.

My brother draws in a deep breath and looks out at the roadway ahead of us. Traffic is getting thicker, and a few cars have slid into the space between me and Dustin. He's four or five lengths behind us now. When the roads open up, though, we'll lose him. Or rather, he'll lose us. Tommy knows the way, and Dustin will want to get his mind ready for speed.

"It was pretty fun, wasn't it?" he says.

I glance his way, my face pinched. He shrugs.

"Growing up, I mean. The three of us. We had a pretty special thing."

I consider his words, letting my mind drift to the slideshow of memories I keep close to my heart. In the story of my life, Dustin and Tommy are the co-stars. And for the most part—maybe ninety-nine percent of it actually —it *was* fun. The only times that lacked were those when Dustin suffered, and the last twelve hours.

"Yeah, it was pretty fun. I'm lucky to have you," I say,

holding out a fist for my brother to pound. He stares at it for a few seconds before letting his mouth inch up in a crooked smile and pushing his knuckles against mine.

"I'm sorry I overreacted," he finally says.

The apology takes me by earnest surprise, and I know my face reflects my reaction. My eyes widen and my breath falls away.

"Don't make a joke," he adds, shaking his head and looking away.

"I'm not, I'm. . . I guess, surprised, is all." I say.

He doesn't respond, and I don't want this moment to slip by without being celebrated—rewarded.

"Seriously, Tommy," I say, grabbing his forearm. I squeeze it lightly until he turns to face me again. "Thank you. It means a lot."

His lips form a tight smile and he breathes in deep through his nose, his shoulders lifting and freezing, hunched up, before he blows out and lets them drop.

"I still think this is a disaster," he laughs out.

"Hey!" I tease.

"But—" he interjects. "I love you both. And if this is something you both want to try—if you *need* to try this— I'm in your corner. I will be here for you. I won't like it, but I'll be here."

I shift my eyes from the road to my brother and back a few times, my smile growing, lips tight and tingling.

"You kinda like it," I tease.

He lets out a quiet laugh and shakes his head.

"I'm your big brother. I will not like any guy coming near you. But if it has to be someone, it might as well be him." His eyes linger on me for a few seconds, and I know he means it.

"So, mom . . ." he starts, and I roll my head and stretch my neck in response.

"Gah! Don't get me started," I say, holding up a palm.

We spend the next two hours dissecting our parents' personalities, and Tommy tries his best to give me advice on how to handle them when it comes to Dustin. Most of his ideas are shit, but when he suggests I write them both letters expressing all the things I can't seem to say to them without our conversation escalating into a parent-daughter lecture, I agree he's onto something.

Dustin blows past us somewhere around the middle of town. We don't see a sign of the Supra again until Tommy and I peel off the main highway onto the state route leading behind the San Tan Mountains. There's a thin sheen of dust on Dustin's car, which is parked outside the diner we used to stop at with my dad when we rode down to Tucson.

My brother draws a dick and balls in the grime on Dustin's window, and I'm in the middle of chastising him when Dustin's presence moves in close behind me. An arm holding a cold lemonade reaches around me, a long straw poking from the cup. I take the drink and relish in the fact his arm moves in to hug me around the waist.

"I think you're missing some hair on those," Dustin says, pointing to my brother's artwork.

Tommy looks over his shoulder and the two of them stare at each other for a beat. I don't need to hear them speak to know they reached an understanding in that look: no need for apologies or more fighting. That's what a lifetime of friendship does.

"You're right," my brother finally answers, adding a few dots on the window to accentuate his drawing.

"You guys are children," I say, though I'm so warm inside over the fact they're getting along like normal.

Dustin steps up and writes the words SUCK IT to the side of Tommy's drawing and the two of them shake hands like bros, proud of their work.

"You should erase that before we get there," I say, looking around the nearby service station lot to see if there are any window cleaning stations.

"Nah," Dustin says, slinging an arm around my brother and crossing his ankles. "When I kick those rich kids' asses, I want them to know," he says.

"Know what?" I ask.

Both Dustin and Tommy laugh, and I get it before they answer.

"That they can suck my dick!" they shout in unison.

My brother climbs in with Dustin and I move back to my car to follow them the rest of the way to the race site. The sun won't be down for a couple of hours, but this is part of Dustin's routine. He likes to scout the landscape, even if it's familiar. He doesn't want surprises. Then he and my brother dig into the engine and inspect every inch of the car. The Supra will sing like a chorus by race time. And frankly, I don't mind the view while they work. Especially when Dustin peels off his shirt and tosses it to me for safe-keeping.

18

It's easy to fall into our routine. Me and Tommy under my hood, Hannah pacing around us, complaining about the heat until drivers show up and she can talk shit about them. Tommy gets pissed when Hannah says something a little too loud, but a minute later, he joins in, ripping on the lame puttering of some kid's muffler.

"You used to love the loud muffler shit, too, ya know," I tease Tommy.

"*Pfft*, yeah. When I was twelve."

My friend circles the Supra as I drop the hood, his eyes set on a line of cars about a hundred yards down the road. I step in next to him and nod.

"Rookies," I say.

"That's what I thought, too," he answers.

There are four of them, probably friends who grew up watching the *Fast & Furious* movies so they think they know shit about racing. Definitely punks from money because their rides are tricked out like mad with custom wraps and high-dollar wheels and shit. Nothing so far says fast to me, especially the drivers.

My friend is reaching for his wallet, a sign that he smells a sucker the same way I do. Tommy doesn't like the money part of this game, but when it's easy . . . like this? It seems foolish not to invest.

I wipe my hands clean from the little tune-up work we just finished and trek across the street to welcome the new guys. Hannah saunters down the middle of the road, her lemonade cup refilled with water she got from one of the guys we know from the tracks down south. Every one of those newbie assholes turns their heads, and while one of them whistles, another makes a joke—probably about her ass—while leaning into his friend's ear.

I'm gonna fuck them up on the road.

My eyes on my targets, I reach out as Hannah gets closer and snake my hand around her body until my palm finds her ass. I pull her into me. My gaze stays on the competition while I kiss her, and three of the four assholes instantly avert their eyes. One of them, though—the one with the pointless-ass designer sunglasses perched on his probably-permed hair—keeps right on looking.

"You find your guy?" Hannah says as our kiss breaks, her mouth hovering around my ear.

"Sure did," I say through a smug grin.

I move my focus to her and she lifts up on her toes to brush our noses together, wrinkling hers and bunching up her lips in the cutest way. I'm sure Tommy is catching this little show and wants to punch me again, but he's gotta prefer his sister being with me over one of these douchebags.

"I'm gonna start the race," she says, slipping back down to her heels.

She drops her sunglasses on her nose and slinks her hand around my chest, then bicep, as she walks around me. I swear, those denim shorts did not show off that much of her ass cheeks this morning. I'm hypnotized by them as she walks back toward her car, the only thing to break me out of it Tommy's firm palm flat on my chest as he pushes me a few steps back.

"All right, that's enough. I can only be *so* cool with this. Besides, you need to save that focus for sundown. We got some bets to make," Tommy says.

I spin until I'm walking in sync with him, acutely aware of the tightness in my jeans, an aftereffect of his sister's sexy-as-hell exit. I roll my shoulders while we walk to shake off the tingles left from her hand, and shove my hands in my pockets as we approach our targets.

I know a few people out here. It's hard not to run into regulars when you race this circuit. But we all follow a code —nobody jacks with anyone else's game. Everyone has something going. Like Jimmy, the guy with the Dodge Challenger who I've beaten so many times he flat out refuses to race me. We make eye contact as I pass, and I catch the slight tick in his lip, a flash of a smile that lets me know he's already made a bet with one of these rich dudes. As far as they know, though? None of us know each other. We're all just a bunch of gearheads who want to drive fast.

I'm headed right for the guy who watched me kiss Hannah with a little too much investment. Every fiber of my soul wants to flex and show my cards early just to make him feel small, but I keep it in check, balling my fists in my pockets and forcing my voice to come out meek.

"Hey, guys," I greet them, plastering a toothy smile on my face that makes me feel like such a fraud. Tommy shakes beside me with a short, silent laugh and coughs to cover it. He's always had a hard time keeping a straight face when I play the part of a sucker. I'm going to have to change it up a little this time, only because my mark saw me kiss Hannah. My normal *character* wouldn't flaunt something like that.

"What's up?" The guy I've picked out lifts his chin to acknowledge me, then pushes up from leaning on the hood of his car. His eyes flick over my shoulder, probably to Hannah laying out on the top of her car. I curl my fist to release the need to punch him in the eye, then pull my hand free.

"I'm Dustin. Mind if I check out your rides?" I hold my open palm out, same stupid grin on my face.

My mark closes the distance, squinting as he sizes me up. I'm about an inch taller than he is, which I bet he hates, so I slouch to make it less evident. He takes my hand and I let him go ahead and squeeze just a little harder, waiting for the flicker in his eyes when I know I've got him. He holds it back, longer than I expect. I have to give it to him, but it comes when our handshake ends.

"Your girl over there. She's . . . something," he says. I pass him and move toward his car, mashing my molars together.

"She's my sister," Tommy grunts, and I'm glad he stepped in so I don't have to.

"She's hot," one of the assholes says, laughing at his boldness. My chest fires up and I'm willing to drop this charade now for the pleasure of punching him.

"Yeah, but she's a real bitch," Tommy says. I laugh to myself, my face turned away from the new guys. Tommy is both pretending and being honest. They love each other, but like siblings who spent a lot of time together growing up. Sometimes, he legit thinks his sister is a bitch. I wonder if he knows the things she calls him.

"That's a pretty sick wrap job," I say, running my finger along the matte green that covers most of the Subaru. I bet it's silver underneath, and I bet his daddy let him drive it right off the lot and into some detail shop that overcharged him for the job. My finger snags on the sharp edge under the mirror and I smirk, knowing this shit is going to peel by the time June rolls around.

"Yeah, had to do something to show off the two-point-four liter twin turbo the right way." He rattles off probably the only thing he knows about his car. And I bet among his friends, it's celebrated and awed over, as if he's some bad-ass because he bought a stock car that goes fast. And it is fast. But not fast enough to beat me.

"Siiiiiick," I say, exaggerating my response to the point that I catch Tommy again trying to stifle his laughter.

"I know, right?" the guy says, popping his hood for me to take a look. What an idiot. If he was playing me, he wouldn't give me access to the inside of his ride. Tommy moves in next to me and we both glaze over, our suspicion confirmed.

"Nice," Tommy drones. The guy doesn't catch the hint of sarcasm in his tone.

"Real nice," I add on, just to layer it thick.

Tommy and I briefly make eye contact as we back away from the engine. It's been awhile since he set something up with me. Out at the Straights, drivers pony up because that's how it's done. It's a respect thing. We're all upfront, and most of the people who race up north are serious about the craft. Racing me on the Straights has become a sort of honor, and a lot of the drivers have side bets going about their times or how close they can come, so they make cash even if they lose.

Down here, though, racing is a hobby. It's playtime for prep-school assholes. May as well give these guys the full experience.

"I don't know, Dusty. I think maybe you can take this car. What do you think?" Tommy says, setting me up.

I grab at the back of my neck and turn to look at my Supra, that to the layperson—which these guys totally are—looks like a piece of shit.

"I don't know, Tom. My car's pretty old. They build these new models so fast," I say, gleefully cataloguing all the custom work going on under my hood, things these guys would be clueless about. Hell, I bet I could pop it and show them what's going on and they'd only see a mess and think I was a joke.

"That a Supra?" one of the guys asks. I shift a little on my feet, uneasy that one of these guys knows enough to at least understand what the body of my car is.

"Yeah. I bought it on OfferUp. What did it cost me, eight hundred?" I fake ask Tommy.

"I think it was nine, but you overpaid," Tommy says in a wry tone. I wink at him, loving the extra effort he's giving to this con.

"I might be able to match that thing on the road"—I gesture toward the bright green car—"but hell, I'll probably blow a gasket before we make it halfway through the race."

"You think? I bet it'll hold just long enough," Tommy lies, rubbing his chin as if really thinking about it. If anyone is blowing a gasket today, it's one of these four assholes.

"You up for a race, man?"

And there it is. I cover my mouth and pretend I'm

considering his offer, but underneath my fingers, I'm grinning like a fool.

"I don't know. Maybe?" I play on, pulling out the cash in my pocket. I have two hundred bucks to my name, money I've kept stashed in my center console as emergency funds. I unfurl the bills and turn to look at Hannah. She's sitting up on the car now, resting back on her elbows. She lifts a hand and waves to me and my heart literally sings.

"She's gonna be so mad if I lose the money," I say, putting the bait out there.

"Maybe you won't lose," the guy says.

"Yeah, maybe you won't lose, Dusty," Tommy repeats.

We are all going to laugh so fucking hard about this later.

I turn back to face the guys, pinching the two hundreds in my fingers, staring at them as though I'm really mulling this over. I roll my head a little and push the money back in my pocket, then step back toward my enemy.

"All right, sure. Two hundred on the race," I say, holding out my hand again. He takes it, chuckling through our gentleman's agreement. His friends try to hide their own arrogant laughter behind his back. They think they've conned me, and it's going to feel so good to smoke this guy in the first six seconds on the road.

"What did you say your name was again?" I ask. He actually didn't say, and he knows he didn't.

"Aiden." He lowers his glasses to the bridge of his nose, though the sun will be down in a matter of minutes.

"Aiden." I repeat his name, nodding. "Nice to meet you."

"Yeah, you, too . . . *Dusty.*" Their laughter spills out as I walk away. They ate my character up and it is so satisfying to hear them be so confident. Tommy and I bump elbows, the move innocuous enough that it doesn't appear to the guys behind us as if we're gloating. But we are gloating. And we're going to enjoy every minute of this. Now to go make some side bets and really rack up the cash.

T his isn't my turf, so I wait my turn. The night's starting to drag on, though, and for a few minutes I am nervous the Scottsdale boys are going to bail.

Bless Hannah and her extraverted personality and her legs and hips and those way-too-short-shorts. She slips into the crowd of guys running the order and manages to move me up. I think they mostly want to see her kick things off, and while I want to punch the rookies for staring at her ass as she slips between my car and the Subaru, I'll settle for ruining their rep out here on the road.

Oh, and taking their money.

And then, maybe, a punch in the face.

"Gentlemen!" Hannah juts her hip out as she shouts, and Tommy pats the roof of my car as he backs away.

I roll the window up and narrow my focus so the only things I see are the reflective dots that fade out down the road and Hannah's long, slender arm in the air.

It's less formal out here. Nobody shouts "start your engines" because our cars are already revving and our windows are up. It's a matter of anticipation, and watching for the hair trigger sign that the starter's hand is about to fall. I have the edge because I know Hannah, and I know she likes the drama. It's one of the reasons everyone loves Ava Cruz starting races out on the Straights. She has a way of making something benign feel rare and special, filling the air with crackling anticipation that bubbles under the low hum of the engines.

Hannah's created that spark here, tonight.

My lip ticks up on one side because I like it.

My hands feel the grip of the wheel and I move my right palm to the gear shift, my hold on it loose and ready. My pulse settles in at a rhythm I like. Originally, I planned to make this close. Or *closer,* at least. But then those dickheads gawked at my girl's ass, and now? Now I'm going to embarrass them.

Hannah's hand falls just as my eyes blink, and I let instinct take over. It's clear Aiden doesn't know how to handle his car, and within seconds, I've cleared his length. A quick glance in my mirror lets me know he's struggling to handle the steering while trying to push his way back into a chance in hell.

That chance left the minute I got behind the wheel, asshole.

I'm at one-twenty faster than I've climbed there before, and my body swells with dominant blood. There's nothing now but me and the road. My gaze zooms ahead, to the marker, and I play with the edge of the gear shift as I approach it, flirting with how I'll make this turn. My lead is so long that Aiden will have to watch, so I want to make it special.

I punch the brake and flip around, barely skidding offline before passing Aiden and roaring back ahead. I imagine him swearing and shaking a fist out his window, and that cartoonish visual amuses me as I sail back to the place I started, not even bothering to roll through the finish line at top speed. I downshift and pull to the side in time to make room for the Subaru to speed through the line of cars, and I'm out of my car before Aiden slows enough to turn.

"Uh, I thought we were going in subtle," Tommy says, clapping his hand on my back.

I shrug.

"I decided to make a point instead," I answer.

"And that point is . . ."

I turn to walk backward as we head toward Hannah and Aiden's friends. There's a flash of green in her hand, which relaxes me because it means the guys paid up and I don't have to fight for my winnings. In the past, when I've shown guys up, they've gotten defensive with the money. There's an unwritten rule about welching on bets on the streets, and once you do it, it's damned near impossible to get let back in. That doesn't sink through for some people, though. I'll give the Scottsdale boys this—they know enough to not fuck around with the cash.

"Nice race," Hannah says, her lashes low and eyes hazed above her proud, faint smile.

Tommy exaggerates an eye roll and gives us some space. I pick her up and swing her around in a complete circle while I kiss her. She wraps her legs around me and tucks the roll of money into the breast pocket of my long-sleeved T-shirt, patting it twice for safe-keeping.

"You've got company," she says in a low voice, glancing beyond me.

I set her down and instinctively move her behind me as I hear the rumble of the Subaru pulling up.

"Yo, that was bullshit!" Aiden says, stepping in close enough that I smell stale smoke on his breath. Fucking cloves.

"Not sure what you mean there. I thought you drove that thing pretty well," I say, playing up the naïve nice-guy routine.

The grin on my face is stretched with fakeness, and I work hard to keep it plastered there while Aiden turns and laughs toward his friends.

"This guy," he says, thumb pointing to me over his shoulder.

Someone else would probably take his fist in their teeth, but I've been hit plenty of times so I see it coming seconds before he twists and fires away.

I dip so his arm sails over me and his balance falters, then I rush forward and knock him to the ground, my knee in his stomach and my hand around his throat. I'm not pressing hard, but enough to let him know I can if I want to.

"You've got a learning curve, Aiden. That's all. You bought a nice car, but if you're going to race it you need to get yourself a good mechanic, or take some auto shop at school. Maybe make some new friends who know how to do more than put stickers on perfectly fine paint jobs." I hold his glare, his teeth showing as he grunts out his labored breath. I give him a wink and let him go, making sure to take a few steps back so he can't sweep my legs. People are always brave a few seconds after an attack. His head will clear, though, and he won't want me embarrassing him again.

"Fucking hustled me, you prick!" He spits at me, the kind that sprays and splatters innocent bystanders. He's made even more enemies now, so he's left to stumble back into his car and drive off with his friends scrambling to catch up.

"My lips to God, Dustin, that shit never gets old," Tommy says, slinging an arm over my shoulder. I shake my head.

"No, it does not," I agree.

I get a subtle nod from Jimmy, who's about to obliterate someone else with his Challenger. We never speak, part of the code, but it feels good to earn that silent respect.

Nothing against the hobbyists who come out here; one day most of these guys will look back on their lives and reminisce about those times they drag raced out in the desert. I bet their stories get embellished in the retelling, and I bet getting smoked by guys like me never comes up.

But for guys like Jimmy? I'll be part of their stories. Like that nod of respect, when they talk to their grandkids about coming out to the desert to race, they'll mention how they once lost to Dustin Bridges. Their kids and grandkids won't have to ask who I am. They'll know. *Everyone* will know.

I'm comfortable in the fantasy, and with my arm around my girl, sharing laughs and smiles with my best friend, for the first time in a very long time, everything in my life feels damn near perfect.

Thing about me, though? Feeling perfect has always been a warning sign of the hailstorm of shit about to come. The sensation raises the hairs on the back of my neck first, and before I can fully turn and slip from Hannah's warm embrace, the cruel and cold creeps in to steal my fantasy.

"Let's see how fast you are now, asshole!" Aiden shouts. His arm hangs out of his car window as he cruises by, what appears to be a nine millimeter Glock—same brand as the one Colt sometimes carries—gripped in his hand and aimed right at my passenger side back tire.

The crack of the first shot echoes across the desert, the reverb playing off the nearby mountainside. My hands search behind me for Hannah, relief coating my stomach when I feel her arms and am able to back into her chest and shield her completely. Tommy rushes to stand at my side, helping to block his sister.

Hannah's body jolts against me at the second shot. This one has Tommy sprinting toward Aiden's car, a wrench from his tool set clutched in his hand. I let my friend show the aggression, not that my body isn't seething with it. Right now, though, Hannah is my priority. Second on that list are the two flat tires that are going to cost a goddamn fortune—more than the couple hundred bucks won tonight—to replace.

Tommy hoists his wrench at the Subaru as it speeds away, falling short several feet only to spark as it clanks against the asphalt. My friend stares at the bright green car covered in stickers as it grows smaller in the distance, soon the only thing visible the glow of two tail lights.

"Shit!" my friend shouts, kicking at the road as he turns to face me. He's threaded his hands behind his neck, and his teeth grind with anger. I should probably look just like him, and I'm a little surprised I don't.

"How are we getting your car home?" Hannah croaks. I turn to look at her over my shoulder and reach out a hand. She takes it tentatively, probably waiting for me to lose my shit like her brother. I won't, though. No sense in that. I'm used to haters. I was raised by them.

"I'll use your donut, and I'm sure someone here will give me one of theirs. We'll get home fine. *Slow,* ha! But . . . we'll get home." At my joke, her hand sinks comfortably into mine and I bring her into my chest, hugging her and swaying her a little to calm her racing heart.

I always thought the day would come when clashes like this wouldn't frighten me. I thought I'd be older, but I guess seventeen is the magic number. I'll be eighteen soon; what better time to feel invincible.

19

All I kept thinking as I followed the boys home at a painfully slow pace was how proud my dad would have been of the way Dustin handled himself.

He had every reason to lose his cool. I was mentally prepared for him to grab someone's keys and speed off after those assholes to run them off the road, if only to pull that Aiden guy out of the car and pummel his face bloody.

Guns have never stopped Dustin from getting in fights. Hell, all of Camp Verde carries, and target practice sometimes happens in back yards around here. But Dustin didn't even show an itch to retaliate.

Despite my best plea for him to park his car at our house and spend the night, he followed through with his own new rules about sleeping at my house. And as much as I missed him last night and worried about him sleeping in his car on two tires that won't get him very far, I'm kind of relieved he opted out of my house now that I'm staring at my dad's disgruntled, stoic face.

He was waiting downstairs for Tommy and me as we came down for breakfast. Mom, apparently, went to work early. I have a feeling she ran away to let my dad get this out of his system without her around getting "all emotional"—his common term when he's in this sort of mood.

"Two a.m." After ten minutes of silence while Tommy and I mill around the kitchen and pour cereal, eat said cereal, and move on to brewing coffee, this is my dad's big opening line.

"I'm sorry?" Tommy says over his shoulder as he pours a cup of steaming caffeine bliss.

I wince as I sit across from my dad at the table. My brother knows exactly what he's talking about. It's the time we rolled in, on a school night. Which for Tommy isn't a big deal because he's eighteen. Personally, I think he gets different rules because of his penis, but whatever.

"Tell me you weren't out with *him*, racing, at two in the goddamn morning," my dad says, his voice a low boil as he flattens his palms on the table and slides them forward, along with the frame of his body, to narrow his gaze on me.

I hold my dad's stare for a moment, letting the panic make its way through my chest so I can offer a smart response.

"Do you mean was I out with Tommy? My brother? Because, yes, I was." I fold my arms over my chest and lean back in the chair. My dad's thick eyebrows lower. I glance behind him to catch my brother now leaning against the counter, smirking as he takes a sip of his coffee. He loves it when I'm in trouble and not him.

"You know *damn well* what I mean!" My father's hand

comes up as he shouts, and he smacks the table to punctuate his sentence. I can't help it. I flinch.

My heart is racing now, but it's less about being in trouble. No, I'm indignant. My lips twitch with want and need to react, but I'm careful—thoughtful. I need to say the right words if I want to make a point. And I do want to make a point. One that won't be flattering at all to my father, and I hate that because despite this very childish display, he's still my best friend.

I swallow and relax my shoulders, letting my hands release their grip on my shirt as I slide back in the chair. Once I say what I am about to, I'm going to need to leave. It's what will be best for both me and my dad.

"Unfortunately, I do know what you mean," I say. My father lets out a breathy laugh, and I can tell he feels smug, maybe a little relieved. He's not going to like the rest of what I have to say, but it doesn't mean he doesn't need to hear it.

"You mean because I'm a girl, I can't do the same things Tommy does. You mean you don't trust me to make my own choices for who to love, or who to believe in. And you mean Tommy can still be friends with Dustin, but I can't, because somehow . . . *now* . . . that's different. Basically, Dustin's never been family to you at all, which makes you kind of a liar."

I push away from the table as my dad's jaw shifts and his head tilts. I grab my bag and make my way to the door, ignoring his grumbling as well as my brother's amused smile. I caught enough of that while I was making my speech.

I've never actually said the exact thing I wanted to say when the moment called for it, and my chest feels full and my body teems with an almost prideful energy. I guess my parents can ground me if they want, though Tommy and I have never been grounded once in our entire lives. I'd point out all of the times my brother's gotten away with things far worse than driving down to the Valley on a school night.

"We're not done with this conversation, Hannah."

That's the last of what I hear, though I'm sure my father had more to say. I wouldn't say I slammed the door shut behind me, but I definitely made sure it closed. I get to my car and turn my music up loud enough to drown out the sound of my phone, and shoot my brother a quick text so he knows I'm picking Dustin up this morning and he's taking Bailey to school.

As I pull away, I'm hit with a wave of sorrow. Maybe even a sense of mourning. If I knew the last time my brother and father and Dustin and I were all together was going to be the last, I would have appreciated it more.

Dustin is sitting on the back of his car, his hair wet, when I pull up. He hates showering at his parents' house, but I guess he's forcing himself to get used to it since the welcome mat to my place has been taken away.

The sight of him eases the ache that was beginning to fill my stomach and chest. One crooked grin as he shakes his head, flipping his hair from his eyes, and everything I said this morning and all of the battles that lie ahead become worth it.

Nobody will ever make my heart pound with love the way this boy can.

I turn so the passenger side is closest to him and roll down my window.

"Hey, goin' my way?" I say, squinting against the sun.

Dustin's mouth ticks up as he slides from the back of his car and picks up the backpack between his feet. He walks toward the open window in this slow, sexy way, then leans forward, resting his arm on the windowsill.

"Ma'am, I don't care where you take me as long as I get to be next to you." He winks to layer on the cheese, and while I laugh and call him stupid, I swoon a little too.

I pull onto the main road as Dustin buckles in. I don't know what he's going to do about his tires, but I don't want to bring it up because he still seems so calm and happy. I know how important that car is to him, though. It's more than just his way around. It's his life's work and a means to bigger ends. If Dustin can't race, he can't grow and get into the circuit.

"Have you checked to see if the scrap yard has hours again?" I ask. He doesn't answer right away, and I mash my lips together, admonishing myself for bringing it up.

"They might have a weekend or two, yeah. I'll ask," he sighs out.

I glance his way with a smile, and I'm relieved when his is still in place. It's not as relaxed as before, though. I added kindling for his anxiety, and now all I can think about is whether or not to apologize for it. I decide against it because it will only prolong the topic, so instead, I switch gears to something I have been *dying* to talk about.

"I'm going dress shopping with Bailey today after school," I say. I glance at him again and laugh when I'm met with his wide eyes and exaggerated smile. I smack his thigh and he grabs my hand in both of his, pulling it to his chest and kissing my knuckles.

"I'm just kidding. I'm looking forward to prom. Truly. I cannot wait to see how hot you're going to look." His eyebrow flicks up and down with his words and I jerk my hand away.

"One track mind with you, Dustin," I tease. My thighs tingle at the thought of his hand creeping up my leg in a short mini dress, though, so I decide that I'm definitely buying something short.

"Your parents still going to let you go with me?" he asks.

I bite my bottom lip and suck it in. Dustin shifts in his seat so he's facing me more.

"Hannah? Your parents know I'm taking you to prom, right? Like, I can show up and pick you up and give you flowers and all that shit?"

My chest tightens.

"Uh huh?" I mutter. "I mean, yeah. Sure! Of course!" I smile through my bullshit, but it's useless; Dustin sees right through my sad attempt.

"Hannah. Your parents have to be okay with this. I'm not sneaking you out for prom. Your dad would hunt me down and take me to one of those places in the middle of nowhere he likes to hike." He twists back in his seat and runs both his hands over his face then through his hair, his thumbs pausing at his temples to rub small circles.

"I will tell them. We are going . . . *together.* And my mom will want pictures, even if my dad shakes your hand with a death grip. Prom is a non-negotiable."

Dustin lets out a short laugh and shakes his head as I pull into the student parking lot.

"Okay, Banana. Whatever you say," he jokes, getting out of the car and rounding to my side to wait for me.

I purse my lips at him when I get out. I can't count the number of times he's uttered that phrase to me over the years, and he always says it when he doesn't fully believe me. I forgive him a little, though, when he slings his arm over my shoulders and pulls me in tight. And when his mouth covers mine—a display put on for every girl our age in Camp Verde—I forget his teasing doubt. One more kiss like that and I'll completely let him off the hook for prom.

20

Dustin

Hannah's parents forbidding her from prom wouldn't be the end of the world. All I could think about after she mentioned the dress shopping was the money it was going to cost me to go. Money I don't have.

Money I have no way to get now that my car is down two tires.

I hate that money is a barrier. As much as I don't want my life to be about money, it seems I'm always desperate for it. Two hundred bucks from last night's race isn't going to stretch far, and I have a lot of bases to cover. Tux rental, prom tickets, dinner somewhere fancy, pictures, flowers. Hannah would pay for it all, but she shouldn't. I don't want her to. But damn, at this point, I can't even pick her up in my own car.

Hannah will be out with Bailey most of the afternoon. She might be a tough girl who likes dirt tracks, but she's also a sucker for all things pink and frilly. She could honestly show up in a sack for a dress and she'd be the most beautiful girl at the prom. In the town. Fuck, in

Arizona. But she wants this to be a dream kind of prom, and though her parents won't be on board at all—despite what she says—I'm going to do my damnedest to make her night perfection.

Tommy pulls up to my house, shifting into park a couple trailers away from mine. He's done this enough times to know the drill. If Colt's around, it's better that he doesn't hear a car pull up. He likes to mess with Tommy, probably because he gets off on making my friend nervous.

"I'll be in and out," I say, patting the windowsill twice before walking toward the quiet trailer at the end.

The normal flash of the television isn't shining through the crack in the blinds, which means my mother is either asleep or not at home. If she isn't home, it's possible she was able to get herself to work. It's a miracle she hasn't been fired from the job at the gas station. I think they're so hard up for people that whenever someone who isn't the owners can come in, they jump on it.

I fish my keys out of my pocket and use my hip to crack the door open completely. The lock doesn't line up right ever since Colt kicked the door open one night and I had to replace it. There's a small light on in the corner of the living room, but other than that, the place seems dark and empty. I push the door shut behind me and quietly move into the center of the room.

"Mom?" My voice is even. Not loud, but quiet enough not to stir her if she is asleep. The ashtray on the coffee table is overfilled, so I carry it to the kitchen and dump the debris into an old coffee can. Mom set fire to the garbage once, and since then, we're careful with her ashes.

The place smells like cat piss, which probably means she's taken in a stray again. I search the corners of the kitchen and the back bathroom to see if there are any traces of an animal. I find a fairly full litter box, so I nudge it with my foot, shaking fresh litter to the top.

I leave the bathroom door open behind me in case the cat is hiding somewhere. I don't want to get in the way of a cat and its shitter. My eyes scan the counters, table, and sofa as I work my way to the back rooms, looking for anything out of place. Nothing seems off, though, so I let my guard down a touch as I enter the hallway. Mom's bedroom door is open, and the oscillating fan hums inside her room. I dip my head in for a quick peek, relieved when I find her sheets twisted on top of her empty mattress, a few dresses laid out on her floor. I stare at the pale yellow one for a beat, the floral pattern scratching at old memories. My mom took me to church once and she wore that dress. I was maybe three or four, but I can pull the visual of her long, blonde hair and the way the skirt of that dress blew in the wind as she stood on the church steps with me in front of her. The material flapped around me as I hugged her knees. The dress looks more like a rag now.

I blink a few times and leave her open door behind before slipping into the room that's technically mine. There aren't many things worth much in this room, but I grab the few items I can sell from the top drawer of my dresser, like the Oakleys I haven't worn in a year and the platinum money clip the Judges bought me for Christmas. I let the weight of those things sit in my palm as I hold my breath and make the slow turn toward the closet, pausing at the door to allow a few more seconds to pass to ensure I'm here alone.

Eyes squeezed shut, I press my empty palm to the door and slide it over, delivering a silent prayer that the money I saw in here last time hasn't been taken. When I spot the wrapped bundle, I let out an actual giggle, quickly shoving my knuckled fist in my teeth between my grin.

My heart is pounding and as I lift my free hand to pull the money bundle down, my fingers tremble. I squeeze then flex them to calm myself enough to get through this next part. I thought about this all night long. It's the solution to everything, and it's also just and right. I'm only taking the money that's rightfully mine—the money Colt stole from me. Two grand, and we'll call it even.

I kneel down, setting my sellable items on the floor so I can unwrap the money bundle carefully. I pick at the plastic seam with my thumbnail and peel it back, flipping the brick over four times until bills are exposed. My breath hitches at how accessible the answer to all my problems suddenly is.

Temptation sits in my throat, burning like a swallow of wasabi. Is two thousand so different from three? I could run up to Vegas and get a race this weekend maybe, turn that cash into six and put it back before Colt ever notices.

A sudden thud behind me rocks me back on my ass and I clutch my chest, expecting a blow to my head. When it doesn't come, I twist my neck to find the source of the noise, relieved to find the heavy book flat on the ground behind me. Stretching along the floor to reach it, I glance to the space underneath the dresser and am met with a pair of glowing eyes. I abandon the aging copy of fairytales nobody ever read to me and turn my focus on the tiny kitten quaking under the bottom drawer.

"Hey, little guy," I whisper, rubbing my thumb and forefinger together softly in an attempt to draw the animal out. He purrs after a few seconds and eventually slinks his way from under the furniture until he's rubbing along my leg, looping under my knee and crawling on top of my thigh.

"Yeah, I see how you suckered my mom into keeping you," I say through a crooked smile. I rub his head with my thumb a few times, my soul quenched by the welcome affection.

"You deserve better, buddy," I say, pulling him to my face and touching his cold, tiny nose to mine.

A faint *meow* slips out so I set him back on the floor between my legs where he continues to curl into a tighter and tighter bundle until he's coiled and satisfied enough to shut his eyes. Why couldn't my mom have rescued something like this when I was a kid? I would have loved to not be so alone in this house. A pet like this would have saved me.

I indulge in nearly a full minute of kitten cuddling then cut myself off, deciding it's best I don't push my luck with the cash. I slip out two thousand bucks in hundreds and rewrap the bundle, slipping the bills in my pocket before sliding the brick of money back in its place. I close the closet, grab my glasses and money clip, and scratch the kitten on top of the head one last time before leaving my room and this hellhole of a home.

I'm careful to leave everything as I found it, shutting the door quietly and locking it before sliding the planter back to the right to block the door from swinging open. Both Colt and my mom think having an object in the way of the door will deter people from trying to get in. I have my doubts that the kind of people Colt is worried about are deterred by a dead aloe vera plant and some dry-ass dirt in a clay pot, but what do I know?

Tommy seems anxious by the time I get back to the car, so I stave off the attempt to mess with him and tell him Colt was inside. I don't mention the cash until we're on the highway, halfway back to his place.

"Mind following me to Earl's so I can drop off the Supra?" My question catches Tommy off-guard and it takes him a minute to realize what I'm implying.

"You found your money?" he responds, genuinely relieved and happy for me.

"Well, there was money there, and he took mine, so—" I leave out the important details, like the money I found was wrapped up, ready for a deal exchange.

"Hey, his fault for not hiding that shit better after stealing it from you, bro. Yeah, let's go get some tires." Tommy holds his fist out for me to bump. I do, but an uneasy feeling washes over my insides. Instead of letting it bring me down from this high, though, I block it from my mind and imagine how gorgeous Hannah is going to look in whatever dress she picks out today.

21

"Do I get to see your dresses?" my mom asks as Bailey and I clamber into the house with bags on our arms. It's a family dinner night, though I feel nothing like sitting down for one. I'm not much in a position to refuse family time, though, since mom gave me the credit card without lecturing me about my choice of prom date.

"I suppose so," I say. Everything about my tone is fake, and my mom can see right through it. Our eyes meet and her brow draws in with apology. If she were truly sorry, she would admit she and my dad were wrong to react the way they did in the first place.

"I know you'll be shocked to see this, but . . . I went with pink," I say, revealing my dress with a flourish as I pull it from the bag.

"Oh, that's . . ." My mom trails off, wiping her hands clean on a towel so she can touch the delicate skirt fabric.

"I know, it's short. But I swear it covers everything," I say before she can ask.

She flits her gaze to me and plasters on her fake, *I'm-a-cool-parent* grin.

"I wasn't going to say that." Her sing-songy tone says otherwise. "I was going to say *beautiful fabric.*"

She runs her hand through the draped skirting again, and her smile softens. This is supposed to be one of those cherished moments between mother and daughter. I won't ruin it if she won't.

"I really love the color," I say, holding the dress to my body and stretching out the side. It's an empire waist cocktail style dress made of a gauzy champagne pink silk accented with delicate beadwork near the bodice. Thin straps crisscross along the open back, and Bailey managed to find me strappy heels that match it perfectly.

"Show her yours, Bailey," I say, wanting to put mine away before Dad walks in and says something to ruin this moment.

I leave Bailey in the kitchen with my mom and head up to my room to stash my dress deep in my closet. It's not that I'm hiding it, but I don't want there to be an accidental viewing by my brother or Dustin, assuming he enters this house again anytime soon.

As if the universe is spying on my thoughts, though, the familiar growl of Dustin's car fills my driveway. I rush to my window and push open my shutters, shocked to see the Supra roaring up behind Tommy's car. With two new tires. Maybe we'll get to hit the Straights tomorrow night after all.

I skip down the stairs and pass my mom and Bailey on my way outside, practically leaping across the driveway and into Dustin's arms as he steps out of his car, a confident grin on his face. He holds me about a foot in the air, then lets me slide down the length of his chest and into his embrace, rocking me side to side as he plants a kiss on top of my head.

"Well, that's a pretty great greeting. Not sure what I did to deserve this." He laughs.

"Never going to get used to that," Tommy says, holding up a palm to block his view of us as he walks by. He's teasing, and it warms my heart to see my brother coming around to the idea of Dustin and me as a couple.

"Are you staying for dinner?" I say, leaning back in Dustin's arms.

"Oh, uhm." He pauses, his lips tight. He shoots a gaze to Tommy and I look to my brother as well.

"Dude, I want no part of this decision." My brother holds his hands up and wanders to the other side of Dustin's car, kneeling down to look at the tires.

I wait for Dustin to drop his gaze back to me; I sense his worry and hesitation in the tightness of his jaw.

"Please?" I ask, drawing my hands to the center of his chest and bunching his shirt in my palms.

"Oh, man. I mean, what's one more round of ego-pounding with your dad, I guess," he relents, and though it makes me a little sad to hear him put it that way, I'm glad he's staying. It wouldn't be a family dinner without Dustin at the table.

Not wanting to spar with my dad too early, Dustin takes a step back to put distance between us when he catches a view of my dad's truck making the turn down our street. I decide not to push things either and fall back a few steps so I'm standing closer to my brother than my boyfriend.

My dad's focus remains straight ahead as he navigates his way up the driveway, parking between our cars and the house. He takes extra time getting out of the truck, wrestling with his cooler in the passenger seat and sorting through something in his center console. When he's out of distractions, he finally gets out of his vehicle. His shoulders lift and fall in a big exhale before he turns around. Unlike my mom, Dad doesn't have the ability to fake his emotions. It's clear from the stiff jawline and straight-lined mouth that he's not looking forward to interacting with any of us. With the way I left this morning, I guess I'm the last person he really wants to see. But my dad has never been the type to ignore elephants in rooms. And that's what Dustin and I are—one big-ass elephant.

"Gentlemen," my dad says, nodding in the general direction of Dustin.

"Hannah."

That's his greeting for me, along with a quick glance in my direction.

"You, uh, staying for dinner?" My dad rubs the back of his neck as he asks, only flitting his focus up to Dustin once before bringing his attention back down to the driveway.

"If that's all right. I'd like to, Mr. Judge."

It kills me to hear Dustin sound so formal with my dad. He shouldn't have to.

"Yeah. I mean, it's family dinner. I'm sure Amanda made plenty of roast. And there's those mini potatoes you like, so . . ." My dad's words are stilted. He's clearly uncomfortable, and Dustin shoots me a quick glance, probably hoping for a life raft. I'm not sure what to say that won't be mean or snarky.

"You see the new treads?" Tommy finally pipes up, changing the subject to one the three of them are always comfortable with—cars.

"An upgrade, huh?" my dad says, moving closer to the

back passenger side. He gives it the preverbal kick then squats down to admire them closer. "You went with the Mickey Thompsons. Pretty sweet."

For a tiny slip, my dad is being genuine.

"Yeah, I'm swapping out the front two tomorrow," Dustin says, kicking the worn front tire near him.

My dad stands, nodding and admiring the rubber. He pops his head up suddenly, meeting Dustin's gaze, and there's a shift in his mood. His brows draw in and his lips part but hang open, as if he's carefully choosing his words.

"Those aren't cheap," he finally settles on.

My dad knows Dustin races for money. Hell, that's part of the culture in this town, and my dad raced on the Straights back when he and Mom were in high school. But it's never been big money out there, not the kind that can front Mickey Thompson radials.

"Yeah, good thing someone taught me how to save," Dustin says, his delivery convincing enough to appease my dad. For now.

"Tommy could learn a thing or two about saving," my dad teases, patting my brother's chest as he turns. Tommy overexaggerates the impact, coughing as if his wind is knocked out.

"I know how to save. I just know how to spend too," my brother says, winking at me.

"Yeah, how many cell phones have you busted? What is it, four? You're good at spending on those," my dad throws back at him.

We follow my dad's lead toward the house, and this walk that we've done so many times, all four of us tumbling into the kitchen after talking about car stuff while my mom has food ready for the table, suddenly feels strange. As normal as my dad pretends everything is, I'm very aware of how much it isn't. I want to fast-forward to a time when my parents are good with me dating Dustin, when they see how wrong they were about everything, and when I can walk into my house proudly holding his hand, knowing they won't stare at it as if it's impending doom.

Like they are now. At least, my mom is.

I feel Dustin try to untether our fingers but I curl mine to urge him to stay with me, to hold my hand despite the judgement. Our time will come.

A quick glance to the set table shows how little my mom was prepared for the additional guest, despite the fact we have set a place for Dustin for as long as I can remember.

"Bailey, would you mind?" my mom says under her breath, handing a plate and a napkin wrapped with a set of silverware to my friend.

"Oh, sure," Bailey says, shrinking her head in between her shoulders. She makes eye contact with me as she rounds the table, and I can tell she's uncomfortable by the way she doesn't blink. Like, at all. I walk to the other side and take the plate from her.

"I got it," I say, purposely scooting the chair that is usually my mom's seat to the side to make room for the one I'm about to add. I pull the spare chair from the closet and slide it between where I intend to sit and where my mom can choose to or not. I glance up as I arrange the silverware around the new setting and my mom looks away hurriedly when I catch her staring at me.

"There. Perfect," I say, clapping my hands together.

Tommy snort laughs because he's amused when I'm extra.

Despite the rough start, when everyone is sitting at the table and shoveling my mom's pot roast into their mouths, things actually start to feel normal. My mom amuses us all with stories about local politics, like the man who filled out forty-seven public comment cards and spent the entire council meeting reading excerpts from his science fiction novel that he's been working on for twenty years to a captive audience funded by tax dollars. My dad complains about one of his land cases, but cuts himself off when he realizes Bailey's father might become the lawyer for the other side. My brother dodges questions from my mom about when he's going to commit to Northern New Mexico University, where he has a full ride waiting.

I am on edge for his answer to that too, and I can tell Dustin is eager to say something to my brother about it. Tommy still doesn't know that Dustin overheard him the night he admitted to having second thoughts about spending a year racing and putting off college. That's, of course, a plan he never ran by my parents either. Funny thing is, I doubt my father would even flinch at the idea, and he'd be so supportive, he'd bring my mom around, too. Of course, all of that was before *me* and Dustin, and maybe that put a strain on all things in the future.

By the time dinner is done and Bailey's gone home, the five of us sit in our familiar places in the living room— Mom in her rocker, Dad in his recliner, and Tommy, Dustin and me piled on the couch. We keep with the routine, with Tommy in the middle, and it seems to keep the peace as we tune in the Diamondbacks game in time to watch them blow a four-run lead. I almost forgot things aren't easy, but the evening reminds me, and when mom decides she's tired and ready to head upstairs, the weight of expectation that Dustin now leave slams into my chest.

"Right, well . . ." Dustin fumbles his words, slapping his hands on his knees then standing from the couch.

"Just let him stay," my brother says, waving his hand in my parents' direction. It's greeted with a steely, emotionless and silent response.

"It's fine, Tommy. I respect the rules of the house," Dustin says. It stabs at my heart because the rules have changed for him, and that's because of me.

"Thank you, Dustin," my dad says, using his *official* voice. "Be sure you bring the Supra over when you get the other set on. Maybe we can take it out for some drifting, break 'em in right."

Dustin flashes a short-lived smile on one side of his mouth.

"Sure, Mr. Judge."

Everyone exchanges these strange, stilted nods that seem to ink a silent agreement that it's time for Dustin to go. I slip from the couch and take his hand in mine, tugging him toward the door.

"I'm going to walk him out," I say.

My mom makes brief eye contact with me then fakes a yawn. I can tell by the way she hovers her hand over her mouth to accentuate it. It's barely eight-thirty. She'll be up reading until eleven.

"Come inside soon," she orders over her shoulder. Sure, her voice is syrupy sweet, but it also isn't the real her. I don't bother to respond, and instead salute my father, earning me a scowl before I head out the door to the driveway.

"Why did you have to throw that in," Dustin sighs when the door is closed behind us.

"I couldn't help it. Besides, a salute is a show of respect," I reply.

He huffs out a laugh.

"Yeah, I'm sure you were being *real* respectful just then."

I wrap my arms around his bicep and rest my head on his arm as we walk to his car. His lights flash as he unlocks the car with his fob and pulls his door open, sinking inside with his legs out the door. His fingers dance along the tips of mine as I stand between his feet, not even close to ready to go back inside.

"How about we just camp out here in your car?" I lift my eyebrows, sadly hoping he'll like my idea. I relent at how desperate it is when he chuckles.

"I am pretty sure any time I spend with you alone when the moon is out is going to earn me very few brownie points," he says through a laugh. "But . . ." He holds up his palm when he senses I'm about to argue. "I don't really like brownies, so I'm willing to lose a few along the way."

He tugs me down to his lap, turning me so my back rests on his seat and my knees draw in so I'm curled in his lap. His arms circle me as his nose playful brushes against mine a few times before his gaze falls to my mouth. My lips buzz with anticipation in the few breaths before his mouth covers mine. I don't think I will ever tire of the way Dustin kisses. He's attentive, passionate yet tender, rough and soft all at once. His teeth nip at my upper lip and a slight growl vibrates in his chest as I wiggle against his lap, feeling how hard he is against my thigh.

"Careful, Hannah. I don't have many brownies to spare," he says, breaking our kiss, his hand on the middle of my thigh.

"Don't you, though?" I tease, shifting my knees apart just enough to encourage his hand to slide toward my inner thigh. He holds my heated stare with one of his own, giving in to temptation after a few heavy, shared breaths.

"This is a bad idea," he hums as I move my forehead to rest on his. My eyelashes flutter, my core swollen and ready to fall apart just from the idea that he may let his hand travel a little farther.

"I'm full of bad ideas," I say, parting my knees a little more. Just enough.

Dustin's hand trails up the inside of my leg, under the ripped hem of my denim shorts to the very wet strip of cotton between my legs. His fingers run along the center, stroking my swollen skin underneath and I sigh, letting my eyes close and my mouth fall to his ear.

"Touch me, Dustin. So I can sleep tonight," I beg.

His chest fills with a long draw of air, his hand still sticking to this line he's drawn, that somehow the thin layer of my panties makes what he's doing chaste.

I bite at his earlobe, holding it between my teeth as a whimpered breath escapes my lips. That tiny sound seems to be enough to break his self-imposed rules, and in a breath, my panties are tugged to the side and his finger sinks into me, the entry sharp and sweet.

I clutch him, gripping his shoulders and tasting his neck with my tongue as he presses against my insides. His mouth moves to the curve of my shoulder and his teeth graze along my skin as his finger slides out then back in, picking up a slow rhythm that urges my hips to roll against it. I moan, careful to keep it quiet enough that it's only a performance for him.

My hand slides down the tight space between us, down the center of his black T-shirt and against his stomach muscles until I find the snap of his jeans and tug them open. Dustin's breath and movements halt, and he draws back slowly, gaining a few inches between us so his gaze can meet mine.

"Hannah," he says, shaking his head.

I mouth the word *please,* and a fire burns behind his

eyes as they flare wide, just for a beat. I move my hand lower, dragging his zipper down, then slip my hand inside until I'm met with the warm hardness of him underneath his boxers. His groan is unmistakable this time, and he's unable to keep his eyes open.

Running my hand along his length through the soft cotton, I feel him flex under my touch, and his hand moves again between my legs. With every pass of my touch along him, he reciprocates, and when I slide my hand under the band of his boxers, touching his bare, hot skin, his touch on me grows in a satisfying force. He presses into me with his thumb as his finger slips in and out, and I run my hand along his length, using his breath—or lack thereof—as my guide to let me know if I'm doing it right. My body surges with a rush of tingles and spasms as his finger slips out a final time and he rubs small circles along my swollen center. And just when I feel I may not be able to take the intensity much longer, my breath halts and every nerve ending that makes me fires at once. I bite at Dustin's shoulder, muffling my heavy breathing and desire to moan as his cock flexes in my palm, followed by a pulse and the warm, wet proof of his orgasm.

Several seconds pass as we hold each other, our hands still touching our most private parts, our bodies damp with sweat.

"Holy fuck," Dustin finally says, and his blunt, adorable compliment draws a slightly embarrassed laugh from me.

I recoil my fingers from him and close my hand into a fist, both proud that I was able to make him feel as amazing as he did me and embarrassed that this boy I've known my entire life has now *done things* with me—*to me! We did things to each other.*

"I should probably get off your lap and maybe get inside

before my dad murders you," I say, burying my hot cheeks in his chest.

Dustin wraps an arm around my head and kisses the top of it.

"I would very much like to remain alive, so we can continue doing things like this," he says, and I giggle and squeeze my eyes shut harder. I can't believe Dustin Bridges has now seen and touched so much of me.

I bite my lip as I slide from his hold, my face burning again when I see the tip of his dick poking out of the top of his boxers, his jeans still unzipped and open. He must notice my blush because he links his fingers with mine before I can completely slip away and he tugs me close for one more kiss.

"Hey, don't be embarrassed," he says, sweeping a few stray hairs from my face before dropping a soft kiss on my nose and then my mouth. He leaves his hand under my chin, forcing me to look him in the eyes.

"When you feel like we do about each other, physical expression isn't something dirty or to be ashamed of. I want to admire every beautiful curve of your body, inside and out, Hannah Judge." He ends his words, lips parted, and I hold my breath waiting for more—waiting for him to say the L word. He practically did, and I know it's not a term he's familiar with. After a few seconds pass, I accept that *feelings* is as close as I'm going to get from him for now, and it's enough.

Body buzzing, I step into him one last time, pressing my lips to his, tasting his tongue, and memorizing his scent.

"I'll see you tomorrow, Dustin Bridges," I say, before stepping away from his door and wishing him good night.

22

I'm drunk on Hannah. All of my blood has been drained and replaced with her essence. She owns me completely, and the more time we spend together—just us —the more I realize she always has.

I trust her. I give her my entire heart, completely. I never thought I would find anyone who wanted it as wholly and completely as she does.

Hannah.

Just Hannah.

I can't stop smiling, and I don't even feel the itch to speed down the dark, empty highway as I head home. I'll sleep in my car tonight, happily, and I'll find a way to make things right with her parents, to show them I'm worth their daughter's love and attention. I'll be her advocate, her pillar—her motherfucking hero.

By the time I pull off the main highway and onto the hidden side road that leads to my trailer, my body is teeming with energy and my heart beats with a will to fight for this. As much as I love the thrill of racing, that's how it is with Hannah. I love her more.

I love her.

I love her, I love her, I love her.

"I love you," I practice saying out loud, laughing at the ridiculous way I must look and sound. God, if anyone were able to see or hear me now, they'd see a young man so absolutely whipped and owned.

I'm dizzy with her memory, the smell of her—of us and what we did—still clinging to my body. It drives me wild, fills my head with dirty thoughts and my own mental slideshow of how she looked shirtless and lying on top of Tommy's car, how her legs parted in my lap, how her voice broke with pleasure in my ear.

The fantasy takes over so much of my mind that I don't register what I'm looking at for the first several minutes I sit, engine off, in the gravel driveway of my parents' trailer. The front door is askew, the top hinges ripped away from the frame, a direct line of sight to the inside of my family's home staring me in the face.

I blink.

My pulse picks up, the drumming in my chest so hard its reverb takes over my muscle control. I snap out of my daze enough to check my mirrors and sink down in my seat, aware that anyone could be outside watching, waiting for me—for Colt. This is extreme damage, even for him. He's not strong enough to cause destruction like this on his own, even in a fit of rage. The porch light is smashed, which makes the stream of light slipping through the open gaps in the doorway that much brighter. It's a yellow-tone, probably my mom's lamp.

My mom.

My eyes scan to the right, to Colt's truck, his windshield blown out, an ax left on the hood, the point dug in to the center where someone stopped digging a ragged valley through the metal.

"Shit," I mutter, crouching lower in my car, so low I can barely see above the dashboard. I'm legitimately scared. Beads of sweat tickle my forehead and my mouth continuously waters with the need to vomit. I reach to the passenger side, flipping open the box and praying to find a knife inside. There was one there for a while, a weapon I stole from dear old Dad. I never gave it back to him, but I was fairly sure he took it back himself. I never had plans to use it. It mostly gave me comfort when I slept in the car at night. And I figured it was better in my hands than Colt's. I stare at the insurance papers and registration in my glove box, no knife in sight, and my stomach rolls with an ominous sense of dread.

There's nothing I need here. Hannah's parents would understand, and I'd offer to sleep in my car, or in their garage. Or maybe Bailey's parents would let me stay there. I only need a safe place to park and sleep for the night. In the morning I can sort out what went on here, check on my mom, contact the police.

The police.

How does something like this happen without someone hearing? The answer is simple—it doesn't. Which means . . .

I flip in my seat and peer out my back window in time to catch the glow of red and yellow streaming toward me. I'm going to throw up for real.

I kick open my door and puke the second my head clears the floormats. The Judges' family dinner splatters on the gravel and I cough, stemming the nonstop contraction of my gag reflex.

Stumbling my way out of my car, I spit on the ground a few times to rid myself of the taste. I get on my knees and hold my hands above my head as the beams of headlights illuminate my face, my body, blinding me before my face is smashed to the ground. I've been around Colt enough times to know the best way to survive these situations, and I do as I was taught. I remain silent, minus the obedient "yes, sirs" I repeat every time someone gives me an order.

I crawl to a stand when they command.

I pull my hands together behind my back when they insist on cuffing me.

When a heavy palm pushes down on my head, I duck as I'm shoved into the back seat of a squad car.

I'm alone, locked behind bulletproof glass and metal, cuffed between two doors that only open from the outside, and though it's hot as fuck in this thing, my breathing normalizes for the first time since I drove up to my parents' home. Somehow, I just know: I'm safer in here, locked away from him.

Minutes pass before it happens, but the moment they drag Colt from the trailer, his face bloodied and body bruised, his eyes find me. His mouth is crimson red, but he smiles through it, his teeth glowing beneath his snarl, like a rabid dog ready to tear into meat. He lurches at me, and though he's under the tight grip of two very large sheriff's deputies, I flinch. Even behind my protective shield and under the guard of what I count to be a dozen armed officers. He's still able to terrorize me, and I hate him so much for it.

My thoughts go to my mom next, and despite my many vows to disown her, my heart still tears in two at the unknown and the many scenarios playing out in my mind.

Two officers climb into my squad car, and I try to make sense of everything they're saying.

"We're securing the scene. Bring in ATF," the one in the driver's seat says.

"What's happening?" I call out, scooting myself forward as close as I can get to the glass. The officer on the passenger side pounds her fist against the glass, never looking back at me.

The canine handler opens my car door wide and the dog circles one side while another officer with a bright flashlight pulls apart the interior of my passenger door.

"Hey! No! I don't live here. Or I do, but I just pulled up—"

Her fist crashes against the glass again, and this time when I turn she glares at me.

"Shut the fuck up," she says.

The familiar heat brews in my chest. Of everyone here tonight, I'm only afraid of one person—Colt. And he's locked away in a car like mine on the other side of the street.

"I'm just their fucking kid! I've got nothing to do with this!" I shout.

She doesn't blink, simply continues to stare at me, sizing me up, sorting out my words to see which are lies and which are truths.

The car moves and my panic returns. I haven't seen my mom yet. I twist, jerking my head to see the scene we're leaving.

"Is my mom okay? Is she inside? Where's my mom? Mom! Mom!" Sometime in the middle of my terror-strewn pleas, I realize my face is soaked with my own tears.

As the miles tread on, I give up asking for answers. My crying stops too. And in the depth of my conscience, I come to terms with the fact that the two thousand dollars I took from that stack of bills in my closet is at the root of everything that just happened. If my mom is dead, it's not because she overdosed. It's because I traded her in for new tires. How the fuck am I supposed to live with that?

I t feels as though I've been lying on this concrete bench for days. Holding cells are nothing like in the movies. The room I've been in for hours is small, but not dirty. It's void of feeling, almost sterile, and I'm alone. There's an intercom on the wall that's always on, like a baby monitor for detainees. I said "hello" into it when they first left me in here, and when a man's voice boomed back a "yeah, what?" I jumped. Maybe I'm in a room like this because I'm a minor, or maybe they've already rooted out the truth and realize I wasn't lying when I said I had no part in what went down at my house. That I'm just a kid.

I'm just a kid.

Whatever the reason, I'm glad I'm nowhere near Colt. I never want to see him again.

I would like to see my mother, though. I need to know she's all right, whether she's alive.

The intercom buzzes and I wait for the deep voice to tell me what's next, but instead I hear steps outside my door. I push back against the far wall and draw my legs in as the door jerks open.

"Someone's here for you. Come on, Dustin," the officer says. This is a new guy, older, hair graying on the sides. My eyes dart around him suspiciously.

"Let's go," he barks.

More like it.

I get to my feet and rub the cuts on my wrists from where the zip-tie cuffs dug into my skin. I follow the man who came to get me down a long hallway. I don't remember seeing any of this on my way in. But I was manic and scared, so the last several hours is lodged in my memory much like panels in a comic book.

We reach the end of the hall and he buzzes his badge against a pad by a thick metal door. When it opens, he nudges me inside. And when my eyes focus on Hannah's dad's, I blurt out more tears and fall into this man who is the closest thing I have to a father figure, relieved when his arms embrace me right back.

23

"Waiting at the end of the driveway is not going to get them home any sooner," Tommy says.

I don't bother to answer. My brother is as anxious as I am. He's pacing the same driveway I'm sitting in.

I was the first in our house to know. Bailey wakes up earlier than any teenager should. She likes to run in the mornings, before the Arizona heat sets in. She had no reason to turn the television on, but it was cloudy and she wanted to see if the morning show was on yet, maybe catch the weather. Chance of rain is a big deal around here. That's when she saw the clip of the crime tape and the reporter camped outside the familiar trailer park. She called me on repeat until I woke up and answered.

My stomach sank and my heart went into panic rhythm as I raced down the hall to my parents' room and shook my dad awake. He spent the morning getting the details of what happened, a partial puzzle with too many holes. It all came together when he got a call from an old friend. And that's what I keep coming back to as my mind spins with repeating thoughts: What if all of life's dominoes didn't line up just right? I can't help but wonder if Dustin would have been lost to us for good.

My dad went to law school with someone in the county prosecutor's office, a guy who'd been to a race or two back in the day and followed my dad's posts about his son and *like-a-son* on Facebook. So when Dustin's name came through the system, he looped my dad in. Suddenly, me and Dustin holding hands at the kitchen table didn't seem so important. Dustin is family, and we take care of our own.

"I think I see Dad's truck," Tommy says, hopping off the retaining wall by the garage that he climbed up on for a better view.

I get to my feet and move to the middle of the street along with my brother. It's a late afternoon sun baking us and the clouds have cleared, so the pavement sends up waves of heat. Despite that, neither of us moves. I stare through the glass on the passenger side until the reflection of the sky clears enough that I can zero in on Dustin's eyes. I cup my mouth, covering my silent gasp the moment I do.

He's a shell of himself. There's a blankness to his eyes that fills my chest with suffocating fear. This has changed him, more than everything he's been through in his life. He'll always be different now. I'll still love him, no matter what, no matter who he's become.

My dad parks closer to the house and I run to the passenger door before Dustin opens it. He's slow to move, almost as if every action he takes hurts. His head rolls to the side and our eyes meet, mine full of tears, his still empty—void of *anything.* He pushes his door open and steps outside, his limbs seeming too heavy to hold up, his legs to numb to move.

"I'm so sorry," I say, words way too small for all he's been through. I move into him, sliding my hands under his arms and around his back before flattening my cheek against his chest. He holds me back, but it's flimsy—fragile.

"Let's get inside," my dad says, his tone serious. Not stern, and definitely not unkind. But there's a hint of immediacy that makes the hairs on my arm prick up a little.

My brother rushes to the door ahead of us, opening it wide, signaling how welcome Dustin is. I think he's over-compensating for the way my parents have behaved and maybe a little how he did at first as well. It doesn't matter, though. None of that matters. My parents woke up and remembered how much they loved Dustin when he needed them most, and I'll cherish that forever.

I thread my fingers through Dustin's and hold his bicep with my other hand as I guide him inside to the table where my mom has a sandwich waiting and his favorite cherry soda. I take the seat next to him and slide myself close.

"I'm really okay," he croaks, and what I think might be a slight attempt at laughter follows. "I'm not the one who got the life nearly kicked out of him."

His eyes flicker to my dad and I follow his gaze in search of some clue to what really happened. All I know is what we pieced together from the news and the things my dad shared when he took off to get Dustin. Someone Colt was in *business* with came to collect. Dustin's mom wasn't home. She never came home from her shift at the gas station store. She basically vanished. Dustin is worried her disappearance means the worst. I can't help but have this feeling she's safe, that she maybe knew what was coming for Colt and purposely removed herself from all radars.

"I'm so glad you didn't go home earlier than you did. If you showed up when whoever did that to Colt was there . . ." I choke up and Dustin squeezes my hand tightly.

"I'm okay. I promise," he says. Again, his eyes flit to my dad. It fills my body with an uneasy poison that is possible to ignore.

"Did they tell you anything about Colt? Are they charging him?" Tommy pipes up, his eyes darting between Dustin and my father for answers. My dad eases his weight back on the edge of the counter as he folds his arms over his chest, his brow pulled in tight, as it's been since he got the call about Dustin being held at County.

"I'm not sure what the charges are, but there are several. My buddy couldn't tell me everything, and I probably got more out of him than I was supposed to."

My dad's answers seem purposely vague and I can't help but feel he's protecting my delicate ears, and perhaps more so my heart, by not telling me everything.

"What about the guys who beat up Colt?" I ask, my instincts telling me this was the source of my dad's forehead lines.

My father draws in a long breath, one brow raising as he shakes his head.

"They don't know much. They're interviewing witnesses, but mostly people only heard the noise when everything went down. I can't imagine anyone stepped outside to get a better look, but maybe someone saw something," my dad says.

I shift my gaze to my brother's face, reading his eyes for answers I don't seem to be getting from our dad, but he looks as lost as I feel.

"You're staying here, right? Dad? He's staying with us

for now." Tommy's insistence eases my ache. I'm glad he's the one who asked.

"Of course he is," my mom says, slipping into the chair directly across from Dustin. She slides her palms forward on the table and Dustin lifts his head from his plate that he hasn't touched to give her a forced, tight smile.

"Thank you," he utters. His throat labors on a swallow.

A thick silence settles in, a combination of me and my brother not knowing what to ask, Dustin not wanting to talk, and my parents satisfied to not talk at all. The longer it lasts, though, the more questions brew in my gut. I listen to that faint voice in the back of my head that says it's not the time to dig deeper. I need to trust this silence, that it's purposeful, and Dustin will share his pain with me when he's ready.

He picks at his sandwich, and my parents delve into some logistical conversation about making a few calls and getting some paperwork done. My dad called in a lot of favors to keep Dustin out of the system. It helps that he's almost eighteen. Two weeks shy exactly. And my parents are in possession of more of Dustin's personal papers than his own parents are. We've held on to his birth certificate since my dad entered him in his first solo kart race when he was seven.

After another hour, my brother gives up on the idea of learning more tonight, and dismisses himself to his room. I can tell by Tommy's silence that he's worried, and maybe later tonight he'll come down and talk to Dustin for real. We both will.

Colt has been a threat to Dustin's wellbeing since the moment our friend—my love—was born. That's the vision that tortures me now, too. That threat carries the potential of taking his life. In the back of my mind I always worried that one day Colt would punch Dustin a little too hard, would be a little too drunk or high to know what he was doing and think his son was his enemy. Would take his life.

My body shakes at that thought and my voice breaks without my permission. The slip in my veneer is enough to trigger Dustin out of his trance, and he abruptly pushes away from the table.

"I need some air. I'm sorry, but . . . I need a minute," he says, ducking his head as he bolts to our front door.

My eyes flash to my dad in search of answers, but my father is watching him go. I stand to follow him.

"Let him go, Hannah. He's been through a lot today, last night," my dad says, his eyes on the now closed door Dustin just tugged shut behind him.

I stand by the table, torn between believing my father and wanting to be there for the boy I love when he's hurting. Dustin's pain wins out and I shake my head.

"I'm sorry, but I can't. I can't just let him go," I say, jogging to the door and rushing out to the driveway where I find Dustin standing at the end by the road, his palms pressed against his crying eyes.

"Dustin!" I cry out. He spins and drops his arms helplessly, his tortured, red eyes finding solace in mine. His lips part as they stretch wide with the need to cry. He's caught in this limbo where he's too tough to show his emotion, but the pressure building inside his all-to-human body is dying to explode with everything he feels.

"I can't, Hannah. I just . . . I don't know what to do," he says, and I throw my arms around him. This time, he does it back.

"You've got time. It's okay, Dusty. It's okay," I say as his weight crushes me, his chin falling into the crook of my neck as his spine curves and his frame shrinks to fit with mine.

I hold him tight, letting him quake against me, his body warm under the weight of his black zip-up hoodie and his black jeans. The sun drops below the horizon, and we stay where we are, eventually sitting on the concrete driveway. The air cools, a mix of warm currents in the slight breeze brewing from the desert, but I don't suggest we change a thing. If this is where Dustin wants to be, it's where we will stay until he's ready to go inside. His head hasn't left my shoulder in an hour, and the only clue I have that he hasn't fallen asleep is the rare utterance of "I'm sorry, Hannah" against my ear.

"You have nothing to be sorry for," I keep repeating. I hate what Colt has done to him, what his mother has done. If she left, knowing what was coming, and didn't bother to take her son with her, she is more shameful than I thought her to be. Who could do that to their child? To anyone they claim to love, even if they choose their addiction over that person. There has to be a thread of humanity in her soul that remembers she is someone's mother, that she has a son—a son who is becoming such an amazing man.

Night comes, and we stay as we are. My dad occasionally comes out to check on us, each time encouraging us to come inside. He doesn't press, though. He gives Dustin the time he needs, and he doesn't insist I leave him alone any more. Maybe he realizes it's useless. Or maybe he sees how I'm holding our boy together. I'm thankful for this compassion.

Little by little, Dustin comes back to me. His hands knead mine, his fingers drawing tiny circles on my palms, his arms coming alive enough to hold me tight. His legs curl around my body as we sit, he scoops me into his cocoon, and finally—*finally*—his lips find the place where wisps of baby fine hair line my temple. I'm soothed by the strokes of his hand in my hair, and his heart isn't racing in his chest.

Still, though his body has calmed, he insists he's sorry.

"I'm just so fucking sorry, Hannah," he finally expands, as if somehow this gives it meaning.

I pull back enough to hold his head between my palms. Our eyes dance, his focus less manic than before but still not the restful expression I'm used to from him.

"I love you, Dustin Bridges. You did nothing wrong. And I love you for you. I love you," I say. I'll repeat these words until he believes them, until he hears them in every part of his body. I'll say them to anyone who asks, to anyone who dares to question where my loyalty lies. I'll pronounce my love for this boy in a court of law, in the face of death, at the line of fire. I'll love him for always because I know, whether he can say it yet or not, he loves me back. He loves me, and I won't let go.

24

SIX HOURS EARLIER . . .

"My mom. Where's my mom? Is she okay?"

I followed Mr. Judge to another small room, this one more like an office, after I soaked his shirt with tears and snot. I didn't realize how hard I'd been holding on to everything until I saw him standing on the other side of that door. He let me cry it out, and I cried so fucking hard. I feel so lost in my head right now, and I have so many fears and questions colliding in my brain, leaving scars and cuts and so much damage. But I can't move on until I know whether or not my mom is all right.

"I don't know where she is, Dustin, but . . . please, sit down." He flattens his palm on the center of a desk in the middle of this room. There's a line of leather cubes against a wall across from the desk, so I decide to sit there instead of the chair across from him. I don't know why. I feel trapped at that desk, I guess, and I've been trapped for way too many hours now.

"Okay, I'm sitting. You don't know where she is, but—" My voice comes out threatening, shaking with frustration, and I regret the way it sounds. I hold up my palm and take a deep breath. "I'm sorry. I'm just . . . I'm sorry."

"It's okay. Take your time and just breathe," he says.

He pulls his hands together on the desk, folding his fingers together, and I stare at the zigzag line formed by his linked knuckles.

I do as he says and fill my chest, holding it that way until a satisfying wave passes through my body. That felt good. I blow it out and do it again.

"Nobody seems to know where your mom is, but she went to work today. The manager at the gas station said she clocked out on time and he saw her get in one of those ride-share cars about fifteen minutes later. Authorities are tracking down that driver, and I'm sure they'll find her," Mr. Judge says.

I lean forward, resting my elbows on my knees, and nod before letting my head fall into my hands. None of that makes sense. My mom doesn't have friends. We don't have relatives other than my mom's brother who lives in Oklahoma. He basically disowned us because he got sick of my mom asking for money. She has no place to go, other than somewhere new to get drunk or high. Maybe she took on another job? I laugh off that thought almost the second it passes through my mind.

"I'm more worried about Colt, Dustin. We need to talk about things, but I need you to be present with me for this conversation. I want you to process things first, to relax," Mr. Judge says, and I laugh out loud in a knee-jerk response.

"Sorry," I say, staring into his disappointed, sloped eyes and stern-lined mouth. "It's kinda hard to relax given, well, all of this," I add, waving my hands around the room and toward the door that leads to whatever the hell this place is where I'm being kept.

Mr. Judge nods slowly and looks down at the sterile desk.

"Give me a minute," he says, knocking on the wood before standing. He rounds the desk and before exiting the door, holds up a finger as assurance he'll be back. The clicking mechanism grinds when it shuts and I can tell I wouldn't be able to just open the door like he did.

I spend my few minutes alone taking in the details of the room. I've been in a place like this before. The two-way mirror behind me confirms it. This is the kind of place where CPS meets with delinquents and kids they want to throw into foster homes. I'm not a kid anymore. I don't need this shit.

I stand so I'm ready to protest when Mr. Judge comes back, and when the door beeps with a clearance badge, I ready myself to tell him to leave me in that vacant room I was in before for the next two weeks. I'll check myself out when I'm an "adult," as if I haven't been one my whole life.

"Let's get out of here," he says before I can get my words out.

My brow draws in tight, and it takes a few seconds to process what he's suggesting. Finally, he jerks his head, urging me to follow, and my feet move.

We stop at a security desk where a woman who clearly doesn't know how to smile hands me a plastic bag with my keys, wallet, phone, and two sticks of gum that they confiscated from my jeans pocket when they brought me in. I sign for my belongings and Mr. Judge signs next to my name under the line labeled GUARDIAN. The woman buzzes us through a thick glass door, and it slams shut behind us. I glance back and note the layers and layers of security between where I was and where I am now. I don't belong here.

I follow Mr. Judge down some steps and into a parking lot filled with squad cars and police SUVs. His truck is parked between one of those armored trucks used by SWAT teams and what looks like an unmarked vehicle, a Dodge that I know is built to go a lot faster than it appears.

"You hungry?" he asks me across the hood of his truck.

I nod as my stomach grumbles. I'm actually kind of sick, but I think having actual food under my nose could change things.

We climb in the truck and take a silent trip several miles toward home, stopping at the Waffle House off the main highway. We take a booth in the back corner and Mr. Judge orders himself an omelet and me a big stack of pancakes. The waitress fills our water cups and we slide the coffee mugs her way, indicating we'd like some. Our eyes meet and we both huff out breathy laughter.

"You boys tired, huh?" the waitress says, pulling her bifocals down to the tip of her nose as she pours coffee in my cup first, then Mr. Judge's.

"Been a long night . . . and day," Hannah's dad adds, as though realizing night passed a long time ago.

She leaves with a cursory smile, leaving the pot behind so we can take care of our own refills. I'm glad we stopped here, far enough from town to not be inside the gossip ring. This place is a truck stop, everyone transitory, and Colt Bridges' messed-up kid isn't on anyone's radar.

We take careful sips of our coffee, setting the mugs back down on the table in sync, which makes me smile. Mr. Judge leans forward, rubbing his hands together on top of the table, his eyes down, brow pinched, and jaw flexing as if he's holding back words I fear might be hard to hear.

I mimic his posture at first, fisting my hands together and reminding myself to breathe through my nose. It's a trick I've learned in racing, something that forces my heart rate in check. My leg bobs with nerves, though, the longer it takes Hannah and Tommy's dad to break his silence. Eventually, I interrupt it for both of us, slapping my palms on the table and sliding them back as I fall into the seat back of the booth.

"Let me have it. Foster care, right? But only two weeks, so—"

"Dustin, Colt is in serious trouble," he interrupts.

I shut my mouth, realizing my worries are bigger than getting stuck in a system. His eyes flit up to meet mine, and he does that thing where he doesn't blink. He used to deploy this technique when Tommy and I were in trouble for breaking something.

"I mean, I gathered." I shrug. Flashes of my dad's face race behind my eyes and I wince outwardly at the memory of his bloodied face, his snarled smile.

"I have to know, and I'm serious about this, more serious than I have ever been my entire life, about anything," he begins.

I swallow down the instant dryness in my throat and lean forward a little, enough to sit upright, good posture for a good person. That's my thought process, despite the one thing I keep coming back to is the two thousand dollars I stole from Colt's stash. I know in my gut that's at the heart of all of this. The remaining eight hundred bucks burns a hole in my pocket. Money I changed out when I bought the first set of tires, self-laundering money I knew was bad.

"Okay," I croak. I blink a few times, my focus on the small pocket on his polo shirt, the imperfect crease in it that says he grabbed it from the dirty clothes and raced to county holding to get me. I move my gaze up until I reach his eyes, and staring into them is as hard as I knew it would be. I won't lie to this man.

"What do you know about your dad's business?" he asks.

"Can we . . . can we not call him my dad?" I respond, squirming a little in my seat. I break our stare briefly but offer a tight smile when I return to his eyes.

"Okay." He nods, his voice soft and soothing. Understanding.

"Thanks," I say.

In through the nose, hold, out through the nose.

"I found his money a couple of days ago. I mean, he's always had cash around, but this was serious money. Hundred thousand, maybe more," I admit.

Mr. Judge remains calm, probably because he knows the real number for the cash. Which means he knows what was with it.

"And there were drugs, like a brick of something. I figured heroine," I say with a shrug, my face flashing hot. I hate that this is my life, that I'm the son of a man who has shit like this stashed in his kid's closet.

Hannah's dad stutters in a sharp breath and his eyes flutter as he leans back in the booth. He looks out the window and grabs the back of his neck with one hand. Maybe he didn't know so much.

"They're gonna lock him up, though, right?" I ask, assuming. I've never thought it would be anything different. Hell, some nights I prayed for this.

Mr. Judge grimaces as he brings his gaze back to me.

His mouth holds a tight line as the waitress moves in with our hot plates. As delicious as my hotcakes smell, my stomach turns from the news I sense coming the minute our server leaves our table. She drops off an extra set of silverware and some syrup, then heads to the other end of the diner to attend to a couple who just walked in to sit at the counter.

"Dustin, they're gonna offer your dad a deal," he says.

I pull my plate close and focus on my pancakes. I pick up the fork knowing I won't eat a damn thing on this plate. I just need something to do. I swirl butter around the top as I say "oh." After several seconds of silence, though, I drop the charade, and the fork, and push my plate away.

"So, he'll be out soon?" I feel the invisible stranglehold of terror grip my throat.

"I wouldn't say days. But weeks? Yeah. And depending on how fast they want to move, maybe days."

"But then he'll serve time, right? He doesn't get a free pass without *something*, does he?" A mental slideshow of all the awful things Colt has done—to me, to my mom, to people—plays through my mind.

"Oh, he'll serve time," Mr. Judge says.

I sigh with relief, but it's temporary.

"Not a lot, though. Maybe eighteen months, maybe six. I don't know the deal. He's small fish compared to the guys they're after."

"So after all this, he'll still get out?" I don't want the truth to sink in. I understand it, I just wish I didn't.

"He will, Dustin. He'll come home."

Home.

I nod and drop my gaze to the table between our two pointless plates.

"That's why I need to know, Dustin. How involved are you? How much do you know about your dad's business?"

I shake my head, processing for a few seconds before I speak.

"Nothing beyond what I told you. I swear," I say, denying my suspicions even though I'm certain they're right.

"You swear on your life?" he pushes.

My eyes move up to find his waiting and I nod.

"I swear, sir," I say, sliding my plate to the side and moving the coffee back in front of me. I pull the mug to my lips and take a bigger drink this time, needing the jolt of a strong, black brew. The taste is bitter and perfect, so I go in for more.

"Your dad . . . Colt, I mean," he corrects. "He got in with the cartel. And from what my friend could tell me, Dustin, he's been working with them for months, maybe almost a year. Something went wrong with this exchange, though, and I'm guessing it went *really* wrong. Colt probably thought he could out-maneuver the guys he was in contact with or something, but those guys always have bigger guys behind them, as do those guys, and so on. Until it's *the* guy. And that guy? He doesn't give a shit about anyone."

I rub my hand over my tired, numb face as Mr. Judge confirms what deep down, I always knew was true.

"I took some of the money," I blurt out. I swore I wouldn't lie to this man, and I won't.

"Shit, Dustin!" he whisper shouts. He covers his mouth and leans back, looking out the window at the busy rush of traffic.

"I know. It was stupid. But he owed me, and I needed to take care of some things." I fumble for an explanation that makes my actions okay.

Hannah's dad leans forward and waves his hand.

"It doesn't matter. Forget that. It doesn't matter," he repeats.

"O-o-kay," I stammer out.

I can't fathom how it doesn't matter, but I'll follow his logic for now.

"The DEA is working with the FBI, and they're going to use Colt to get to his guy. You understand what I'm saying?" he asks.

I nod, though I don't know what that means bigger picture-wise.

"Dustin, I need you to understand the gravity of this. Your dad—Colt Bridges—is going to be a dangled carrot to lure some really fucking heinous men."

I flinch at his brashness. And then, my pulse ratchets up. I'm starting to understand everything. Why we're here —*why he's here.*

"I feel sick," I say, laying my head on my arms and pushing my ass back in the booth so I can stare at my lap. "Oh, God, I'm gonna be sick.

"Go if you have to," he says. "Bathroom's right there."

In through the nose, hold, exhale.

"No, I'll be okay." I won't. I never will be again.

A weight hits the table, the thud enough to push my forehead up from my arms. I glance up through my lashes to find a massive book, a notebook with it, along with a stuffed business-sized envelope.

"Is there a test?" I lift a brow. My stomach rolls.

"It's twenty thousand dollars, Dustin. Take it, and the book so it doesn't look like I'm just handing you cash at a truck stop." His voice is low, and for the first time since we got here, it quivers with nerves.

I blink my focus to the bundle as he pushes it toward

me and I do as he says. I pull it all into my lap and turn the spine of the book to read it—*Moby Dick.*

"What do I do with this?" I ask, hugging the envelope, tucking it against my stomach and behind the book and notepad.

"Amanda and I are going to be your guardians. A few papers need to be filed, but for two weeks, until you're eighteen, you'll be ours." He pauses with his mouth open and his eyes drop. This is where the *but* comes in.

"I need to go," I say in a low whisper, the words coming out slowly.

Mr. Judge nods, his movement stilted and slight. His eyes flit away from mine, the guilt of looking me square too much to take now that the cards are on the table. He's paying me to leave; to leave *Hannah.* I can't blame him.

I pull the envelope out and drop it on the table.

"I don't need your fucking money," I bite out.

He pushes it back to me and holds it at the edge of the table, about to fall into my lap.

"Don't be stupid. Dustin, this isn't a bribe, it's what we can do to help. You can get started with this, find a place, get a job somewhere far away from Colt and his taste for revenge. You can break free of his shadow. Get a good truck body, build it out. Join the circuit and win your way to greatness. I believe in you, Dustin."

I can't help the laugh that spills out of my mouth when he says that last part.

"I do, Dustin. Truly."

"Fuck this," I say, sliding from the booth. He steps out before I can stand, though, grabbing my arm, wrapping his fingers around my wrist. The envelope of cash falls to the booth behind me and we both glance at it before staring each other in the eyes.

I'm so goddamn hurt right now. And I'm angry. But I can't take that out on him. I just can't, though my instincts want me to be violent, to throw this fucking whale book in his face. To hotwire his truck and peel out of here. What good would that do, though? I'd be just like Colt. I'd really be buried alive then, more than I am right now.

"You want me to leave Hannah," I finally say.

His eyes flash with the truth and he nods, just once.

"That's the deal, Dustin. I can get you out of here, out of this." He leans his head to the side as if that signals the trap I'm in with Colt and the law. "But you've gotta leave my baby girl alone. You'll destroy her, Dustin. The target you've got on you is so hot, so big. It's not only you at risk anymore, and I can't . . . I can't . . ."

He runs the side of his palm under his tearing eyes as he sniffs. I relax my muscles and he loosens his grip, letting me slide back into the booth. I pull the envelope back into my hands, and I swear it burns my skin to touch. It feels dirty.

"What about the DEA or whatever? Aren't they going to want to know where I am?" I can't believe I'm considering this.

Mr. Judge leans to one side and pulls a small folded paper from his pocket, opening it and holding it out for me to take. There's a phone number jotted in pencil. I don't recognize the area code.

"Your Uncle Jeff, he's in Oklahoma. I'll take care of the rest, represent you and make sure the right people know you aren't running, that you're with kin. You're not the one in trouble here, Dustin."

"It sure feels like I'm in trouble," I respond.

I refold the paper and slip it into the pocket of my jeans. I've never met my uncle, or at least not when I was old enough to form a memory of it. Why would some man who worked really hard to put miles between him and his sister want anything to do with me?

"Two weeks. When I'm eighteen?" I reiterate. I meet his eyes briefly and he nods.

The silent agreement sits heavy at the table between us, and long minutes pass.

"You can't tell Hannah," he finally says, bringing the knife down completely and driving it through my heart. My eyes close on automatic.

"I understand," I say. And as angry as I am, at her father, mine—the world—he's right. Hannah will follow me. And I love her too much to let her.

PRESENT...

Hannah wouldn't leave my side all night. It's half the reason I stayed outside in their driveway. I figured out there, her dad wouldn't make her feel guilty for being with me. He owes me this time with her. I think he knows as much.

I carried her inside after she fell asleep curled in my lap, head against my chest. I lay her on this couch where I've sat for the last hour with her hair trailing over my thigh like satin ribbons. This is it. This is the last time I will ever get to see her angelic face, her soft pink lips, tiny and parted as she breathes. She's so at peace like this, and it's the way I want to remember her.

I can't stay in this house for two weeks knowing everything I know. I'll never survive it. I won't be able to hold the secret. I'll break because I'm weak and I don't want to leave her. I don't want to leave this fucking town. I hate it here, yet it's my entire heart. The reasons for my hate are all wrapped up with the reasons I need to go.

God damn you, Colt Bridges. You gave me this life and have done nothing but threaten me for as long as I've walked this path.

My phone in my palm, I hover over Hannah's face and snap a quiet photo, locking her image away somewhere I can see it whenever I want. *Whenever I need her.*

I tossed around the idea of writing a letter, but really, how cruel would that be? She'd pick it apart, if her dad even let her have it. And Tommy. What about Tommy? He's going to hate me, and for real this time. But he'll be free of burden, free to go to college and live for his dreams, not mine. I can't hold that against him anymore. If anything, I understand better. I want so much for him. For all of them.

I slip away from the sofa, holding my breath when Hannah stirs. I wait until her breathing falls back into its peaceful rhythm and slink my way into the laundry room, to take my last shower for probably the next few days.

The hot water hardens my resolve and hides my tears. I only grant myself a few. This chapter of my life has to close, and it needs to be a definitive finish.

Their dad was planning to get my car back for me, and he hoped he'd have it by my birthday, but I've come to terms with that too. My days in the Supra are done, which means I'm going to have to take a bus to Oklahoma. I won't screw Mr. Judge over so much that I completely fall off the grid. I'll go where I promised, and I'll make sure Uncle Jeff communicates what he needs to. I can't put leaving off. It has to happen now if it's going to happen at all.

I rummage through the laundry room, taking the few things I recognize as mine that Mrs. Judge cleaned for me, along with a few shirts of Tommy's that I've always kind of liked. I smirk as I bundle them all in a hoodie, wondering how long it will take him to realize they're missing. Hannah's yellow race shirt catches my eye and I grab that too, holding it to my face and breathing in the scent of lavender fabric softener and her. She bought this shirt in Tucson, the last time I raced there. I aged out the next day, and she got shirts for all of us to celebrate my birthday. Tommy's became an oil rag when he outgrew it, and mine never fit but I felt too guilty to tell her.

I tuck her shirt in my back pocket, letting it hang, then run my gaze along the shelves in their storage closet in search of one of Mrs. Judge's cloth shopping bags. I find one that's plain and blue, something that won't stick out or draw attention, and dump my things—along with the items I'm stealing—inside. I grab Mr. Judge's key from the counter and duck outside through the back door, rounding the house to the driveway so I can grab the cash and the stupid whale book from his glove box. I pause, looking at the notepad, and decide to bring it in case I get the urge to write Hannah something I'll probably never send. I'm going to have a lot of hours on a bus. I am going to need to somehow work out the trauma from this.

I laugh silently to myself. My high school counselor would be proud. She was always trying to get me to journal.

I put the key back where it belongs and cinch up my bundle after splitting the cash between my two pockets, my wallet, and the bag. If someone is going to mug me, I've at least got to make it hard.

I know this isn't how Thomas Judge planned this. I don't pretend he thought any of it would be okay. He knew it would be hard when he hatched this plan, but he also knew it would be necessary.

With a final stop at the end of the sofa, I kneel down and allow myself five more minutes of time with her. I won't kiss her good-bye. I can't afford to wake her up. I'm pushing things by stalling. When I feel the sting of tears, I get to my feet and nod, silently bolstering myself for all that comes next.

I head straight for the back door, deciding that's the quietest route. Denying myself a glance over my shoulder, I stifle the sound of the door shutting by pulling it slowly and bracing it with my other hand. I slink against the walls of the house, avoiding the motion-sensing lights, and when my feet find the pavement of the road, I break into a slow jog, heading for the highway where I'll hitch a ride into Phoenix.

Good-bye heart. Good-bye home. Take care of the Straights, and God watch over this girl.

25

My eyes blink open. The bright room startles me. It's unfamiliar at first, all of it. I flail my arms around, tossing the knitted blanket to the floor as I realize where I am. I sit up in a flash when I do, my hands flattening on the cushions of the couch on either side of me. My hair is ratted and covering my eyes as I blow at it to clear my view.

"He's gone," Tommy says.

"What?" I grumble. I run my fingers through my hair, taming it into place. My brother is sitting on the arm of my dad's recliner, and the front door is wide open. I point at it and Tommy glances over his shoulder.

"Yeah, he's gone," he repeats. "I guess he took off in the middle of the night. Dad's pissed."

My body rushes with adrenaline, my mouth waters, and I sprint to the back bathroom, pausing with my arm folded over my mouth as my feet feel the damp evidence left behind on the tile floor. Dustin took a shower in here, and it could not have been that long ago. I hunch over the toilet and heave out bile.

Tommy appears in the doorway, leaning against the jamb. I flip the lid of the toilet down and flush, laying my arms over the seat and resting my cheek on my arm as I blink at him, wide-eyed and terrified.

"What do you mean he's gone?" It's a stupid question, and leave it to my fucking brother to call me on it.

"Uh, he's not here? Va-moose. Poof!" He snaps his fingers.

I stand and shove him out of my way, rushing to the driveway where my dad is closing the passenger side of his truck.

"What happened?" I blare out.

My father grumbles and presses his key fob, locking his truck as he marches past.

"Dad!" I shout, getting his attention. He spins on his heel, his open mouth snapping shut to stop himself from blurting out a knee-jerk answer that probably wasn't going to be kind. He shakes his head instead.

"I don't know, Hannah. I just . . ." His eyes move to the highway, and before he can stop me, I run inside, grab my keys and race back to my car. I'm peeling backward in my driveway when my brother slaps the hood of my car, causing me to punch the brakes and screech to a stop. He pulls the passenger door open and hops inside.

"I'm going with you," he announces, buckling up. "It's better if we're both looking."

I nod to him in panicky agreement. We tear down our street, ruling out everything we can think of. Tommy calls Dustin's number over and over, every call going right to voicemail. My stomach feels tight again, but I don't have time to throw up, so I swallow down the burn and stress bubbling up my esophagus.

"Why would he take off? Where would he go?" I keep asking these same questions, over and over, mile after mile, and my brother is kind enough not to answer and not to stop me from asking them.

We barrel into the gas station, cruise by Dustin's trailer, the entire park now roped off with police tape. We zoom through the center of town, to the Straights, which are empty and desolate in the bright light of day.

School. Restaurants. The grocery store, the small urgent care, Earl's garage—each place comes up empty. His car is still in the impound lot, both doors torn apart from whatever the police did to it. He has nothing—*nobody.*

My heart sinks with each passing minute, and as those minutes turn into hours, my grasp on hope falters. My parents call my phone, but I send every attempt to voice-mail. Finally, Tommy answers on his phone and stares at me through their one-sided conversation.

"Yeah."

"We did."

"Okay."

"Okay."

"She is."

He hangs up, tosses his phone in the cup holder, and reaches forward, gripping at my dashboard before letting out a monstrous growl. The sound of my brother breaking stops my heart, and I pull to the side of the roadway. The rush of cars heading north for the weekend whizzes by us, the wind from eighteen-wheelers shaking my small vehicle as they roar past.

"Dad wants us to come home," my brother finally says.

"No," I blurt out.

He nods.

"Okay."

We sit in silence, not even my radio on to fill the space. Every engine that rumbles by makes me think of him. Every car that's shaped like his brings his face to my mind. Every beat of my heart reminds me how he could make it rush. My lips burn from missing him. My hands curl along the steering wheel, wishing they were holding his hands instead of this plastic piece of shit circle.

"He's really gone," I finally admit after several long minutes of quiet.

My brother doesn't answer out loud, but I hear his thoughts.

He is, Hannah. He's family, and he fucking left.

"Let's go home," I say, not bothering to look at my brother again as I check my mirrors and signal. I pull onto the highway, and about halfway through our trip, Tommy flips my stereo on, turning it all the way up and losing himself to his own thoughts.

TWO WEEKS LATER...

"Why don't you come with us? It'll be fun," Tommy says, though he knows it won't. Being a third-wheel date with your brother and some girl you barely know for prom is pretty much the bottom of the barrel. Even Bailey has a date. And her dad is letting the guy pick her up and take her to dinner first.

Milestones are happening left and right, and I'm wearing the same sweatpants for a fourth day in a row, along with Dustin's old Checkered Flag T-shirt that he won at a race in Nevada.

My mom has quit begging me to get out of my funk. I caught her crying two nights ago, and though she played it off as allergies, I knew better. She misses Dustin, too. And she is probably torturing herself over the way she treated him in the weeks before he left.

"You're sure?" my brother asks one more time, leaning over the sofa and staring at me upside down. I reach up and pretend to grab his nose, the way our parents did when we were little kids.

"I'm positive. Now, go on and get out of here before Mom makes you let her take more pictures in front of something else," I joke.

My brother laughs, and we smile at each other with mouths that don't quite stretch the distance. Our emotions haven't reached our eyes in days, not since Dustin left. He took our lights with him when he left, and it's going to be a while before they burn again.

I notch up the volume on the TV as my brother dashes out the door with his date, and settle into the nest I built on the couch for my next TV show binge. My dad's been working on a new case, and while I suspect it has some-thing to do with Dustin, I don't let myself pry. If he's helping him, good. But if Dustin is talking to my dad and not to me? I also don't want to know. I'd rather go along with the terse answer my father gave me the first time I questioned the folder stuffed with pages he closed the second I entered the kitchen.

It's just a bunch of pain-in-the-ass paperwork. Story of my life.

That paperwork seems to be reaching its end. He just

headed out the door after Tommy left to drop one last filing in the mail.

"You sure you don't want company?" my mom asks, hovering over me the way Tommy did a minute ago. I force a smile on my face.

"No, Mom. I'm happy. I promise." I don't bother crossing my fingers anymore. She knows I'm bluffing, but calling me on it will only make me mad, and then we'll fight. We've all fought way too much lately. We're all tired from it. *I'm* tired.

"All right," she says, grabbing her tablet from the side table to binge read while I opt for the more passive form of entertainment downstairs.

I start the first episode of some show about killer squids taking over a ship, and let my eyes glaze over and focus on nothing but the vapid dialogue and terrible casting. There are six seasons of this thing, and it's so popular they're mass printing T-shirts with quotes from the show. I don't get it, but after a full weekend with nothing but *Mr. Squid* and the couch, I intend to.

I make it through about thirteen minutes of Episode 1 before I slap the remote and hit the pause button. I don't think a squid shirt is in my future. Maybe massively fattening snacks will make it better.

My stomach a bland container that's barely processed anything over the last two weeks, I let it growl at the thought of popcorn and decide that might be the key to making it happy. I pull one of the packets from the box and toss it in the microwave, then spend the next two and half minutes walking in circles around my kitchen and downstairs.

I play a game with myself where I'm not allowed to step on cracks, which gets harder as the tiles get smaller in the hallway. I close the bathroom door behind me and prepare myself to feel everything I tend to when I'm in this room. The plastic wrap draped over my prom dress behind me catches me off guard, though. I spin and pull the hanger down from the spring stop at the top of the door.

"Oh, you beautiful dress," I whisper to myself.

Without hesitating, I pull the plastic from the hanger and slide the straps free, letting the slinky fabric wind through my fingers. Closing my eyes, I imagine the way the silkiness feels on my body, how it would have felt to have Dustin's hands roaming over the skirt, the top, his fingers sinking into the open back.

I pull my shirt over my head and kick my legs free of the giant sweatpants, slipping into the perfect dress. I spin and look down at the skirt as it splays out into a bell shape. It sways when I make a hard stop, and I run my hands down the bodice and gather the soft folds at my hips, clinging it to me. I lift my head to take in the full picture in the mirror. I've never felt more beautiful in a piece of clothing in my life. Even now, as hideous and empty as I am, this gown somehow makes me feel like a princess.

"Why?" I hum. My fake smile falls fast, the weight of heartbreak dragging it farther. My eyes dim and I let my attention fall away from the mirror to the beaded glitter decorating the front of my body.

Why did you leave, Dustin? Where did you go? Why aren't you here?

The questions never seem to stop. I don't think they ever will. And I'm so damn afraid the day will come that I will want them to. I'll pray for the thoughts to leave. I'll beg myself to quit caring. It hurts so much, but that hurt, it's what I have. It's him. If I don't hurt from missing him, then he's really gone. He'll be gone for good.

The microwave beeping echoes in the kitchen, snapping me out of my indulgence. I take off my gown and hide it under the plastic sheath where it belongs, safe and guarded, ready for next year, when Dustin comes home and takes me to my prom, and proves to everyone how wrong they were about him.

About us.

ONE YEAR LATER . . .

"Are you sure this is where you want to spend your prom? I really am cool going to the actual dance, you know?"

Michael Bosa is the most compliant prom date in the world.

"I'm seriously okay with being here instead," I say, roaming my hand over the cold metal knob of the shifter. My eyes lower as we pull up to the Straights.

I graduate next week, and I'll be out of here in days. I opted to start at Northern for the summer session. I'm sick of this place. Sick of turning around and expecting to see someone who is never going to show up.

What a fool I've been.

"It's just, you wore that dress, and you look. . ." Bosa trails off. He's still a little intimidated by me. He thinks I'm still Dustin's girl. I haven't been her in a long time. Maybe I never was. I was naïve to think I belonged to him so completely.

"How do I look?" I ask coyly. I bat my lashes, feeling the weight of the deep black mascara I layered on. I wanted to be someone else tonight. No, to *become* someone else. This girl doesn't fall for anyone. She captures hearts and holds them in her hands for a while, but always sets them free. Love is an illusion. I'm not even sure my parents actually love each other anymore, and I always thought they were this perfect union. I've been watching them closely, though, over the last few months. They hardly talk, and when they do, it's more like a messaging service.

Dad tells Mom what he's picking up for dinner.

Mom tells Dad that Tommy called and he'll be home for the Fourth of July weekend.

They discuss paying my tuition, what's left after my scholarship. They divide tasks and work well as a team. But is that love?

"Go on, Michael. Tell me how I look," I say, drawing my tongue over my bottom lip to lure him. I won't kiss him tonight, and I think deep down he knows it. I won't kiss anyone ever again. I'll flirt, to feel the heat of attention. I've learned that I like the rush I get from the control. Anything more than that, though, comes with a risk.

"You look hot," he finally answers, his words tumbling out amid nervous laughter as he rubs his likely sweaty palms on the knees of his slacks.

"Good boy," I say, reaching over and tapping his nose. I look away before he has a chance to make anything more of it.

"Now, let's find a race," I say, shifting into first and idling my way through the crowd. We're not the only couple who opted for this over some dance at the Union Hall. I used to wonder if Dustin and I would have ended up here on our prom night. Now, I don't care.

He was the ruler of this place. A legend of the lanes. Now, he's a ghost. And I've got his precious car. I'm not entirely sure why Dad let me keep it when he towed it home from the impound lot. Maybe he felt guilty for being so hard on our relationship. Funny how right they were, though. My parents knew he'd hurt me.

Tommy did the wrap job for my birthday a few weeks ago, my eighteenth. I wanted the car to look nothing like it did when *he* drove it. Tommy made it midnight blue, almost black. The only hint at color can be seen under the right light, by the right set of eyes, thanks to the matte finish.

I spot our mark halfway down the gathering, pull into an open space and shift to park.

"Be right back," I say, kicking open the door with my white Vans. I tossed the heels in the back the minute Michael and I left my house after my mom snapped about a million photos. *Like I'll ever want to remember this night.*

"You want me to come with?" He leans across the center console, his blue eyes blinking up at me. I dare say, he's handsome. Just not handsome enough. Not broken enough. He's safe.

He works at his cufflinks, rolling up the sleeve on one arm, his jacket long abandoned to the tight back seat.

"Oh, I've got this. I'm a big girl."

He lets out a smitten laugh, so when I shut the door I decide to cool it a little on the flirting. I can't have him getting the wrong idea.

I'm not sure whether Aiden remembers me or not. I look a little different than I did a year ago when he shot out the tires that used to be on this car. My brown hair is closer to black now, and I'm wearing a lot more makeup than normal. Plus, I don't think Aiden ever really looked at my face the night he fucked us over. I flash him a fifty dollar bill as I walk up and he looks beyond my shoulder, probably for my boyfriend. I shift so his eyes have to meet mine.

"Nope. Just me," I say, giving him a crooked smile.

He chuckles and looks to his friend. I don't recognize this guy, but he could have been there that night. Aiden, though, him I will never forget.

"Sure, honey," he says, taking my cash and handing it to his friend for holding.

"Can I trust him?" I cock a brow.

"Either that or find yourself a different race," Aiden says.

I hold his stare for a few seconds, and for a moment, there's a glint in his eye that makes me wonder if he recognizes me. I nod finally and turn to walk away.

"No, I'll take the race," I toss over my shoulder.

Aiden's learned a thing or two since last year. He's probably been burned for cash. That's the only reason he would make a big deal out of my question. Truthfully, I couldn't care less about the money. The way I see it, I just bought myself about four minutes of unadulterated euphoria. It's worth fifty bucks, win or lose.

I think I'll win.

I've gotten pretty good out here. Tommy taught me how to tighten my shifting, and he spent time with my footwork so I got gear changing down to about three seconds. It's nowhere near the two Dustin could pull off, but it's faster than any girl I've ever seen out on the Straights besides Ava. She complimented me last month too. That must mean I'm doing something right.

"We're on," I say, climbing back in the car.

I'm sure Michael says something in response, but I don't hear him. I'm already lost to the road. My legs tingle with the rumble as I reverse, giving the car a little gas to let people know I'm serious.

I flip around and line up at the usual start, my eyes

glued to the empty stretch of roadway ahead as the Subaru, still covered in those goddamn stickers, crawls up next to me. A guy who used to lose to Dustin out here on the weekly passes between our cars and gets our nods, a silent acceptance of the rules. He makes his way out to the yellow dashes that jet out from between us, and stops in the glow of our headlights. His hand lifts, a white bandana tied around his wrist to make it easier to see.

My eyes haze, and my mouth curves. The smile is faint, and I feel drunk. Later, I will be. Never too drunk, but enough to tamp down the threat of feeling anything. I tarnish the memory of us every time I go to a party, every time I light up with my brother at a bonfire, and every time I sneak downstairs when my parents are asleep and I'm fighting with my demons. At this point, if Dustin Bridges shows his face anywhere I am, I'll be unrecognizable.

When the bandana falls, I punch the gas and do as I've been taught. My hand moves slower, but it doesn't matter. I'll pass Aiden in the stretch, halfway back to home. And if I don't, fuck it. Because this feeling right now? This is my love. This is my bliss. And it's the only kind I'm ever going to get.

EPILOGUE

THREE YEARS LATER, TULSA, OKLAHOMA

Virgil isn't Tommy.

I say this every damn race, and yet I can't seem to let myself part with the man. He's fifty, and wears a John Deere hat over his salt-and-pepper hair every day of the week. He's a shitty mechanic, though. I think there's probably some daddy issues at play with our relationship and my inability to let him go. I mean, he's fine for a guy changing oil and filters and crap, but he's never going to get me beyond the B-level races out here in the sticks.

"All right, give that a go and let's see how she does," he says, dropping the truck hood with a heavy clunk.

I've dropped a lot of cash into this modified Chevy pickup, and the best it's done is fourth place. Yeah, I'm getting attention, and I'll probably pick up enough sponsorships and wins to slide into the circuit for stock after this year, but I sure would like to feel the thrill of winning again, just one damn time.

"Alright, Virgil. I'll treat her right," I say. He winks at me and I remind myself again that I can't ever drop him. The man is too good, and my life is too void of that stuff.

The ride feels choppy already, and I know a belt is too tight. I wait until I get out to the track before I step out and give it one tiny adjustment. Hopefully Virgil doesn't see this. I hurry back inside to find my rhythm, my heart not quite ready for the final thirty laps of this stage. If I can just hold on to the top five, I'll earn out. I'll be able to pay off the advances from Tulsa Motors and get Uncle Jeff the rent money we agreed I'd start to pay.

I'm too old to be living with my uncle, but I don't know yet where I would go. Everything around the city is too pricey to handle on my own, and since I left Arizona, I'm not much of a people kind of guy. The idea of picking up a random roommate sends shivers down my spine.

In through the nose. Hold, and exhale.

My ritual doesn't work as well as it used to. Nothing does. I know I did what I had to do, and I know it was for the best.

Colt's been out for two years now. He'll probably find me someday, and by then I'll probably have earned things that are important to me. He'll take it all, too. But he won't take Hannah. She'll be okay, and so will Tommy. And that's all that matters. That's why I keep Virgil. That and the man insists on making me mix tapes for every race. I'm the only asshole out here with some garage-sale tape player buckled to his passenger seat because his only friend is fifty and lives in 1984.

I press play, curious what song will hit me out of the gate. I chuckle at the first few notes of Tom Petty's "American Girl." It's a classic, and Virgil didn't have to teach me this one. It's not his fault, but only a few seconds in, the song has me deep in my thoughts. The Judges loved Petty, and Hannah and Tommy's dad used to play his greatest hits on the drive down to Tucson. "American Girl" was always Hannah's favorite.

It's her theme song. Every verse of it.

"Alright, Han. I guess this one's for you," I say, flipping down the visor to get one last look at the image of my sleeping beauty. I used Uncle Jeff's printer to run a copy of the photo I snuck of Hannah the night I left, and it's fading. I've lost the original, though, in a devastating phone incident that involved me, a bit of whiskey, and a river. So much for not following in my mom and Colt's footsteps. I've been drunk every Friday and Saturday night since I left Arizona. I had to do something to survive, and it turns out alcoholism loves company.

I press two fingers to my lips and close my eyes, remembering how hers looked the first time I let her ride along for a race. Nothing has ever been so pure. She was a calm in a storm, a bigger storm than she bargained for, and I'm sorry for that every day I breathe.

My vision of her is still with me when my eyes open. I press my kissed fingers to her photo and push the visor up to keep her safe.

I'll always keep her safe—from me, from Colt, from my demons. But I'll never quit looking for her everywhere I go. You can love something and deny yourself the pleasure of it. That's real love. That's the kind of love that matters, the kind that lasts. Love from afar, it can't get hurt. It can't be broken. And if that's all I'm going to get in this life, I'm sure as hell going to protect it.

"Hey, you hear me, Dust?" Virgil gets a kick out of the headset.

I get a kick out of how amused Virgil is.

"Roger that, V-man," I say.

"Huh?"

I shake my head and laugh quietly.

"Nothing, I was just trying out some lingo."

"Oh, right. I mean, ten-four," he says. I smile at his attempt.

"Hey, you got a call from some woman named Bailey. She said you could call her after the race if you want. You know her?"

I think maybe a full minute passes before I answer. I'm stunned lifeless at first, but soon, I'm scrambling out of my truck and signaling that I need into the pits. Of all the blasts from my past, Bailey is the last one I expect to ever hear from, and there could only be one reason for her call.

Hannah.

"Uh, Dust? You've got like ten minutes till go," Virgil says. His voice is breaking up through our connection, but I'm almost to him anyhow.

"It's fine, Virg. Just let me see my phone."

I startle him when he realizes I've crept in behind him. His wide eyes look panicked, so I rest my hand on his chest.

"Virgil, this race is sponsored by a chicken wing shop that only has six locations," I explain.

"Yeah, but. . ." Virgil stammers. I hold up my finger now that my phone is in my hand, and I'm already dialing Bailey's number. She answers on the first ring, thank God.

"Dustin? Is that you?" she asks.

"Yeah, Bailey. What's wrong? Is Hannah okay?" My mind races through a dozen different scenarios, from accidents to illnesses.

"Dustin—" Virgil breaks in again. I shush him this time, and he must sense by my expression that this call, it's serious. I pace a few steps away, plugging my ear to cut out the engine noise as much as I can.

"Are you at a race?" Bailey asks.

"Yeah, but it's fine. Bailey, tell me!" I plead.

"Oh, God. I didn't want to tell you this before a race. And Hannah didn't want you to know at all, but—"

"For fuck's sake, Bailey! What is it?" I demand.

"Colt's dead. Your dad. He . . . passed away. The manager of your old trailer court found him. I guess he'd been in there a few days, and I, well, Hannah's been torturing herself with the news all weekend, debating whether or not to tell you."

I fall back on my ass. For most people, the next phase to hit them would probably be grief, but all I can seem to do is cry out in laughter.

"That's it?" I say.

"I'm really sorry, Dustin." Bailey knows my life story. She wouldn't think I would be destroyed by any of this.

"Don't be. God! *Oof!*" I blow out. I hold my hand to my forehead then give Virgil a thumbs up. His face is still full of worry. I love that he cares.

"I'm just glad it's not Hannah. I was worried—" And then something new hits me. "Wait, Hannah has my number?"

I got a new phone number when I left. I knew if she could text or call me, I'd give in. I later learned she did the same.

"Yeah, but don't . . . Dustin, don't let her know I told you. She'll be so mad, and you can't call her."

"This is her phone you're calling me from?" I shout. I haven't been this close in so long, and suddenly I find myself wanting to drive across the country. Colt's gone. My mom hasn't shown up anywhere since she disappeared the day hell went down on Earth. There's no longer a threat, or a reason to worry.

"Yes, but please, Dustin. Please. She would kill me if she knew. She would *kill* me. She won't call you, and it took her so long to get herself right," Bailey says. I fall back to my ass again. So many goddamn ups and downs. This one is a heavy blow, and it cuts out a cavity in my chest. Hannah had to get herself right.

I hurt her. Like her dad said I would.

I knew it would be forever when I left, but damn hope in the form of a phone call.

"No, no. I get it. I won't, Bailey. I . . . thanks for letting me know, though."

"You're welcome, Dustin. I hope you're okay. I . . . I better go," she says, and after a short good-bye, the line is dead.

Virgil is tapping on my shoulder now, and my body teems with so many toxic emotions, I jerk around and bark "what!" at him.

"I'm sorry, Virg," I apologize right away. I run my hand over my face and pinch the bridge of my nose. My head is pounding. There's no way I'm going to drive well. There's too much to process.

"That's Robert O'Keefe behind you, the owner of Tulsa Wings," Virgil says, leaning into me and doing his best to whisper. Thanks to years of smoking, though, his whisper is more like a growl, and it's completely audible from everywhere.

Add one more crushing weight to my fragile, barely-held-together ego.

"I'm so sorry, sir. I just . . . that was news from home." I can't very well blurt out my dad died, not after I giggled with fucking glee. I wait while the man studies me, tugging the lapel of his oversized suit jacket. I shouldn't make fun of the fit. It's a nicer coat than I own.

"Just get in the goddamn truck, Bridges, and drive. And maybe fucking win tonight." Mr. O'Keefe's thick, gray eyebrow lifts up on one side, like a checkmark on his forehead.

I nod and leave him with Virgil, reminding myself of my mechanic's charm, which is one more reason I accept his failures underneath the hood. He'll smooth this over, but I got the meaning of our sponsor's undertones just now. If I don't win, he's pulling his money. If he pulls his money, I might not get out of these shithole races for another two years.

But none of that matters. Hannah knows where to find me, and I have faith that when she's ready, she will. She's my love. My bliss. And the only love I'm ever going to have.

To be continued

CONTINUE READING WITH WRECK
AND BURN, BOOKS 2 AND 3 OF THE
FUEL SERIES, RELEASING JULY 2021!

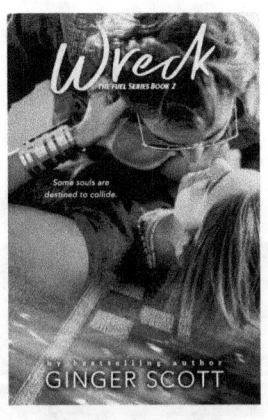

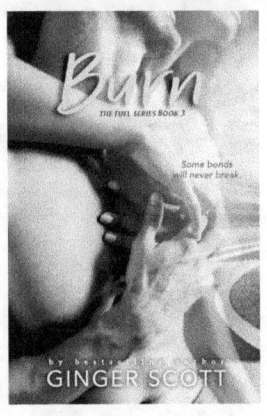

ACKNOWLEDGMENTS

Phew! Am I right?

This series has been such a rush to write. I cannot wait for my readers to experience every moment of it. I wanted you to have something special this summer. Of all summers, this one called for something big. I hope this book hits the spot for you.

I have a lot of people to thank for helping me get this baby over the finish line. (Get it?) As always, Autumn, you steer me in the right direction. I am forever grateful for your expertise, but even more for your friendship. Aly Stiles - you are more than a critique partner, you are literally a life coach. I'm not sure I know how to write without Rebecca Shea sitting across from me at a Panera. My betas for this baby, Jen and Shelley, you were patient and guided me so much. And Brenda Letendre, YOU were my Rusty Wallace. You kept me going when I was running on empty, and this book shines because of your editing. I'm so deeply proud of it, and I have you—all of you—to thank for that.

Mom, boys, and my gear-headed brother—you are the

soft and chewy center of this book. But my sweet Lesley, you are the heart. It beats with your spirit. This series—it's for you. Even if you're too shy to read the saucy parts lol!

Thank you for taking this journey with me. If you enjoyed this book, please consider leaving a review, talking about it with a friend, forcing it in someone's hands, shouting about it out the car window—pretty much anything. (Only kidding a little.) My readers are the only reason I get to do something with these stories in my head, and I am profoundly grateful. Now, back to the race. ;-)

ABOUT THE AUTHOR

Ginger Scott is an Amazon-bestselling and Goodreads Choice and Rita Award-nominated author from Peoria, Arizona. She is the author of several young and new adult romances, including bestsellers Cry Baby, The Hard Count, A Boy Like You, This Is Falling and Wild Reckless.

A sucker for a good romance, Ginger's other passion is sports, and she often blends the two in her stories. When she's not writing, the odds are high that she's somewhere near a baseball diamond, either watching her son swing for the fences or cheering on her favorite baseball team, the Arizona Diamondbacks. Ginger lives in Arizona and is married to her college sweetheart whom she met at ASU (fork 'em, Devils).

FIND GINGER ONLINE: www.littlemisswrite.com

facebook.com/GingerScottAuthor
twitter.com/TheGingerScott
instagram.com/authorgingerscott

The Harper Boys

Wild Reckless

Wicked Restless

Standalone Reads

Candy Colored Sky

Cowboy Villain Damsel Duel

Drummer Girl

BRED

Cry Baby

The Hard Count

Memphis

Hold My Breath

Blindness

How We Deal With Gravity